ALL IN A DAY

Gloria Cook titles available from Severn House Large Print

Out of Shadows
A Whisper of Life
A Stranger Light
Keeping Echoes
Never Just a Memory
From a Distance

ALL IN A DAY

Gloria Cook

Severn House Large Print
London & New York

This first large print edition published 2009
in Great Britain and the USA by
SEVERN HOUSE PUBLISHERS LTD of
9-15 High Street, Sutton, Surrey, SM1 1DF.
First world regular print edition published 2008 by
Severn House Publishers Ltd., London and New York.

British Library Cataloguing in Publication Data

Cook, Gloria
    All in a day. - Large print ed. - (A Victorian Meryen saga)
    1. Cornwall (England : County) - Social life and customs -
    19th century - Fiction 2. Large type books
    I. Title
    823.9'14[F]

    ISBN-13: 978-0-7278-7773-4

Printed and bound in Great Britain by
MPG Books Ltd, Bodmin, Cornwall.

*In memory of my dear brother Ted,
now fishing for a much larger catch
from a far greater river.*

One

Bang, bang. Shudder, thump. Fierce winds driving in off the downs were harassing the front gate in a series of nerve-jarring thuds and jerks. The solid wood gate could not simply have blown open; it had been made and set by craftsmen and it would take a far stronger tempest to loosen the iron latch. Someone had opened the gate and neglected to shut it.

Until now the howling down the chimneys and whistling round the corners of the sprawling isolated property, Chy-Henver, had not bothered Rachel Kivell as she sat in the snug office of the six-bedroom cottage, built fortress-strong, as was the carpentry workshop, stores and stable across the backyard. Let nature do its worse, she thought. Slates could be replaced, downed posts righted, and the garden she was so proud of was protected by stone walls, trees, willow fences and privet and box hedges. She was eager to finish the business paperwork, to slip up to her room and re-read James Lockley's love letters, every one of his loving messages to her, permeated with wonderful promises. To dream about the future they would have to-gether – that was as soon as James, the village doctor, had found a way clear of the one complication that stood in their way.

Putting down her pen, tapping her fingers on the kneehole desk, she waited for the untimely caller to knock. A harsh gust drew the wildly dancing flames in the register grate to leap towards the chimney top, sending back down soot and debris to scatter on the rug. The wood smoke made Rachel cough and stung her eyes. She dashed off a note to send for the chimney sweep, since she oversaw the domestics for her brother Jowan and their cousin, Thad, master carpenters and cabinet-makers, the owners of the business.

The gate slammed against the immovable granite post. Rachel heaved a sigh. Why no summons at the door yet? Whoever was imprudent enough to arrive on business or to call on her in this heathen weather was taking their time.

Her impatience vanished as quickly as it had taken a hold. It might be James! He might have dropped his doctor's bag or something, causing the delay. She lived in hope that he might turn up at any moment. She jumped up and fussed with her appearance in the hall mirror. Her lynx-eyed, flushed reflection shone back at her, proof of how James made her feel, happy and warm, and so excited that sometimes she could hardly breathe. Since falling in love with him she daydreamed about him all the time. Jowan and Thad teased her laughingly about being so absentminded. They would be furious if they

8

knew the real reason behind it.

At the door she twisted round a silver bracelet on her wrist in anticipation, but there was no knock. It wasn't James. He would never loiter, playing games. The disappointment was crushing; she would never get used to it, but it was something she willingly endured. James could not be easily available to her. He had a busy profession and he had a wife.

In times like this her eyes lost their fierce blueness and her shoulders flopped. She raised her eyes accusingly to the ceiling, where she could hear Dora, the daily general housemaid, making the beds. 'I suppose I'll have to see to the gate; you certainly don't intend to.' When she had hoped it was James she would have been dismayed to hear Dora coming down, since she was apt to babble and pry.

Rachel knew Dora's reasoning. The woman wasn't lazy, but she refused to do anything outside her province and that included the front garden. Rachel couldn't blame Dora for not wanting to venture outside. She had complained she'd been blown along every inch of the road from the nearby village of Meryen, the copper-mining community where she lived. 'Air out there's as thick as porridge and as dark as Hades,' she had declared. 'Something sinister lurking in it, if you ask me.'

'I can well believe it,' Rachel muttered, shrugging on her short coat and wrapping a shawl over her head. She took a deep breath and braced herself. Even with the copious shelter in the garden she was about to be buffeted about like a twig. The weighty front door was nearly pushed in on her. On the other side she had to tug on the brass knocker to get it shut. Holding on to an upright in the porch, she shielded her eyes and peered through the shrubbery all the way to the gate. It was being rocked, seeming to rise and fall on each forced journey before being violently slammed against the post, the wind seeming intent to tear it off its hinges.

Clutching the shawl about her face, her head lowered, she started off along the paved paths. Nearly all the blooms of the camellias had been blown off. Bushes were being blown this way and that, like groups of lurching drunken men, snagging her full skirts. Her eyes drawn against dust and grit, she urged herself on. The gate was broad, its bars thickly constructed. It would take a strong arm to hold on to it with the elements using it as a battering ram. Not a particularly hard task for Rachel, she was strong and had the necessary determination. It wasn't as if the men could be summoned to do the job. Jowan and Thad, with the two men and two boys from other branches of the family, were in the church, installing newly carved pews.

There was much thrashing of foliage and Rachel hated every moment. She had never felt so cold and had been foolish not to have tied on a bonnet and pulled on gloves. As if a scratchy limb of a bush had suddenly reached out for her she was tripped up by the ankle and she fell, her arm and brow striking the ornamental stone border as she hit the hard pavement. 'Owwah!' she screamed in shock and pain, then exclaimed in anger, using words that would shock her menfolk.

She lay sprawled, catching her breath, waiting for the pains that would signify the extent of her injuries. Doubtless she was bruised and had a cut or two. Damn it all! Then she realized she should be pleased; she would exaggerate her hurts to give a perfect reason for James to attend her.

She looked up through the corridor of her shawl and felt a trickle of blood wetting her cheek. She pulled her head back sharply. 'Ugh! What on earth!' A face was staring at her – a dirty, crazed face, with huge wild, yellowy eyes, and tats of hair. Rachel gagged at the stench of the creature. The shock made her scramble to her knees. A moor spirit had pounced on her. The superstitious, especially among the mining folk, whispered of fantastical and dangerous creatures coming forth from hellish dens in these kinds of destructive conditions. This aberration had deliberately brought her down! In her present mood Rachel was angry rather than scared. 'Get away from me!' She snatched up a handful of stones, raising her hand in threat.

The creature shot back under a hydrangea bush, curling into a ball, throwing its clawing hands in front of its face. 'No miss, no miss,' it blubbered.

Rachel's temper died away. This was nothing

supernatural. It was a woman, some homeless wretch, quite young, thin and bony and in rags, and most definitely an imbecile. Rachel got to her feet cautiously, feeling darts of pain here and there. She gazed down at the intruder. 'Did you leave the gate open? What do you want?' Both questions were unnecessary. Of course the woman was responsible for the banging gate and she was here looking for shelter. She had probably been too afraid to come to the door and ask for help; instead through her retarded mind she had reached out in an unfortunate manner. Now she was scared and whimpering, and probably fearing a beating for making 'miss' take a tumble. Many would feel the right to deal her a few blows and turn her away. Rachel's heart, however, was touched with compassion. 'Do you want food? To get warm by a fire, is that it?'

'Please miss, please miss.' The woman played her scraggy fingers along her thin, blistered lips.

'Wait there. I won't be long. I must close the gate before it drives me mad.'

The gate was swinging towards the post when Rachel reached it. The powerful force of the wind made it easy for her to end its journey, but she had to shove on the gate with her body to hold it in place while she lifted the trigger of the lock and let it fall back in place. At last the gate was shut firmly. She returned to the beggar.

The woman had emerged from the bush and was up on her filthy bare feet. She was unsteady on bowed legs, her trunk stooped. She was bobbing as if bowing in subservience. Altogether she made the height of an average twelve-year-old. Her horrible eyes, red-rimmed from some infection, were agog and on Rachel pleadingly, but suspicion and fear was uppermost. More than hope of a little charity, she was expecting a brutal rejection. One would be hard put to discover a more pitiful creature.

Anger against her past tormentors welled up in Rachel. Her own hurts were forgotten. 'Come with me. I'll take you inside.' Her movement towards the beggar was met with a timid trembling retreat, the woman wrapping her scarecrow arms round her scrawny body, ready to curl up again in defence.

'Don't worry. I'm not going to harm you.' Rachel used a firm tone, which she felt the woman was more likely to respond to. She stepped past her. 'Follow me. I'll find you some food. You may shelter in the kitchen till the wind blows itself out.' She sensed the air. The wind was easing off, as if it had suddenly exhausted its prolonged fit of temper.

Rachel went on a little way then looked back. The woman was hunched over on the same spot, darting her head at the porch and then the gate, as if unable to decide whether to take up the offer of hospitality or flee. She was probably frightened her fate would take a cruel twist once she entered the cottage.

'It's all right,' Rachel called above the soughing lament, beckoning to her. 'You can trust me.

13

Come along now. It's too cold to linger out here.'

The woman was clearly petrified. Her sight was on Rachel and was full of pained uncertainty. Rachel thought the dreadful fear and longing in those wretched eyes would haunt her forever if she was unsuccessful in helping this pathetic scrap of humanity. She went back to the woman. She must take things slowly. 'It's all right to come with me. You'll be perfectly safe, I promise you. Do you understand me?'

The woman nodded, to Rachel's relief.

'My name is Rachel. What's yours?'

'Miss Rachel! What on earth are 'ee doing out there?' Dora shouted from the doorway, letting a small channel of lamp light escape from inside. 'I couldn't believe my ears when I heard the door go then felt an icy blast whooshing through the house. "What's she up to now?" I said to myself. Oh, you got someone with you, have you? Who's that then? Someone in trouble, is it? Can't think of another reason for being out on a day like this, when even the angels wouldn't care to flutter a wing outside heaven.'

Once Dora got started she'd rattle on and on. Rachel ignored her. 'Are you coming inside?' She spoke soothingly to the woman as if to a child. 'That's only Dora by the door. She and I will look after you. You can have some nice hot chicken broth, and I'll fetch you something warm to wear. Would you like that?'

'Yes miss,' the woman gasped at last, nodding

14

like a cork on a string. 'I come, I come.'

Trying not to mind her rank smells, Rachel stretched out a hand and was pleased the beggar allowed her to help her along. 'Just a little way to go, then we'll go into the kitchen and you can sit down. We must do something about your poor feet.'

'Yes miss, thank 'ee.'

'Good grief!' Dora stood aside to clear the way into the hall, waving her hand in front of her crinkled nose. 'That's Eva Bowden you got there. She's daft in the head, as I'm sure you can tell. Her mother had a bad birth, that's how she's like she is, although her mother is a heavy drinker too. What's she doing here, for good-ness' sake? How did she get here?'

'It's easy to see,' Rachel said. 'She ran, as best she could; there's mud splashed up her legs.' A lot of Eva Bowden's crooked legs were on show, her skirt a long time in tatters.

'She can rarely be coaxed out of doors. Never been this far in her life, I'm sure. Aw, she smells like a privy and is crawling with lice, but then that's no surprise to me or to anyone else in Meryen. Ugh, she's got boils on her neck. Glad I don't live near her family.' Dora closed the door. 'Aw, Miss Rachel, you've got blood on your face. Did she hit you? She's usually a terrified little thing, but she might lash out, I suppose, in fright. Her brother's got some ter-rible temper on him. He's a brute. There's—'

'Bowden?' Rachel interrupted. 'I heard some-thing about a miner of that name dying

15

recently.' Watching Eva shiver and shake, with her arms wrapped about herself, probably a defensive habit, sadly out of necessity, Rachel took off her shawl and swung it around the woman's slight body. 'This will help you keep warm, Eva, dear.'

Eva's vacuous eyes fluttered in surprise then she clutched the shawl about her, rubbing her sallow cheeks against the soft plaid wool in childish delight.

'Aw, Miss Rachel, Mr Jowan gave you that,' Dora tutted. 'What's he going to say? Yes, you're right. A Bowden did die, just a fortnight ago. 'Twas this creature's father, hung himself he did – suicide, shameful. But p'raps I should not be too hard in his case, not after what went on in his house all the time. There was always men—'

'Shut up, Dora.' Rachel aimed irritation at the servant. Short and rubicund, Dora was as curious as a cat, and bluff, with an inclination to find glee in others' troubles. Each Monday morning she rushed in to work and before she'd tied on her apron, blurted out a breathless account of the gossip gleaned from the chapel pews the day before. Rachel usually didn't bother to listen. She had no burning interest in the ordinary copper-mining folk, but she did in Eva Bowden, who came from such stock. 'Have some consideration in front of these poor ears. Heat up the broth, please. Then you can tell me about Eva's life – discreetly. I take it she's unable to speak properly?'

16

'Well, I'd say that was more 'n obvious, isn't it?' Dora sniffed, but kept her voice low and led off to the warm roomy kitchen. 'She lives down below Edge End, in what can only be described as a hovel. Her mother had a large brood, but all except for Eva – and Silas, the first born, a miner at the Carn Croft – they all quickly followed one another to the churchyard. That was just as well, since the whole family's not right in the head, although I always belonged to be a bit sorry for the father. He was a quiet, God-fearing man in his youth.'

Rachel ushered the shuffling Eva along and placed a chair at the hearthside. 'Sit down, Eva.' Instead Eva lowered her wobbly balance down on a carved three-legged stool; it was for decoration rather than a seat. She hunched up, pulling on her ear lobes, her mouth sagging open.

'Glad she knows her place,' Dora muttered. 'I won't have to wash her stink off the chair.'

'Have some charity,' Rachel hissed. 'The poor thing looks as if she's never known a kind word in her life.'

'Why do you care?' Dora dragged the pot of broth on to the hob of the range. 'You nor none of your family have ever bothered much with anyone 'cept yourselves. Well, you've taken something on now, mark my words. Eva Bowden coming this far like this can mean only one thing. Trouble. She's run away from something that terrified her. Got to be Silas; he must have given her a thrashing. You might end up

17

regretting helping her.'

Most employers wouldn't tolerate such blatant disrespect but Rachel did not mind having someone to spar with. She made a face. Dora's first assertions were true. The Kivells had been resident in the area centuries before the village had sprung up and had kept to their own land and self-contained community of Burnt Oak, a mile and a half from the village. Originating from the Norman invasion, they had intermarried with the lawless and gypsies, evolving into a dark, brooding, suspicious clan. Nearly a decade ago, with the world branching out into industry and opportunity, they had begun to network into society and move away, including overseas. Kivells had taken over many of the businesses in Meryen. Rachel was one of the Kivells who was not happy to stay put. To start afresh in some distant place would be necessary if she was to have a future with her married lover.

'My family may not tend to seek out people in trouble but we have never refused hospitality to those who turn up on our doorstep.' Looking down at the huddled shivering mortal stinking out the kitchen, she felt more and more sorry for her. 'It's different when you're faced with someone like Eva, poor little thing.'

'Little? She's nearly up to her twentieth year.'

'Well, that makes it even more sad. I hope she's not being interfered with – you know what I mean.'

'Doubt it's that.' Again Dora crumpled her

18

nose at Eva's repulsive condition, but a fleeting moment of sympathy appeared under her squiggly eyebrows. 'But you never know. Silas is always drunk and has any number of rogues in the house. 'Tis a God-forsaken place, always violent quarrels going on. The father left his wife, Judy, with child again. That's a shame. She's always drunk on rot-gut gin, no mother at all. Be better if this baby's another that don't survive.'

'It seems a crime to allow Eva to go back to the life you've described.' Rachel sighed, cutting thick slices of bread and lavishing them with butter. 'But we've got no right to keep her here. After she's eaten, I'll send her home. Do you think she'll be able to find her way back?'

'Debatable.' Dora frowned.

'Well, I'll take her back. Make sure everything is all right for her to go inside.' Rachel brightened at an idea. 'I'll take her along to Dr Lockley. He can prescribe something for her sores and boils and to get rid of the lice. I need to see him anyway, I'm hurting all over.' She gingerly stretched her painful arm.

'You can't take her there!' Dora was appalled. 'You'd be wasting his time and your money. Eva hasn't got the sense to take pills, put on potions and make up poultices, and her mother won't bother to do it for her. And Mrs Lockley wouldn't thank you for turning up on her doorstep with someone so filthy and disgusting. She's a refined lady, comes from the upper class. Married down the scale she did, that's why she's stuck out here where she don't belong. Anyway, one of your uncles is the apothecary. Are you sure you're up to a walk to the village, Miss Rachel? Why not let me ask the doctor to call here on my way home.'

'Thank you, Dora, but I'm sure I can manage the walk. I suppose you're right about taking Eva to the doctor. Well, we'll have to do our best for her, and I'll get something from my Uncle Henry. As for myself, I'll see how I feel when I get back.' Rachel decided to have James call on her; she didn't really want to chance coming face to face with Charlotte Lockley. She watched Dora ladle soup into a tin bowl – the good china could not be risked on Eva. Taking the bowl, she put it on a small wooden tray with the bread and butter and a spoon then tapped Eva on the shoulder. 'Sit up straight,' she intoned slowly to break through the woman's mental fog. 'Eat this all up.'

In shocked audience, Rachel and Dora glanced at each other as Eva rapidly gobbled down the food, making slops down her front, which she licked off before scrabbling for every crumb of bread, even those that had hit the floor. 'Poor thing is starving.' Rachel was unable to repress a shudder. 'We'll give her some more. You pack up some food to take with her, Dora. I'll make up a bundle of my old clothes. I've kept some things from my younger days, which should fit her of sorts. I knew people lived in terrible poverty but I had no idea some lived in such a degrading manner.'

'None of us see what we don't want to. Well, I don't advise you to go inside her home, Miss Rachel. That will open your eyes even more.'

Shortly afterwards Rachel was dressed in her warmest outdoor things and back in the kitchen. 'Got the food ready, Dora? Good. Put these stockings and boots on her feet.'

'Why me?' Dora bristled, backing away as if she was about to be contaminated with pestilence. 'You brought her in here. Get a live-in servant if you want someone to go that far. I'm only paid to do the housework, and it's time I got on with it. I'll be late going home at this rate anyway. First off, I'll have to light a lot of scented candles to get rid of the beastly smells in the house. I'm not having your visitors saying I'm a poor housekeeper.'

Rachel glared at Dora, then looked down at Eva's feet, flopped and spread out on the mat. She couldn't imagine a more gruesome sight – hard brown flesh, fungal-infected nails, weeping blisters, protruding bones. She swallowed. 'I'll pay you double for today if you do it.'

Dora pulled the footwear out of her hands. 'Double it is and will be no more than I deserve! You're tough as nails most of the time, Miss Rachel, but this shows up the squeamish side in you.' Dora took a mighty breath, held it in, then sank to her knees in front of Eva. Eva was oblivious at first to someone trying to push a woollen stocking up over one of her feet. But then, aware of sudden pain Eva shrieked and lashed out, swiping Dora across the top of the

21

head. Dora flung the stocking down and jumped up, red-faced and gasping and waving an angry hand in front her nose. 'Ruddy creature! I'm not trying that again.'

Eva whimpered and rocked backwards and forwards, her eyes desperate and on Rachel.

'I'm sorry, Dora,' Rachel said, horrified. 'I should have known better. Her feet hurt and boots would only rub her feet raw and she'd be worse off. You wash your hands and get on with your work. I'll take Eva away from here. How do I find her house?'

'It's a hovel, not a house, don't forget. I still want my extra money. Miss Rachel, you just be very careful. Don't be gone long or I'll start worrying about you. You'll need to go all the way down Edge End, the row of houses just past the greengrocers. Her place is a little crumbling cob cottage set back on its own. You'll smell it a long way before you reach it.' Looking at her hands in disgust, Dora sped to the back kitchen and the carbolic soap.

Left alone with a snivelling Eva, Rachel glanced out the window. Although the light was better and the wind was now blowing only from the east and would be at their backs, it was going to be a rough journey. She went to Eva's side and tugged gently on the shawl. 'I need to wrap this round you tighter for the walk home, Eva, dear.'

Gazing up out of baleful eyes, Eva allowed Rachel to wrap the shawl round her head, cross it over at the front of her and tie the ends together behind her waist. Eva's fetid odours were unbearable but Rachel braved her way through. 'Up you get now, Eva. I'm going to take you home.'

She was curious about Eva's life and utterly determined to see her right. Eva had reached her heart and at this moment she was her champion. 'Can you carry this?' She held out the bundle of clothes.

'Yes miss.' Eva nodded like a puppet as she wrestled up.

'Good girl. I've got some food to last you for a few days too. Follow me then.'

Two

Once outside on the road, a coarse thoroughfare with little in the way of hedges, Rachel was grateful to have the bracing air cleanse her nose and lungs. The moors and scrubland of Nansmere Downs were bleak this time of the year, stretching away behind Chy-Henver. In view in the near distance were the gaunt workings of the Carn Croft copper mine, the wind carrying the echoes of its thunderous industry. Engine houses of other parish mines were just seen on the far horizon. On the opposite side of the road was common land, and beyond that fields of the Poltraze estate.

23

Rachel patiently adjusted her lively step to compensate for Eva's lumbering plod. She kept slightly ahead, for when she found herself beside Eva the woman eased her pace to remain behind. Apart from that Rachel got the impression Eva was operating merely on instinct, simply obeying a better.

In this way they passed between the wind-blown winter landscape of dips and rises, of scrubby furze and rust-coloured banks of fern, the sweeps of finished heather dull brown and twiggy. The ground was muddy and stony and they had to skirt round the numerous pot holes and avoid the deep ruts made by cartwheels and animal hooves. A few sheep grazed in the shelter of a crop of huge rough boulders. Later there were some thin brown-hided cattle and a couple of small bony goonhillies – wild ponies. A glance behind and Rachel was saddened to see how scared Eva was of these animals, even though they were hundreds of yards away. 'Come along, Eva, dear. You're quite safe with me.'

'Yes miss.'

Before leaving Eva at home Rachel intended to order her mother – her brother too if he was there – to care for her properly. A threat from any Kivell usually accomplished such a task. People knew it was foolhardy to cross anyone in the family. The Kivells may now be prosperous and more respectable, but their surliness and autocratic spirit remained as strong, and sometimes was as hostile as the winter. If one was offended, all were. After that, the instant she got home, she would bathe and treat her wounds, and primp and pamper herself for James's not strictly necessary consultation. In the old days Kivells had scorned the services of those outside their circle, but last year Rachel had suffered a severe case of pneumonia and seemed about to die, and James Lockley had been called in as a last resort. His dedicated treatment of more than the usual linseed poultice had brought Rachel through and back to full health, and because paying someone of a profession was considered a sign of wealth and importance, another Kivell taboo had lost its grip.

James had called twice daily for a week and then regularly after the crisis had passed. Rachel's gratitude to him had turned into friendship. She'd liked his soft and gentle yet strong and confident manner. She'd liked his voice, deep and echoing with a calm resonation. She'd found herself looking forward to seeing him, and to dwell on his lean physique and perfectly formed slender face. He had luscious china-blue eyes, a garland of fair lashes. It was easy to trust him, to be drawn to him more and more, and all too easily to fall in love with him. When James, in a dull, fruitless marriage, had confessed a deep love for her she had been elated. So far they had been successful at hiding their feelings from others. In her family's presence James behaved as the thoroughly modest gentleman he was. They were unlikely to guess the truth anyway; Kivell women tended to be attracted to the rugged, tougher sort of men of their own breed.

They had nearly reached the fringe of the village. Soon they would be passing a few houses and the first of the two Methodist chapels. Rachel knew she and Eva would be seen and speculation about their strange little procession would spread quickly. It was unwelcoming and annoying, yet the rebel in her also found it a little amusing. She led the way along High Street – a pretentious title, for in most places it was wide enough only for one-way passage and it consistently assumed quirky bends. Curtains twitched and shadowy figures stared out, first at her and then at Eva, the eyes of insignificant people sightseeing for something to do.

Up on top of three steep side-on steps, behind a rising iron hand rail, the door was opened and a housewife, small in stature, plain in garb, looking older than her actual years, as most of the ordinary village women did, came outside her quaint solitary little cottage, aptly named Three Steps.

'Miss Rachel Kivell, isn't it? Surprised to see you with the Bowden maid. I saw Eva earlier, tearing along she was, well, going as fast as she could on those poor legs. Weeping like a child, she was. I called after her but it seemed only to frighten her all the more. I can see you've been looking after her. That's very civil, very Christian, if I may say so. All right now, is she? I'm

Mrs Irene Retallack, by the way.'

Rachel paused, but only to glean anything useful. Eva stopped dead, edging off to the other side of the street. 'She'd made her way to Chy-Henver. She was in a state of terror. I understand she lives in the most appalling squalor.'

'Indeed she does,' Mrs Retallack sighed, studying the parcels being carried. 'My son was on the late core down the mine last night, and he said her brother Silas turned up for work in some evil mood then left in just the same way. He went straight home, which isn't usual as he normally heads straight for one of the taverns. He probably terrified the maid. He's some awful cruel to her. 'Tis said he's got even worse since their father hung himself.'

'Has no one ever tried to do something about it?' Rachel raised her chin and gave the house-wife her most penetrating gaze, plied with accu-sation.

'Some have tried, me included, but 'tis a sorry tale to say it was never appreciated. Begging your pardon, Miss Kivell, but you're not taking her all the way home, are you?'

'That is my intention,' Rachel replied stiffly. 'Someone has got to take a stand for Eva's sake. Good morning, Mrs Retallack.'

'Miss Kivell! Don't go yet.'

Rachel turned back impatiently. The dithering was getting too much for Eva. She was be-coming agitated, biting on the cloth tied round the bundle of clothes. 'Yes?'

Irene Retallack was chewing on a fingernail. 'Please don't mind what I'm about to say ... Look, I'll speak plain, that hovel's no place for a lady. You could put yourself in danger if Silas is home; he don't pay mind to nobody. I was wondering – would you like my son to go along with you? I'm sure he'd be glad to. Silas won't get the better of my Flint.'

Rachel was in no mood for the company of what would be, no doubt, an uncouth man who sounded testy. 'Thank you,' she said curtly. 'As it happens I have kin in the church. I shall go there first.'

'I hope all turns out well then,' Mrs Retallack called after her.

They were almost at the turning for Edge End, a terrace of houses running in a die-straight row about halfway through the village. It would be sensible to go on to Jowan and Thad. In fact she had family all around her: Kivell the Ironmongers; Kivell the Watchmakers; Kivell the Haberdashers. There were also women family members who had married local traders: Penrose the Bakers, and Cardell the Apothecary. But stubbornness was deep-rooted in Rachel. Without really knowing what she wanted to prove she was set on taking Eva home by herself, without male strength and presence. So far she had got past unseen by her relations. She hoped it continued, and she could get Eva home without further question.

As if Eva had forgotten she wasn't alone, she headed off down an empty scrap of track.

Rachel grinned; this was good. Eva was taking a route that avoided more doorsteps. There was barely room to put one foot in front of the other but it meant they'd be out of sight. Rachel followed Eva, soon up to her ankles in mud and fighting to keep her balance. At the end of the track Eva slid and skidded down a narrow dip formed by running water. At the bottom she veered off in the previous direction. Rachel slithered and slew down the last part of the dip, sending out a shower of small stones and dirt all the way. Eva shot round. Startled, she nearly dropped the bundle of clothes. She was puzzled and nervous before it dawned on her who the other person was. 'Miss! Miss!' she squawked.

'I'm all right, Eva.' Rachel looked down ruefully at the ripped hems of her skirt and petticoat. She was beginning to look like a beggar herself. 'Lead the way to your house.' Eva just looked vacant so Rachel took the lead once more. A few steps along a well-trod rough path she saw the end house of Edge End. It would be a surprise if Eva had lived in one of these small, well-built houses, but it was a shock to discover, several yards distant and set off at an angle to the row, the crumbling wreck that was the Bowden hovel.

The walls of the single-storey cottage were fragmenting and the thatch was falling out, as if a giant hand had ruffled maliciously through it. A lean-to of sorts, made of wood scraps and corrugated iron, had been tacked on. Rachel felt a chill pricking her spine. This shouldn't be termed a home. The pigs in the village back-yards were housed in better conditions. It was a wonder the cottage hadn't been blown apart by the earlier high winds. Reaching the door, which was splintered as if by several vicious kicks, she grew unnerved and began to expect more than squalor. Instinct warned her that something dreadful was lurking within these wretched walls.

She had come this far, and there was nothing for it but to carry on and hopefully get this over with, yet her acquaintance with Eva would not simply end here. In no way would she forget poor Eva and her plight.

'Well, we'd better go in, Eva.' Rachel reached for her hand, judging rightly that she'd need coaxing to enter her home. But Eva wasn't a little way behind as before; she was cowering under the shutters of the one window. Rachel sighed, wishing now she had gone to Jowan and Thad after all. 'Come along now. I won't let anyone hurt you, I promise. Eva, you must come with me now.' The authority she put in her voice worked and, very reluctantly, Eva, quaking and mumbling fearfully, went to her.

Holding Eva's chapped hand, Rachel lifted the latch of the door. She needed to push hard to get the door open and it scraped over layers of dirt on the roughly flagged floor. She had to fight not to retch at the stench that flew out and she turned to gasp in some much-needed fresh air. Stale alcohol was just one of the beastly smells. She forced herself to peer into what was the only living room. Her fears had been justified; there was no one here but the scene was one of violence, the few bits of basic furniture overturned, and crocks, ale flagons and gin bottles thrown about and smashed. It had been an age since a fire had been lit and ashes seemed to have been kicked out of it. Rachel recalled the smudgy dark marks on Eva's face and legs – some of the cinders had hit her. The walls were filthy and dripping with grease. Rachel felt contaminated just looking over the threshold. She swallowed down her disgust. How could people live without a trace of shame? There was a sense of hopelessness – no light, no life, just utter degradation and depravity. It was no wonder the Bowden father had killed himself to get away from this.

She had to grip Eva's hand tightly to prevent her slipping off, for she was struggling to get away. Who could blame her for not wanting to return here?

'Hello, Mrs Bowden?' The reeking odours thwarted Rachel's attempt to call out in a strong voice. 'Are you there? My name is Rachel Kivell. I've brought Eva home. Where are you?' There was silence, a heavy stillness, brooding and somehow final. Had the other inhabitants of this disgusting place absconded? 'Eva, where's your mother?' Rachel repeated until she was understood.

'Mother!' Eva cried out. Flinging her bundle on the fouled floor she pointed frantically to a curtain hanging lopsidedly on a wall.

Rachel guessed the curtain hid another room, a bedroom, and Mrs Judy Bowden must be in there. Intuition made her fear what the curtain concealed. Eva yanked her hand free and ran to where a makeshift sideboard was tipped over and she huddled down beside it. There was nowhere sanitary enough for Rachel to risk putting down the food bundle. 'Stay there, Eva,' she said, raising her voice for emphasis. 'Don't run away. I'll make sure everything will be all right.' She hoped she could keep her promise. Climbing over the remnants of a chair and other poor quality oddments she reached the curtain.

Her instinct was to recoil, but clamping her teeth to her bottom lip she edged the curtain aside. This second room contained nothing but sacking and a mattress for sleeping on, and down on the floor near the mattress lay a woman.

'Dear God!' Rachel clamped a hand to her mouth, overwhelmed by fear, horror and nausea. Judy Bowden was dead, murdered, with a pick – a miner's tool – embedded in her chest. There were a lot of injuries, blood and mess. Silas Bowden must have come home from the mine and butchered his mother. Eva may or may not have been aware of all that had happened but she had fled for her life. And Rachel had brought her back and put them both into terrible danger.

Rachel found her feet. 'Eva! Come with me! We must leave at once. Take my hand, we must run as fast as we can.'

'You're going nowhere!'

Rachel's heart jerked in terror. In the doorway, drunk and unsteady and blocking their escape, was a stocky, bull-necked man. He was splashed with blood.

'I kicked that imbecile out of here an hour or two ago. You've made a big mistake, lady dogooder, bringing her back.'

'I'm a Kivell,' Rachel hurled at him, gaining a little hope that Silas Bowden was unarmed and his balance erratic. 'If you hurt me you'll have every Kivell in Meryen and Burnt Oak after you. They'll never stop hunting you down. Let me take Eva out of here. I promise I won't raise a hue and cry until you've had time to get away.'

Silas Bowden belched out roars of crazed laughter. 'If I wanted to get away I'd be well past Redruth by now, wouldn't I? I'll be caught whatever I do, but I'm not going to hang for it. My father might have chosen that way out but I fancy going out in a bit more of a spectacle.'

'What do you mean?' Rachel gulped. She closed in on Eva and stood in front of her.

'What a touching little scene,' Bowden sneered. 'The two of you can be found huddled up. You'll be a dead heroine, Kivell lady, a blackened skeleton, clutching on to a worthless bunch of twisted bones.'

'No!' Rachel froze. Bowden was holding out a handful of matches – it would only take one flame to ignite the splashed alcohol. Then she called up her courage and was incensed with rage. She wasn't going to meekly allow Eva and herself to be hurt. Dropping the food she snatched up a broken chair leg and launched it at the brute, looking for the next missile. 'Fight, Eva, fight, fight!' Instinct for survival made Eva obey.

The chair leg struck Bowden on the shoulder. He was so fanatical that while being bombarded with bits of furniture and broken crockery he was howling with laughter and attempting to strike the matches. Needing to do something more drastic, Rachel grabbed the chair seat and, thrashing through the debris, she ran at Bowden. Screaming with effort and desperation, she raised the weapon and drove it against him with all her might. The propulsion hurtled Bowden clean out of doors. He was propelled many steps backward but managed to remain upright, on swaying feet. A lighted match had hit the floor and it ignited a pool of alcohol. Rachel screamed. Seizing the bundle of clothes she spread them apart and jumped on them, suffocating the flames before they turned into an inferno.

Bellowing in rage Bowden careered inside, throwing all his weight at Rachel and before she could sidestep the smouldering clothes he caught her round the neck. Slavering and grunting, he squeezed and squeezed and she felt herself choking but she fought back, kicking out while trying to lever his brutal hands from her throat. A bloodied gash appeared on

Bowden's head as Eva hit him with a piece of crock. Rachel grew light-headed and her blood thundered in her ears. Bowden was getting the better of her. She was going to die and then he'd kill Eva. All she could think of was that her aim to help Eva would result in a painful death for the poor woman, her last moments on earth filled with terror, and that she herself would never see James again.

Suddenly the hands that were killing Rachel were wrenched free from her and, off balance, she fell to the floor. With her sight hazy she could make out Bowden being punched on the jaw by another man. Bowden hit the floor like a rock, knocked out. She and Eva were saved.

Eva scrabbled over to her, throwing herself across her chest, squawking, 'Miss! Miss!'

Her senses clearing, rubbing at her painful neck, Rachel's voice emerged raw and husky. 'I'm all right, Eva. Shush, shush now. We're both safe, thanks to...?' Her grateful gaze at the stranger was rewarded with an angry glare. She fell silent. She had been a fool, had acted on stubborn impulse and it had very nearly brought devastating consequences. She had so nearly selfishly left James to go on without her, although so often he had stressed that he couldn't bear it if he lost her.

'It was a good thing my mother kept watching you, Miss Rachel Kivell. She saw you duck off rather than fetching your menfolk. You were mad to face Bowden by yourself,' the man threw at her in biting tones. He kicked rubbish

CAERDYDD

out of his way to reach her and the now quiet Eva. 'Damned do-gooders.'

'At least I tried to do something for poor Eva,' Rachel croaked, shamed and angry at the stranger's rebuke – he could be no other than Flint Retallack. 'The men in the village could have stopped Bowden bullying her at any time. He's murdered his mother. Her body is in the other room.' She pushed away the big rough hand that reached down to help her up. 'Don't touch me. I can get up by myself.'

'Please yourself. Judy's dead?' Flint Retallack went to the curtain to see for himself.

It took an undignified struggle for Rachel to get herself and Eva upright with Eva clinging to her. Her legs were shaking and her balance was horribly undecided. She remembered what she owed this man and his mother, but she would not forfeit her higher station. 'I thank you for saving our lives, Flint Retallack. Your intervention means Bowden can now rightly face the gallows. I wish to speak to your mother; please take us to her.'

'You're in no position to hand out orders, Miss Kivell. You can wait until I tie Bowden up; don't want him coming round and getting away. Then I'll take you to safety and fetch the constable – and,' he added with cynicism, 'your brother from the church.'

Rachel turned Eva away from the spectacle of her brother being bound up where he was sprawled. 'You'll soon forget about this.' She tidied the woman's shawl about her ugly face,

36

glancing over her shoulder to see how Flint Retallack was progressing. He was swarthy and martial in appearance, with a strong jaw line, more hardy and masculine than James. James was by far the superior, polite and honourable and without the slightest hint of vulgarity. 'Come along, Eva. We'll wait outside.'

Her heart gave a silent cry of emotion to be out of the putrid, evil atmosphere. The bitterly cold air was almost a relief; she prayed it would dissipate some of the mental and physical horrors she had experienced today. Flint Retallack joined them and pulled the door shut.

Rachel knew it was out of the question to reach his home by way of the muddy track, but she was dismayed to have to parade all the way up the twelve-house terrace of Edge End, to run a gauntlet of curious eyes, of women, children, old people, and miners not on core, neighbours alerted by the disturbance. Flint Retallack answered all their questions, and was able to delegate the fetching of the constable and alert those in the church.

Minutes later Rachel knew the merciful comfort of a seat beside the hearth in Mrs Retallack's gleaming clean kitchen, waiting for a hot drink.

'I'm sorry Eva and I are in an unfortunate condition, Mrs Retallack,' Rachel said, shivering now and then. 'I owe you and your son my deepest gratitude.' Eva was perched on a brass box for kindling wood, leaning towards the warmth of the black iron cooking slab.

'What are you going to do with her? With Eva?' Flint demanded, keeping an unfriendly stance on his feet.

'Well, she can't go back to that hovel. It's only fit to be burned down. She couldn't look after herself anyway. I, um...'

'You'll what?' Flint's eyes narrowed in his leonine face. 'She's your responsibility now. Has that sunk in yet? Does it sit on your fine shoulders?'

'Flint, don't forget you're speaking to a lady,' his embarrassed mother chided.

'She's not gentry, mother, nowhere near it. The fact remains that she's taken it upon herself to take control of Eva Bowden, and I'm interested to know what she's going to do about it. Don't suppose her men will want what they'll see as an infested imbecile staying under their roof. They'll want her put in the asylum.'

'Hold your tongue,' Rachel snapped, wincing as it hurt her throat, shooting an anxious glance at Eva, who was thankfully slurping down a mug of warm cocoa she'd just been given. 'The poor soul has probably been frightened many times before by that threat. I am quite willing to do my best for Eva. A Kivell never shirks from their duty and we do have compassion whatever you and others may think.' She meant every word, but if Eva were given a home at Chy-Henver it would make it even harder for her to see James alone.

'Flint, you're not helping,' Mrs Retallack said, her round cheeks burning with embarrassment. 'You get on in the smallholding until the constable comes to question you. The subject of Eva is best left to us women.'

'Best left to Miss Kivell and Miss Kivell alone, don't forget that, Mother.' Throwing Rachel a last frosty stare, he went out.

'Sorry about that,' Mrs Retallack said, handing Rachel strong tea in a cup and saucer. 'Flint has been very protective of me since we lost his father in an accident at the mine and his brother to consumption.'

'There is no need to apologize, Mrs Retallack. I'm sorry to have intruded on you. My brother should be here soon and we'll be out of your way.'

'You're not bothering me, Miss Kivell. I don't get a lot of company unless at chapel or chapel meetings. Flint's either working or out and about most of the time. It's very brave, what you've done, very charitable. Your family aren't much for having a faith, but you go to church, don't you? You've set a fine example.'

'I didn't help Eva for that,' Rachel replied. She only attended the church because James and his wife went regularly. She dismissed the picture of Charlotte Lockley, older than her husband, the one with money in the marriage, a slim, unsure, colourless, eager-to-please sort. It stirred unwelcome guilt to dwell on the lady. Charlotte Lockley was shy but friendly, and was devoted to James. 'I've got to consider what's the best for Eva. Are there any relatives who might take her in?'

39

'None that I know of,' Mrs Retallack disappointed her, eyeing Eva sadly. 'She could go to the workhouse, I suppose, but I don't think the poor soul would last five minutes there.'

'I won't let that happen to her. I could take her home with me, but it's a household full of men, and people are always coming and going to the busy workshop. She might be frightened.' Rachel genuinely wanted to see Eva cared for but she was desperate not to take on her care personally. She couldn't take her along, bringing all the complications, when she went off with James, hopefully in the near future. She had an idea; it was a terrible cheek, but she ploughed on, 'Will you consider taking her in, Mrs Retallack? I know it's a lot to ask, but I'm worried Eva might not like it away from the village. I'll provide for all her needs and pay you for your services. I'm not trying to shirk my responsibility, please believe me but ... well...' Blushing, she had run out of argument.

'It's no job for a lady,' Mrs Retallack said, believing it was what Rachel had meant. 'I understand. You'd hardly know where to start, Miss Kivell.' She gazed at Eva, now snuggled up in her shawl, humming and staring into space. 'She's forgotten about her mother already. Her little mind is only ever on the moment. Once she's cleaned up – and that's going to be something of a battle – I don't suppose she'd be much trouble, but my son wouldn't like it.'

'If you are prepared to show that much

charity, cannot he?' Rachel encouraged. 'Surely you have the right to make this decision.'

''Tisn't that.' Mrs Retallack looked down.

'He'd think I was putting on you? It wouldn't be that entirely, Mrs Retallack. You'd be paid handsomely and I'll pay a lump sum today. You'll have some company. You sounded a little lonely just now. You could take Eva to chapel; what better for her soul?'

Mrs Retallack took a sip of her tea, pondering. 'Flint will say I don't need the money. He provides for us both very well,' she tagged on proudly. She gazed at Eva. 'She's quiet as a lamb, dear of her. Well, I suppose I could give it a try.'

'Really? Eva would be so much better off here than anywhere else. She does look quite comfortable here, bless her. Is that an agreement?' Rachel held her breath.

'I'll tell you what I'll do. I'll take her for a week and see how things work out, but mind you, Miss Kivell, if for some reason I can't manage I'll bring her straight to your door.' In bustling mode, Mrs Retallack put on water to heat up. 'Actually it would be good to have someone about the place. I'll get Mrs Frettie Endean, the midwife, to help me scrub her up nice and clean. Eva can wear one of my night-dresses for now.'

'Thank you so much. You have my word I'll give you all the support you need.' Rachel's relief was so great, coming on the heels of her terrible ordeal, she felt light-headed, and now

41

she seriously considered it, Eva really would be better off here among her own people. She mentioned what had happened to the bundle of clothes. 'I'll get my brother to pass in some more when he returns after taking me home. I'll give him some money for you, Mrs Retallack, enough to also get some boots and shoes measured for Eva and to go to our Uncle Cardell, the apothecary, to get some treatment for her.'

There was a knock on the front door. Rachel sprang up. 'That's Jowan now. Tell the constable he can speak to me at home. I'll call and see how Eva is tomorrow, if I may. I won't disturb her now, I'll creep away or she might fret if she sees me leaving.'

'You'll be very welcome here any time,' Mrs Retallack said. 'Now you go home and see to yourself, miss. You must be worn out.'

'I shall summon the doctor.' Rachel smiled. She appreciated the motherly advice and the way Irene Retallack treated her with respect. Her father, the late, notorious Titus Kivell, a murderous rogue, had taken two common wives in addition to his churched wife and had sired numerous children. She and Jowan were illegitimate. Generally this was overlooked due to them being placed well and hard working, but some looked down on them. She'd had to go through a private baptism to be allowed to join the church.

At last she was on the way home up on the covered business cart, unheeding the lecture Jowan was giving her for ignoring Mrs Retallack's initial advice. She had received a hug and a kiss from him at first, and now she leaned against his strong arm and clung to it.

'Are you hurt?' Jowan softened. The brother and sister were very close, and he was eager she would do well in life.

'It will take a long while to get over all that's happened.' The only way she was going to get the gruesome picture of Judy Bowden's hacked up corpse out of her mind was to see James. She really needed him.

Three

It was after dark when Dr James Lockley arrived at Chy-Henver on his dog cart. 'Please accept my apologies for being unable to attend on you earlier, Miss Kivell. I had been required at Poltraze for some hours.'

In her nightgown, shawl and soft slippers, Rachel was resting against pillows, swathed by a blanket, on the settee in the sitting room. If she had taken to her bed, Jowan and Thad would have stayed close outside the open bedroom door – being territorial about their women was a Kivell trait. Right now they were completing her abandoned work in the office. Rachel assumed James had been called to Mrs

Nankervis, the squire's wife, who, apparently, was enduring a difficult pregnancy, but Rachel wasn't interested in her.

'I understand, Dr Lockley.' She gave him a secret smile. How handsome he was in an immaculate suit of clothes and dark green silk necktie. James responded with the sort of smile that made her insides melt. After hours of impatient waiting she fought down the desire to snatch the moment and reach out for him. He was here at last, and vibrant colour surged into her paleness. James made her feel a whole woman and deliciously alive.

'You have undergone a terrifying experience, Miss Kivell. May I commend you on your compassion and bravery? I'll try not to make my examination traumatic, especially about your neck. Lie prone for me please.'

Pushing aside the blanket, Rachel lay straight and untied the ribbon at the top of her lace-trimmed nightgown. She told him where she was hurt. He came close, bringing the tantalizing smell of his spicy cologne. As his gentle hands glided over her, probing gently, the horrors of her fright began to lose their grip on her. He was entirely professional as he summed up the extent of her bruises, cuts and grazes. Then he glanced at the door and listened for interruption. Rachel listened too. They could hear the other men's low voices a safe distance away in the office. Smiling into her eyes, he whispered, 'My darling girl, I don't wish you such dreadful drama but it's a joy to see you

44

unexpectedly.'

'You say the dearest things.' She leaned up on her elbows and offered him her lips and he took them. He was mild in manner in all things except lovemaking and he kissed her in a most disrespectful manner and pushed his hand inside her nightgown, round and round and down and down, but not for long. Flushed faces and heavy breathing could not be quickly dissipated and never explained. After the harrowing moments of the day, Rachel was happy beyond belief. 'I wish we could be together.'

'I too, so very much. I'll try to get to our special place tomorrow in the afternoon. Will you be there?'

'Nothing would stop me.' She'd go to the house she was renting under an assumed name, after seeing Eva.

Returning to proper conduct, James swept the blanket over her and pulled vials and small cork-stopper bottles out of his fat leather bag. 'In my opinion you have been most fortunate, Miss Kivell. I foresee no lasting physical effects from your ordeal but do let me know if you are troubled. I'll leave you some medication for tonight and a valerian draught to help you sleep, and I shall write out prescriptions to be taken to your family apothecary. I advise you to rest as you feel necessary and to eat lightly so as not to overtax your digestion.'

'Thank you, Dr Lockley.' She retied her ribbons, then whispered, 'I love you, James.'

'And I— Good heavens!' He leapt back from

45

her in guilty fashion. 'What on earth was that?'

'It's someone at the front door.' Rachel was cross at the second repetitive banging of the day. Unlike this morning, it started off the dogs barking in the kitchen. She pulled her shawl on, sat up straight and tucked the blanket about herself demurely. 'Someone in need of your urgent services, I'll warrant. It can't be anything else.'

'Mrs Nankervis...' James muttered worriedly, repacking his bag hastily.

Jowan and Thad Kivell got to their feet at the same moment. 'I'll go,' Jowan said. Although the younger of the two, he always took the lead – Thad was unusually quiet and peaceful for a well-built, black-haired Kivell.

'I'll see if the doctor is finished with Rachel,' Thad said.

The knocking on the door turned into a hammering. 'Open up! Open up!' cried a rather refined male voice. Some snobbish servant sent over from Poltraze, Jowan assumed, picking up an oil lamp from the hall side table.

'Hold on there!' He took his time. He wasn't about to beat a drum for a Nankervis. The door wasn't locked until bedtime. He opened it and peered out. 'What do you want?'

He was surprised to be faced not with a servant but a finely attired gentleman, stamping his well-booted feet and rubbing together his kid-gloved hands. Jowan's brows shot up when a lady in a velvet bonnet, travelling outfit and fur-trimmed mantle pushed her way in front of

46

the gentleman. She was holding a tiny brown and white dog, no bigger than a hand muff. 'Why did you take so long to answer? Have you no hospitality to offer distressed travellers? Let us inside at once.'

Jowan never paid heed to uncivil demands, not even from a high-bred female, who was obviously as cold and wind-harassed as her companion. 'What's happened?' he asked the gentleman.

'Must you prevaricate? Let us in out of this dreadful weather,' the lady said, and tried to push her way inside. Jowan refused to budge.

'Leave this to me, Helen, do.' The gentleman used ungainly force to lever her aside. 'We've had an accident with our carriage, sir,' he said, modulating his cut-glass tone into one edged with an ingratiating plea. 'If we may be permitted to step inside...'

Jowan nodded and moved out of the doorway. The lady stepped over the threshold in a huff, followed quickly by the gentleman. Jowan closed the door. He returned the lamp to its place. 'Tell me what's happened?'

'First allow me to introduce us, sir,' the over-fleshed and top-heavy gentleman said, while the lady stuck her chin up in ire, making her pearly-fair ringlets swing. He flourished a hand, as one who was well practised in lavishing out charm. 'I am Mr Ashley Faulkner and the lady is my sister, Lady Churchfield. We are on our way to Poltraze, on an errand of mercy, to support our cousin, Mrs Nankervis, during her confinement. We've come all the way down from Norfolk. Unfortunately, the carriage we had hired to take us there, after we'd rested at the Red Lion Hotel at Truro, came off the road about half a mile away. The coachman hurt his back while he was trying to haul it out and is now quite unable to move. We spied your lights and thought it would do well to find this place and request assistance. I was about to set off alone but Lady Churchfield could not countenance the idea of remaining behind, unprotected from the weather. The carriage is unstable; it's tipping to the side. Indeed we did well to scramble out of it without injury.'

'And you've left the coachman lying on the ground unattended?' Jowan muttered tersely.

'My brother left him in the lee of the carriage,' Lady Churchfield rolled the words coldly off her tongue. 'My maid is with him. He will not fare too badly if you would only refrain from delaying the recovery of the carriage,' she added with extreme irritation. 'The coachman is a fool. Apparently somewhere along the route from Truro he took a wrong turning.'

'He took several wrong turnings to be on this road,' Thad said, joining them. 'I'm sorry for your catastrophe.' He shook his head when Jowan smirked at his use of the last strong word. 'As it happens we have a doctor in our midst. He and I can be with the coachman in a short while. Jowan, will you come too? Perhaps between us we can pull the carriage back on its wheels.'

'I thank you, sir.' Ashley Faulkner spoke to Thad; unlike his sister he seemed to be unruffled by Jowan's lack of charity and subservience. 'I shall go with you. Then we may be on our way very shortly. May I know your names?'

Thad told him, then received a further disparaging ascension of eyes from Jowan by next employing the politest tone. 'May I suggest Lady Churchfield joins my cousin, who is Jowan's sister, Miss Rachel Kivell, in the sitting room?'

Puzzled over who had been admitted to the house, Rachel was looking expectantly towards the door. So was James, at a suitable distance from her. Both were surprised at the distinguished guest who was shown into the room by Thad, who gave the explanation.

Like a ship in full sail Lady Helen breezed to an armchair close to the fireside and sat down without invitation. 'Do forgive the intrusion while you are indisposed, Miss Kivell,' she intoned, making herself comfortable and settling the dog on her lap. 'If you could get on, Dr Lockley, Mrs Nankervis is expecting me and she will be frantic over the delay.'

'I'll do my best for the coachman,' James said in an officious tone. He loathed the way some of the gentry treated him as if he was no more than a tradesman. It was unlikely he would be paid for his trouble. As the second son of a lawyer his position was hard won. This woman lived off the sweat of the poor, whom she almost certainly had no care for. She was a leech, a worthless being. She had no right to look down on him. This was a sore point with James. His in-laws had declared to his face, in front of Charlotte, that he was beneath her, accusing his intentions to use her for her money and to climb socially in Bath, and with little to recommend him he had only secured an inferior post of village doctor and mine surgeon in this backwater part of the most south-western county. Charlotte coped admirably with her family's disappointment in her and their ostracizing of him. Just one aunt, Charlotte's doting godmother, Mrs Eliza Wellbeloved, had offered to help her at any time but Charlotte was too proud to accept and James was too proud to consider it. The Wellbeloveds had humiliated him and he loathed them for it.

'Mrs Nankervis told me she was expecting relatives but she had forgotten quite when you were due to arrive. I'm afraid she has been a little forgetful of late.'

'Oh, then there is no real panic after all.' Lady Churchfield looked about the surroundings.

'I'll bid you good night, Miss Kivell. Do send word if you need my services again. Good night, Lady Churchfield.' He picked up his bag and left on a brisk step.

'What a dear little room,' Helen Churchfield remarked, peeling off her gloves. As her differing surname to her brother suggested, she wore a gold wedding band. 'Ring for some tea would you, Miss Kivell? And perhaps you would allow a little warm milk for my dear little Venetia.'

Rachel was peeved to have lost James's company so abruptly, and she was annoyed to be placed in an inferior position in her own home. 'I don't have any live-in staff, my lady. If you will excuse me I'll go along to the kitchen.'

'You have no servants? Are you not middle-class? How do you manage?'

Rachel was acutely embarrassed. Most Kivells still didn't conform to patterns and trends and didn't always show that they considered themselves a little above the newly emerging middle class. She had Dora's daily services as well as a washerwoman and a part-time gardener. She enjoyed cooking and saw no reason for someone to wait on her every minute.

'A mean decision on the part of your ill-bred brother, no doubt,' Lady Churchfield went on. 'He needs to learn some manners. My late husband had a mean streak. You have my sympathy, Miss Kivell. Is that sherry in the decanter over there? That will do.'

'Over there' was the wine table, mere inches away from the lady, who was not inclined to rise to her richly shod feet to pour the drink, and obviously did not care that Rachel had just been attended by a doctor. Rachel got up awkwardly. The bruises blooming on her arm, legs and side from the fall in the garden were painful. She poured two glasses of sherry and handed one to her guest, who grimaced before accepting it.

51

Rachel didn't care that she had made a faux pas by not serving the sherry on a tray.

Lady Helen tasted the sherry then declared in surprised appreciation, 'Good stuff. Your brother keeps a good wine cellar.' She peered about again. 'But I don't suppose you actually have a cellar.'

'No, we don't,' Rachel muttered, irked that she was compelled to speak to this arrogant creature, which hurt her raw throat. She looked away sharply.

'Oh dear!' Lady Helen exclaimed. 'I've just noticed your neck. I thought you might have a little chill. I didn't realize you've had an accident, or...?' She leaned towards Rachel. 'Do forgive me, but is your brother violent towards you?'

Rachel felt the question had been delivered in a searching way and to provide amusement, and she was furious. 'My brother is nothing but good and generous to me. What makes you assume he is a brute?'

'I'm very sorry I asked.' Helen Churchfield made an expression of faint ridicule and leaned back in her chair.

'Actually, I was very nearly murdered today,' Rachel ground out. What would the unfeeling witch make of that?

'Really? Poor you,' was only the interest given. The lady was concerned only with her own dramas.

Rachel deliberated that she and the other woman couldn't be more different. Lady Helen

Churchill had no true humanity or high values. Chances were against her having shown dear Eva even the slightest pity.

Moments later Helen Churchfield said, as if nothing chilly had occurred, 'I have to say you have some very fine pieces of furniture. What business does your family do?'

'Carpentry and cabinet-making. We get all of Poltraze's commissions for the woodwork and furniture,' Rachel replied briefly, sipping the last of her sherry and longing to go to bed. Her head ached, her throat throbbed angrily and her every bone felt under attack. Thanks to this unwelcome guest she had lost the precious intimacy she could usually hold on to for a while after being with James. She wondered about Eva. Had she screamed and struggled when Irene Retallack and her neighbour had stripped her to scrub her clean? And when the ointments and poultices had been applied? Had she been frightened of Jowan when he'd stopped off to hand in five pounds, a sum from Rachel's savings for when she absconded with James? Was she now tucked up in her new bed and sleeping like the child she was? She hoped the boorish Flint Retallack had not made Eva feel intimidated. It struck Rachel then that she had not thanked the miner properly for saving her life. If not for him she would not be here now suffering the presence of this overbearing madam, and she wouldn't have just seen James again.

'Of course!' Helen Churchfield's indolently

arched eyebrows rose up to her sculptured hairline. 'Kivell. My cousin wrote to me some four years ago, shortly after her marriage to the squire, about a double murder involving the head gardener there and an old woman, both named Kivell. Your family seems to be connected with murder.'

'Indeed it is, Lady Churchfield,' Rachel retorted fiercely. 'Laketon Kivell was a sadistic killer and my grandmother, who was a lady by birth, deliberately shot him in the west wing of Poltraze to prevent him murdering the squire, and others. It's an accepted fact that Laketon haunts the whole house; he is an evil presence there, and people quake in their beds and are afraid to wander the house alone. I doubt you'll enjoy your stay there.'

'Oh, ghosts don't worry me. Mrs Nankervis wrote that Poltraze is sometimes a deathly cold and cheerless place. Do not be so defensive, Miss Kivell.' Lady Helen took Rachel off beat by smiling without her usual sarcasm and adding confidentially, 'Many a fine skeleton jangles its chains in my family's history.'

'Including murder?' Rachel hoped to have her admit this.

'Hasn't every great family?' Helen Churchfield was unconcerned. 'You don't know the squire personally, of course, but what impression do you get of him?'

Rachel sensed the question was important to her. 'Does not Mrs Nankervis mention him in her correspondence?'

'Of course, she does. Well?'

'He's very distant.' To Rachel, Mr Michael Nankervis was a pompous man who processed self-righteously up to the front of the church every Sunday morning, he having lavished money on much needed repairs to St Meryen's and the churchyard, replacing all the pews, the windows with beautiful stained glass, and titivating the Nankervis tombs. His wife was like a shadow, plain and bookish, and bloated in pregnancy. Adeline Nankervis had not been seen out for some time now. The squire might find Lady Churchfield, whose classic features were just a little too strong and denied her being a devastating beauty, quite a draw in comparison.

Lady Churchfield said no more. She seemed submerged in her own selfish thoughts. Rachel groaned. How much longer would she have to endure the presence of this egotistical wretch, whose intense perfume was nearly as offensive to the nose as Eva's disgusting body odours? Her body and mind were suddenly near to exhaustion. So much had happened, all in one day.

Four

'Did you bring the book I asked you to, Helen?'
Adeline Nankervis enquired in her muted
voice. She was looking forward to reading her
umpteenth book since the doctor had ordered
her to take indefinite bed rest. Her cousin had
just flounced into the room, the master bedroom of the oldest part of Poltraze, and seated
herself at the farthest window to gaze out across
the parkland. Helen looked as bored as on every
other of the ten days she had been there. She
had brought a lot of trunks and had worn a
different dress and jewels every day. Adeline
knew she was drab in comparison in a linen
nightgown, cap and shawl, but she was not
envious; rather she found Helen's sparkling
appearance disorganized the quiet order of the
house. Helen, and Ashley too, were causing a
lot of disturbance in the house with constant
demands on the servant and their need to be
entertained.

'Some boring old history book, wasn't it?'
Helen shrugged. 'I forgot all about it. Oh,
Adeline, can you not get out of bed? You may
have had a little bleeding but you've said that
was weeks ago. Come downstairs to the

56

morning room so we can do something to-gether. I have no one to talk to. At any minute your wretched nurse will barge in and order me out. What am I supposed to do with myself day after day? Nothing goes on here. The only visitor you have had is the doctor's plain wife. Surely you don't need all this rest.'

Adeline rubbed her forehead; even a few minutes of Helen's company was a strain. She regretted writing that she was having a difficult time with her pregnancy, which had brought Helen down here. She was the same petulant and utterly selfish girl Adeline remembered from their childhood days during family visits to Norfolk. 'I will do all in my power to ensure I have a healthy child, even if it means I remain here for the next two months. Dr Lockley knows best.'

'Oh, that doctor! He's only ordered bed rest so he can call everyday and earn more money from you.'

'Helen, it took a long time for me to conceive and Michael and I are anxious for all to go well, can't you understand that? Surely you wanted to give Lawrence a child?' Adeline closed her eyes as her head began to throb.

'Perish the thought! Nothing would have in-duced me to endure all that pain and indignity. I would have been ashamed at producing a brat as ugly as he was.' Helen looked away for a moment. She had successfully avoided preg-nancy by keeping marital relations with her sixty-five-year-old husband to just the honeymoon, but not mothering an heir for Fairbrook Hall had proved to be her biggest mistake. Immediately on Lawrence's death, the nephew who had inherited his estate had cast her adrift without a penny. 'Adeline dear,' she cajoled with a pout. 'Please get up, and don't frown so, you will look old before your time.'

'I already do. No one would guess I am but twenty-five years,' Adeline murmured, feeling faint.

'Indeed,' Helen replied, deliberately unkind. The drawing room and boudoir living she was accustomed to, the pampering she'd assured she had received, had given her a dazzlingly fair complexion. Adeline looked about to fade into the gloom of this dull, dull room. Helen had expected life here at Poltraze to be quiet, waiting for her dreary, somewhat reclusive cousin to give birth, but things were crushingly monotonous and Helen resented it. Michael Nankervis was a good catch for Adeline. A former widower, his forebears had acquired wealth from leasing their land for mineral rights, but he was of no particular consequence in Cornwall, and he was unbelievably enchanted with his uninspiring, bleak ancestral home, which was so small compared to what she was used to.

'I can't wait for you to deliver and hand the brat over to the nursery. Adeline, do cheer up. This is all too much for me. Why do you use this room and not the new grand suite in the west wing? I've peeked into it. It's modern and vibrant compared to elsewhere. It's foolish to worry about ghosts and believe the suite holds bad luck. I shall ask Mr Nankervis if I can move into it. Are you listening, Adeline? You would feel better if you did something to brighten this room. It's so terribly austere, hardly a scrap of colour in it, not one pretty ornament. The bed looks more like a giant coffer than somewhere to sleep peacefully or make love in. Order some plants to be brought in and flowers to be picked, Adeline. It would make a start.'

'The nurse wouldn't allow it,' Adeline sighed, her long-suffering look deepening. Helen was wearing her out. 'She says the pollen wouldn't be good for me.'

'Nonsense, I've been in childbed rooms before and they were overflowing with blooms. Surely a mother-to-be will be healthier if she is happier. You allow yourself to be bullied, Adeline. I wouldn't allow anyone to tell me what to do.'

'I suppose I could ask Dr Lockley's opinion when he calls later today,' Adeline said uncertainly. To go against medical advice would be to go against Michael's wishes. She had a different view to matrimony than Helen; she wouldn't dream of disobeying her husband. She loved Michael, not passionately, but with a gentle, devoted love. She was grateful to have won a husband when she had thought – as Helen had jibed for many years – that she would end up an old maid. She and Michael enjoyed the same things: history, books, and a

59

quiet, uncomplicated life. She took the focus off herself. 'Do you miss Fairbrook Hall?'

'Yes.' Helen looked up angrily at the plaster ceiling. 'I miss my lavish lifestyle and high social life.'

'Ashley lived with you at Fairbrook Hall. What is the property you now have like? You did not it mention it very much in your letters.' Letters from Helen had only started after her widowhood, fifteen months ago. How Adeline wished she had never replied. Helen was a thorn in the flesh, and Ashley, although a charmer, was a wastrel. Their elder brother who had inherited the family estate did not welcome Helen or Ashley under his roof, and Helen complained bitterly about it.

'Adequate, I suppose,' Helen sighed moodily, shifting her eyes, oblivious to her cousin's discomfort. 'Well, I shall make myself scarce before the doctor arrives. He's a rather good-looking individual but there's nothing else to commend him. His marriage is the opposite of what mine was. It's the wife who is much older and ugly and has the money – very little money in her case, but I suppose he believes he lives well in this God-forsaken backwater.'

'Backwater? You really don't need to stay here, Helen. And I wouldn't call Charlotte Lockley ugly,' Adeline defended her only friend as she lay fighting off nausea. Charlotte was kindness and compassion itself, whereas Helen, who had virtually taken over the role of mistress here, disaffecting the servants, was self-centred, frivolous and intolerant. 'Helen, you should not be so uncharitable.'

The nurse emerged from the adjoining dressing room in dove-grey and starched whites, and moved swiftly on soft steps over the aging Eastern carpet. Marjorie Floyd, of silver-rimmed eye-glasses, adroit features and ram-rod posture, took one glance at her patient and shot off an order. 'I'm afraid I must ask you to leave, Lady Churchfield. Mrs Nankervis is not looking at all well. Pray do not come back without checking with me first.' The squire had given Nurse Floyd his assurances that she was in charge of the rest room.

'As you please. Rest well, Adeline.' Without a single glance at the bed, Helen glided out of the room.

She took a few dragging steps along the dark corridor, the high panelled walls crowded with lacklustre paintings of bygone Nankervises, a dark-haired, self-aggrandizing breed. The floorboards creaked, disquieting her, and she looked over her shoulder. Despite her assertion to Adeline she was sometimes unnerved by the thought of the house being haunted. There was a heavy, brooding atmosphere, which seemed ominous at times, but it could be, she supposed, because she knew she wasn't welcome here.

She wondered what Ashley was doing, probably still lazing in bed chomping his way through a big breakfast. She pouted. Ashley should make the effort to fit in with the timing of the Nankervis household. She would have a word with him. But, just as quickly, she decided against it. He would only throw her faults at her. He implored her to be more amiable, to show some interest in young Cecily and Jemima Nankervis, Adeline's stepdaughters. She wouldn't find that easy; the girls were irritating, giggly creatures. She and Ashley were both being foolish. They should be behaving circumspectly, making themselves acceptable. Their position was precarious and they were at the mercy of Michael Nankervis. He was their last hope of providing a comfortable roof over their heads. She must change her haughty ways or she would almost certainly regret it. She must think of a way to cheer Adeline without offending her wretched nurse, to show Adeline she would make her an indispensable companion. She wouldn't suggest to Ashley that he change his ways. She hoped Michael Nankervis would eject him. She did not care about her brother at all. She hated him clinging to her. All his life he had never been any use to anyone.

What was she going to do with the rest of the boring day? She had sent letters announcing her arrival at Poltraze to some of the local big houses, including the fairly nearby Tehidy estate – the titled Basset family were among the wealthiest and most important of the old Cornish families. So far she had not received a single reply. It was very worrying. How was she to bag herself another rich husband if she did not have a social life? Two gentlemen had called here but neither had been eligible for marriage. She just *had* to meet someone and get him to fall in love with her. The only thing she had to offer a husband was her breeding. She was a penniless widow who had been dropped by her usual circle. Cornwall and Poltraze, Adeline and her husband were her last resort. She had a worry concerning her maid. She had not paid Simpkins for over a year and she was threatening to find a new post. She would not be able to engage a new maid and that would be utterly humiliating. All she had in the world were the clothes she had brought with her, her sewing things and her jewels. She dreaded having to be forced to sell the jewellery and to have to live without servants in some little house in an obscure location. She wouldn't support Ashley, and she would end up living a wretched, lonely life.

Fear, something she had never really known, for she had always believed her high position was assured, sank its talons into her with full force. She had been imprudent. She had hidden it from herself, how everything had changed, and she had done nothing to beguile herself to the very people she was here seeking to use. She had arrived on a wave of complaints about her ill-fated journey. She had not even thanked the Kivell family for their help, something that had angered the squire because he had a loyal link to them, the elderly Kivell matriarch having saved his life from the murderous gardener. Since then she had antagonized everyone, even

Adeline. She must work fast and make amends or very soon she might end up living a life of hell. She must work to make Adeline like and need her. Adeline wasn't allowed flowers but what else could she do for her? She had an idea and rushed to her room.

An hour later she emerged with her sewing box and a long piece of white silk, part of a petticoat she had cut up, and on which she had started an exquisite piece of embroidery. It was for a baby's gown, and she would finish it with lace and ribbon; she was an accomplished needlewoman. This should cheer and please Adeline, and meet with the squire's approval. She would ask the nurse politely if she could join Mrs Nankervis, promising that she would sit quietly and sew. Or read to Adeline; she would go down to the library and fetch the forgotten book. Adeline would appreciate lying back comfortably while being read to.

Ashley Faulkner had beaten his sister to the library and had entered without knocking. 'Ah, Mr Nankervis, I was hoping to find you here. May I have a word?'

'What is it you want, Faulkner?' Michael Nankervis frowned through every inch of his long, formal face. He had come in here to pick up some papers before heading to the steward's office, but had been unable to resist lowering himself into a club chair to browse through the latest instalment of William Thackeray's *Vanity Fair*. He got up sharply. 'I'm about to go out.'

He loathed Faulkner's flirtatious exuberance, the way he chomped through extra servings at every meal and made free with his wines. It was obvious what he and his insufferable sister were up to. They had become impoverished and feared destitution. They were parasites. Michael tolerated them for Adeline's sake, she being a good Christian and naturally kind, but the moment she'd had enough of them, out they would go.

'I will only take a minute of your time,' Ashley simpered, all fawning smiles. He could see the squire was more than annoyed. He and his sister had outstayed their welcome, which they had not received in the first place from Michael Nankervis, but Ashley was hardened to this sort of reception. He knew it was time to make a shrewd exit from Poltraze. 'I have come to ask if I could I prevail upon you, Mr Nankervis, for the loan of a carriage to Truro? While I was there recently I arranged a business meeting. I won't bore you with the details, just to say that I am confident that the outcome should set my sister and I up very nicely for the future. If all works out well, I shall, I'm afraid, be asking your forgiveness, for I shall be sending for my sister at once. I hope she has been of some comfort to dear Mrs Nankervis during our stay, and I shall pray for a happy outcome to the confinement. Um, this is a trifle embarrassing. It seems I am a little financially embarrassed at present. I should be honoured to repay a small loan...' All the while he had wriggled his fingers but without once casting a blush for his down-right cheek and lies.

Michael regarded him as a rake off to commit a swindle, but he would gladly give the order for Faulkner to be driven to Truro to be rid of him, and subsequently his sister. He didn't want them here when his child was born. Adeline was not strong and childbirth was a potentially dangerous experience. He couldn't bear it if he lost a son and heir, or Adeline. They didn't share a great love and he satisfied his lust elsewhere, but Adeline was the ideal wife and stepmother to his daughters. He loved her and respected her for complimenting his quiet ways. 'I fully understand, Faulkner.' His every word dripped off his tongue with disdain. 'Shall we say twenty pounds? I'll have a carriage prepared for you without delay. Do not trouble yourself with the future of my family.'

'You are too kind.' Ashley flourished a formal bow, then ventured, 'I was rather hoping of a little more money, perhaps a hundred?' Ashley showed his crooked teeth in an obscenely wide smile.

'The sum of twenty pounds remains and let that be an end to the matter,' Michael barked, loathing the toadying portly man more than ever. He strode to the door and opened it. 'Goodbye, Faulkner.'

Ashley hid his disappointment at not cutting a better deal but he had much to be jubilant over. 'I thank you for your generosity and your hospitality. I'll go straight up and take leave of

66

my room.' Ashley blinked when the door was shut firmly after him. Thanks to his worthless ways he'd had many doors closed on him.

He found Helen nearly up to him in the hallway. 'Are you thinking of going into the library, m'dear? I advise against it. The squire is within and he's in a very offhand mood today. Well, I've got things to do. I'm about to take a ride.'

'You had better not have annoyed Mr Nankervis!' Helen was surprised to find her brother up so early.

'I was sweetness and light itself, m'dear. You know how he is, rather unsociable.'

'Buffoon,' Helen called at Ashley's back as he hopped away to the stairs. She must shake him off, the sooner the better.

Heeding his advice and forgoing the fetching of the book, she waited until he had cleared the stairs before going up to Adeline. She came face to face with Dr James Lockley as he left Adeline's rooms.

'Good morning, Lady Churchfield,' James said with a dark expression. This damnable woman was causing a lot of disruption and thereby upsetting his patient. Would she be civil to him today? 'I'm afraid it is another inclement day.'

'Yes, indeed, Dr Lockley,' Helen said vaguely, having taken no notice of the weather. As long as she was warm and comfortable she didn't care what fell from the sky. Poltraze had fine woodland and kept its fires well fed with logs. 'Mrs Nankervis was a little pale when I

67

was with her earlier. I hope she is faring reasonably well.'

'If you are intending to go into her I would respectfully ask you to wait until later today, my lady. It's imperative Mrs Nankervis gets lots of rest.' James angled his head to gain the best view of her in the dim daylight. She was not displeasing in looks but every inch of her exuded petulance and snootiness. She could not be trusted, always looking for the main chance. She was to be despised. She was no pliable woman who willingly fell into the arms of a man. She would never offer her body as a sacrifice. She used her temple of flesh either for enjoyment or to further her own ends. She would never give herself over fully to a husband's service or spend long lonely hours aching for a lover's company, hanging on to his promises. She was an uncompromising bitch, an unfeeling termagant and a ruthless witch. She should be brought down, made to squirm.

Helen gasped at his penetrating gaze. He had no right to meet her eyes at all yet the insolent dog was scorning her, leering at her. She glowered and stamped her foot.

James did not drop his eyes but kept a steady examination. Her chest heaved in indignation and he sensed she was not far from slapping his face. Yes, she should be brought down, and he'd take delight in playing a major part in such an undertaking; it would be delicious in the extreme. She should be broken and brought to begging and a little madness.

'Dr Lockley!' Helen lifted her hand. He thoroughly deserved to have his face slapped. The derision on the man's face would be offensive to any woman, let alone one of her station. She would complain bitterly to the squire about him if she had not already made too many objections.

'Lady Churchfield,' Michael boomed, coming up on them fast. 'Have you seen your brother recently?'

'Yes, Mr Nankervis,' she said as she turned to him, taking the opportunity to treat him to a pleasant smile. 'Not many minutes ago as he was coming out of the library.'

'Then I'm sure you would rather be in his company right now. Excuse the doctor and me. I wish to have a private discussion with him.'

'Of course,' Helen said in her most melodious voice, a little puzzled at what he had meant about Ashley. Ashley was taking a ride. Her mind returned to her embroidery and how it would please Adeline.

Michael led the doctor along the corridor in the opposite direction. 'I'm pleased to say the lady's brother is leaving here today, and she soon afterward. Faulkner asked me for money. I knew from the instant I laid eyes on him he was an undesirable. It would only have been a matter of time before I'd have been forced to throw him out. Was Lady Churchfield demanding to see Mrs Nankervis? Is that why she raised her voice to you, Lockley?'

'I'm afraid it was. I prohibited her admittance to Mrs Nankervis. The nurse has informed me that the lady's demands have been greatly unsettling Mrs Nankervis. If I may venture a professional opinion on the matter, Mr Nankervis...?'

'Go ahead. I value all you have to say.'

'If Mrs Nankervis receives any more untoward distractions, I cannot guarantee she will go to full term and come through a safe delivery and produce a live and healthy child. Along with a careful diet, she needs complete rest and absolute peace.'

'Indeed.' Michael exhaled heavily. 'That is precisely what my wife will get. I shall have a footman stationed outside the room to forbid Lady Churchfield entrance. Poltraze will soon be rid of her, one way or another.'

Five

Rachel was in her own temporary little paradise, a house down a quiet back lane from the hamlet of Meadowbank, rented from the landowner under the names of a Mr and Mrs White, who required the house only occasionally when in the area. Rachel and James reached the house by a series of lonely lanes in the opposite direction of Meadowbank. Rachel had renamed the house as Lowenna, meaning joy in Cornish. It was part of her joy of being in love, the only place where she and James could be totally alone, to make love and plan their future. Lowenna would provide her with happy memories after they finally got away.

There was no definite plan for James to join her today, and Rachel passed the time dreamily playing the housewife, clearing ashes from the parlour and bedroom hearths and fetching logs from the woodshed. She assuaged her longing for James by thinking about Eva.

Arriving at Three Steps the day after Eva had turned up at Chy-Henver she had been dreading that leaving Eva with Irene Retallack had been a disaster.

'Come in, come in,' Mrs Retallack had bid her cheerily.

'How has she been?' Rachel asked in the short passageway, carrying an armful of things for Eva.

'The dear maid was lost when you went, and nervous. She kicked up some ruckus when me and Mrs Endean washed her down. She was too scared to get in the tin bath. But otherwise she's been good as gold. I was afraid she'd be scared of Flint but he spoke softly to her and kept his distance, so I think it'll be all right.'

'Is he very cross with me?' Not that Rachel really cared about that.

'Let's say he's not impressed.'

'But he doesn't mind if Eva stays?'

'Not as long as I can cope. Don't worry about Flint; he's a good man, and he'll be kind to Eva.'

'That's a relief.'

'Come into the kitchen. She's been curled up in my chair at the slab since breakfast.'

Eva was rocking and humming in the wheel-back chair, her legs up and her chin to her chest. Rachel was delighted to see her in comfort, on knitted cushions and nestled inside crocheted blankets. She was wearing an old dress and stockings of Rachel's. Rachel took one of the things she'd brought and knelt down to her. 'Hello, Eva, do you remember me?'

Recognizing her voice, Eva lifted her head. She was a curious sight, her hair and skin greasy with herbal ointments to rid her of the lice and boils. Already her eyes looked brighter and less jaundiced. She grinned, revealing her missing teeth. 'Miss!' she squeaked.

'I'm glad to see you looking so much better. Look what I've brought you.' Rachel held up a large cloth doll in colourful clothes. 'It's a doll. You can take her, she's yours.'

Cautiously Eva reached out, perhaps expecting the gift to be snatched away from her. Once she had the doll she grinned again. 'Dolly, dolly.'

'She knows what it is.' Irene clapped her hands like a proud mother. 'I'm sure she's not totally retarded.'

'Does she know how to dress herself?' Rachel asked, smiling.

'More or less, and she knows when she needs to use the privy, bless her. Do you know, Miss Rachel, I think this is going to work out.'

While she dusted the things she had brought to Lowenna for herself and James, Rachel was glad not to have to worry about Eva. She had covered the ancient solid furniture here with runners and chair backs of her own making, embroidered during the many lonely hours she had waited here hoping James would come to her. She had supplied the linen on the bed where they enjoyed each other again and again, uncaring that the mattress was lumpy. Once they had even dared to stay overnight. As a doctor, James could tell believable lies about his absence, and Rachel had fooled Jowan and Thad into believing she had stayed with one of their relatives. They had not slept throughout that night, leaving sated the next day from vigorous passion. As soon as James arrived here, and once or twice when he had been waiting impatiently for her, he'd laid his hands on her, smothering her greeting with his hungry mouth and pulling her where he may, to chair, table, down on the floor. Rachel understood his need for instant relief. He loved her, he wanted her, and he got no such loving consideration at home.

The last time they had been here together she had pressed James for a possible date when they would leave. 'When shall we go, darling?' She was naked, breathless after a fierce tumble, James looking over her hot damp limbs in the glow of the firelight. 'Surely we can decide on a place. You've been saving money and I have some of my own – surely we have enough to go away. The annual rent for this house will be due in the autumn. I'm hoping I won't need to pay for another year.'

'Well, we must not go to Bath or London,' he'd replied. 'Charlotte has family there. Nor to Dorset; that's where my people are.'

'What about Derbyshire? I've heard it's a beautiful county.'

'That's a possibility. We'll need to change our names. It will have to be somewhere capital where I can set up a better practice than my present one.' He'd resumed exploring her body with demanding hands. 'Edinburgh in Scotland comes to mind. It's an important town and a grand castle overlooks it. I owe it to Mrs Nankervis to attend on her until she has delivered her child. The squire has hinted he will reward me handsomely if I see his good lady through to a healthy birth. Think of that, beloved. Is that not worth biding here for a little longer?'

'A few weeks and then we shall definitely go?' Rachel had said with growing excitement, leaning up on her elbow, tenderly caressing his handsome fair face.

He had smiled one of his gorgeous smiles. 'For you, my darling, anything. You are lovely and absolutely perfect. I never stop counting my blessings that I have you in my life.'

'And you always will James, I promise. I can hardly wait for the day when I'll walk proudly down a street on your arm. We'll have beautiful children together.'

'Nothing could be truer. Talking of children, my love, are you late in regard to nature?'

'No,' she had been relieved to say. Twice the onset of her monthly courses had been overdue and James had examined her in an invasive manner, as only a doctor could. Used as she was to his strident lovemaking, and sometimes he would get a little out of control, she'd found the medical intrusion humiliating and painful. But it had unfortunately been necessary – she dare not bring a child into the world yet. If she had conceived from this latest lovemaking it would not matter, as they were soon finally to elope.

She waited all day, running to the living-room window, scanning the path to the lane for sign of James. Defeated again – she had not seen him since the night Poltraze's insufferable guests had parted them – with an aching heart and a void in her soul, she put out the fires. More of her time wasted. Another batch of lies she'd have to make up when Jowan and Thad asked her how she had spent her day. She gazed at the bed and big silent tears slid down her cheeks. She had so wanted James to be here, so she could look at him, touch him, slide into his arms, to lie in his adoring embrace.

She couldn't imagine a worse loneliness than being the mistress of a married man, waiting and yearning for scraps of his time. But she wouldn't change a thing and she wouldn't have to endure this much longer. She and James would soon have a proper home of their own, in Edinburgh.

Over at Poltraze, Helen looked up from her needlework. 'Is it time to change for dinner already?' Simpkins, her maid, had joined her. 'I've been so absorbed working on this for the baby I'd quite forgotten the time. I'll wear the pink satin and tulle, and the rubies.' She hoped Michael Nankervis would not shun the dining table tonight. She would try her hardest to impress him with her new caring character.

'Begging your pardon, my lady, may I have a word with you first?' Simpkins held her orderly frame pert and formal.

'You may; there's not a problem, I hope?' Helen showed patient interest. She had been gracious towards her maid since returning here this morning, where she had eaten luncheon and taken afternoon tea to keep out of everyone's way.

'I was wondering if we are about to leave here. Mrs Nankervis's personal maid has told me that Hankins the butler informed her that Mr Faulkner has had all his things packed and taken a carriage to Truro. He's not expected to return.'

The more Simpkins went on, the more every muscle in Helen's body tautened. Ashley had left without telling her? She was glad to be rid of him, but what on earth was he up to?

'Are we to join him, my lady? Because if we are, I wish to inform you that I have applied for a local post which Hankins has told me about. I'm sorry to be blunt, but if I am not paid my overdue wage in full I shall not leave Poltraze with you. Hankins is sure Mr Nankervis would kindly allow me to stay on until — '

'Never mind all that. I had no idea my brother was leaving. Run to his room and see if he has left me a note.' Helen threw the sewing down. 'I want to know what is going on.'

Simpkins left to perform the task while Helen paced the carpet. 'I'll kill you, Ashley, if you've left me with more trouble.' But this might be the best thing to have happened. Michael Nankervis wouldn't turn out his wife's abandoned cousin. She could save face by weeping that Ashley had absconded with all their non-existent money. Pity would be taken on her. It was perfect. She would play the nicer person and hope that, despite her penury, some gentleman, age and looks of no importance, would be taken with her.

She waited at the door and the instant Simpkins returned she took a sealed note from her hand. She turned her back on the maid to read it. Separating the paper from the red sealing wax, she unfolded it eagerly. She scanned her brother's flaunting script.

My dear Sister,

Truth to tell I have had quite enough of this dreary house and equally enough of your trying company. I know you feel the same way in regard to me. From now on I shall make my

own way in the world. I am confident you will
see yourself well, you always do.
  Yours, never-obedient Brother, A Faulkner.

'He's gone for good, and good riddance,'
Helen told the maid calmly, then turned to some
cajoling. 'Please listen to me, Simpkins. I know
I've been a challenging mistress and neglectful
of your wage, but it was always my brother who
held the purse strings. I am confident that now
he has gone I shall have a place here for as long
as I require it. I give you my word that I shall
treat you with more consideration. I shall sell a
piece of my jewellery and pay your wage in full
and some in advance. I'll buy you new clothes.
Without my brother's influence I know I can be
a different person. What do you say?' Blame
Ashley, that was a good ruse. She would sell
her least favourite and most valuable pair of
earrings.
  Doubt flickered in Simpkins' quick eyes. 'I'll
think about it, my lady.'
  'Good.' Helen took that as read, sure she had
talked the maid round. 'I'd better get ready
now.'
  When Helen was dressed and her hair had
been coiffured at the dressing table she gave
Simpkins the small brass key, secured in a
secret compartment in a powder box that opened the bureau where her travelling jewellery
box was kept.
  'Oh!' Simpkins gasped.
  'What is it?' Helen swivelled round on the

padded stool.

'The bureau has been broken into and the door wedged shut. My lady, your jewellery box has gone!'

'What?' Helen screamed, jumping up. She knew at once who the culprit was. Her face was scarlet and distorted in murderous fury. 'Ashley! He's ruined me. All I have left is my wedding ring and the diamond necklace and earrings I've just taken off.'

Simpkins edged away to the dressing room. 'In that case I'm glad to leave your employ this very minute. Goodbye, Lady Churchfield.' She rushed off to pass the news on to the butler.

'Oh my God.' Helen fixed a hand to her mouth, feeling she would be sick. 'I ... I must see Adeline.' In a terrible dither, trembling from scalp to toe, she snatched up her embroidery and took it with her.

She hurried to Adeline's room. There was a footman there for some reason and he resolutely blocked her way. 'Move aside!' she barked.

His eyes aloft, the footman stiffly stood his ground. 'I'm sorry, my lady. I have orders from the squire not to allow you admittance.'

'How dare you be so impertinent? Get out of my way! I need to see Mrs Nankervis at once.'

Helen was horrified to be banned from seeing Adeline. Did Michael Nankervis know Ashley had gone? Ashley had spoken to him this morning; what lies had he spun? Helen was in the worst panic. Her future was looking bleak and she had very little jewellery left. She could

79

only throw herself on Adeline's mercy. It was paramount she saw her without delay.

She kicked the footman hard in the shin. He yelped and reached down to soothe the pain. Helen took the advantage and thrust him out of her way. She was soon inside Adeline's bedroom. 'Adeline! Adeline! I must speak with you. Wake up!'

From a lightly drug-induced sleep Adeline woke with a dreadful fright. 'Oh! What is it?'

'It's Helen.' She rushed to the bed and shook Adeline to bring her to full consciousness. 'I need to speak to you. I'm in a terrible predicament. You must help me. Ashley's absconded with all my jewellery and I'm quite ruined! Adeline, I need your help!' She was growing ever more hysterical.

Adeline couldn't make out a word or grasp what was happening. She thought she was being attacked and screamed shrilly.

The nurse pelted into the room. In a moment she had encircled Helen with both doughty arms. 'Come away, Lady Churchfield. You are distressing Mrs Nankervis.'

Alerted by the butler that there might be trouble, Michael entered to find his wife whimpering and thrashing about in the bed while her cousin was manhandling her and the nurse was trying to haul the Churchfield woman away from the bed. 'Get that woman out of here,' he ordered the sheepish footman. 'Nurse, see to Mrs Nankervis. I shall recall the doctor.'

Helen was taken by both arms in a vice-like grip – the footman's revenge – and marched out to the corridor. To calm herself she had to take several deep breaths. 'M–Mr Nankervis, I'm so very sorry for my behaviour, please let me explain.'

'Hold your tongue, woman!' Michael hissed, wanting to shake all the bones out of her body. 'Go to your room immediately or I'll have you dragged there every inch of the way.'

The embroidery still clutched in her hand, Helen meekly plodded back to her room, the squire and the footman on her heels. Venetia yelped, sensing something was wrong, and fussed at her skirts. Helen put the dog up on a chair and faced Michael, red-faced and contrite. She knew there was only way out for her now and that was to grovel. First she must allow him to berate her.

'You are not to leave this room on any account. The door will be guarded. Your things will be packed and you will leave here at first light. In the meantime you had better pray your act of gross selfishness does not do my wife and child any lasting harm!'

Helen burst into tears. It felt as if her life had come to an end. 'I ... I know I've just done a terrible thing but that was only because I panicked after Ashley ran out on me with my jewels. I know I've been difficult but this morning I'd made up mind to change, honestly I did.' In a plea for mercy she held up the sewing. 'Look, I'm making your baby a gown. Please, Mr

Nankervis, let me stay. I promise I'll never upset dear Adeline again. Please, please let me stay and be her companion. I promise I'll serve her faithfully. Please, I have no money. I have nowhere to go.'

Michael yanked the sewing out of her hand and tossed it to the floor. 'My child – if it lives after what you've just done, you bitch – will have nothing of yours. Leave tomorrow by the back stairs. A carriage will be waiting for you. I don't wish to set eyes on you again. You will find your brother at the Red Lion Hotel in Truro, although I doubt if he was telling the truth of his destination. Do not write begging letters to Adeline; she will have none of you after you've risked the life of our child. I hope you meet with a just end, Lady Churchfield.'

Six

James took off his dressing gown, folded it precisely and laid it carefully over a chair. His wife liked things neat and he always went out of his way to please her. He joined Charlotte in the low post bed. It was an old bed and not a comfortable one; like all the furnishings it had been dragged down from the attics of Poltraze, owned like the house, which was near the church and draughty early-Georgian vicarage, by the miserly squire. Charlotte had a flair for making the dreary and modest appear top-notch and elegant. She had inherited much fine china and porcelain and had brought impressive drapes and lace, and the home was tolerable for the more important visitor, an infrequent occasion much to James's offence.

It was late, but Charlotte had stayed awake to hear the news about his latest summons to Poltraze. 'It took a while to settle Mrs Nankervis,' he reported, 'but I left her quite comfortable. I shall return at dawn. Hopefully, the confinement will continue without too much problem now the abominable Churchfield woman is to be evicted.'

'It was such a wicked thing to do.' Charlotte tutted. 'Although I saw for myself what an overbearing, selfish individual she was when I called on Mrs Nankervis. Poltraze will be well rid of her. I suppose she will now try to get her hooks into some poor unsuspecting gentleman with the wicked intention of relieving him of his wealth. I hate that sort of thing, James. It's a pity she can't be forestalled.'

'Quite so, my dear, but do not fret; the wicked are inevitably dealt their just reward.' Just wording the sentiment made him burn with the desire to mete out retribution on Helen Churchfield, to see her plunged into utter humiliation. He let the deep, dark moment pass, and whispered in a tender way, 'Charlotte, darling, can I be with you? I'll be very gentle.'

'Certainly, my dear; it is your right and my duty.'

James was pleased Charlotte did not think of lovemaking as a pleasure. She was too respectable to writhe and cry out and rake her nails down his back, like the whore he visited in a certain address in Redruth. He considered himself most fortunate to have three women who fed his lust in different ways. The whore allowed him anything. The use of Rachel Kivell's perfect body was loving and sometimes wild. She was intelligent and strong, but also stupid and gullible to believe he would give up his cosy life for her. Charlotte was the ideal wife for him. He didn't want anyone with spirit who would press him and try to be his equal. Charlotte was dutiful and she doted on him. He had saved her from the disgrace of being a thirty-six-year-old spinster. Thin and bony and nervous of men, he had charmed her by gentle romance into marriage, her one thousand pounds a year the attraction. He had thought he'd find her boring and a tie but Charlotte was good-natured and understanding and he had quickly grown fond of her. He liked to see her content.

He lifted her nightdress and mounted her, holding her hand throughout the few minutes of mechanical motion, in the dark as usual. It was enough to give James relief. 'Thank you, darling.' He kissed her brow – no sensual perspiration there – and gently pulled her nightdress down. 'I love you.' It didn't hurt to tell her this.

'I love you, James, very much.' Charlotte turned her head to him on the pillow.

He sensed she was excited, uncommon for her, and had something important to say. She only talked about household things or asked if everything, like his meals, were to his satisfaction. 'What is it, my dear?'

'James, I hope you are going to be pleased. I haven't said anything before. I wanted to be absolutely sure. I am with child. I'm sure you will be able to confirm I'm two months along.'

'You are?' He was astonished. 'How did I miss that?' But he had never taken any notice of her monthly cycles. Charlotte wasn't too old to conceive but it had seemed unlikely in an older bride. 'Well, I...'

'You don't mind, do you?' Charlotte asked urgently. 'It's what I've been praying for.'

'Mind? Of course I don't mind.' He could truly say he didn't. A child of his own would be wonderful, but now he saw Rachel Kivell for what she actually was, a complication in his life. She was in love with him – a dangerous thing in a mistress – and when she finally realized he had no intention of sneaking off with her, a strong-willed woman such as she was would not take the news meekly and simply disappear into the shadows. She might cause him untold trouble. Charlotte would be pierced to her soul at him committing adultery and she would not easily forgive him. She would not leave him or cast him off, she would stand by him no matter what, but his home life would be irrevocably marred. He couldn't bear to live under the weight of self-righteous condemnation. He had to get Charlotte away from Meryen. 'It's wonderful, darling. But I can't honestly say I want a child of mine living in such close proximity to a mining community where death and disease are prevalent. Meryen was a good enough place for my first practice but now we must think of somewhere more prominent. I want our child to have the best start and to be proud of me. We'll keep the news about the child to ourselves. I shall look into applying for a better practice tomorrow.'

Charlotte went along happily with whatever James wanted, but she piped up the courage to say, 'James, I know neither of us would countenance it before, but now we are to have a child it isn't just us we have to consider. I've been thinking very carefully, so please don't get cross with me for what I'm about to suggest. You know I've kept in touch regularly with my Aunt Eliza and each time she replies to my letters she reaffirms her offer to help us. Could we not now consider this for the sake of our child? I'd so like you to do better; it's what you deserve. You work hard without due appreciation and I know you are not happy. I'm sure Aunt Eliza would be glad to find us a suitable address, and rooms for you to practice in. She has no children of her own and she plans to leave me everything she possesses in her will. Could we not take benefit of that now, James?'

He lay on his back thinking about it, but not

for long. He would have to bow and scrape to the Wellbeloveds but this was the perfect solution to get away from the supercilious Michael Nankervis and Rachel Kivell. He would be ingratiating and he would indulge his rich clientele. When he had made a name for himself, and by God he would, he'd take his family up to London and the Wellbeloveds could go to hell.

He turned to the patiently waiting Charlotte. 'I wouldn't entertain it in other circumstances, but as you've said we have the child's future to take into account. Yes, my dear, write to your aunt and see what she can do for us.'

Charlotte was soon sleeping peacefully but he was denied the same blessing. He went downstairs and drank glass after glass of brandy. He couldn't keep still and paced about like a caged animal. His body was coursing with adrenalin, from anxiety and excitement and an unholy intent. He was in a fever, lathered in sweat, his skin scarlet, his eyes stinging. He felt he was being roasted. It was horrible yet at the same time delicious. Pain and pleasure were excellent partners. His head whirled. He'd leave this stinking parish tonight if he could. Waiting for the Nankervis birth was no longer important. Suddenly he was filled with rage. Following the latest episode of the wretched Churchfield woman distressing Adeline Nankervis, the squire intended to call on a top physician from Truro for his opinion. Michael Nankervis might ask this new man to take over his wife's care. That would be humiliating for James. Damn

Helen Churchfield to Hell! Her livid response at his stares haunted him. She had been about to strike him. The squire was throwing her out, but she deserved to suffer so much more.

James left the house well before dawn. Clad in old clothes procured from the gardening shed – a long cloak of his he had roughed up, a pulled-down wide-brimmed hat, and a scarf ready to pull over the lower half of his face – he drove his dog cart to half a mile from the gate house of Poltraze then concealed it in a small clearing in the woods. His nerves icy calm, he waited behind trees on the road verge for the carriage driving Helen Churchfield away to her banishment.

Common sense forbade him to risk the secure future he had with Charlotte and their child, but he couldn't forget the bitch's sneers or the way she had looked at him as if he was dirt. It gnawed at him and made his guts turn. His hate turned to loathing and wouldn't let him be. Helen Churchfield must be paid back, punished, shown she was the one who was really scum, and he would take absolute pleasure in every moment doing it.

Helen was slumped against the padded seat in the carriage, clutching Venetia to her chest. She stared ahead, cold and numb. She could hardly believe her fortune had plummeted so horrendously in a mere twenty hours. To retain a little pride she had left Poltraze without further grovelling to the fuming squire; it would have been to no avail anyway. She had twenty pounds in her reticule, thank God – at the last minute Michael Nankervis had allowed her the same financial consideration as Ashley, the villain. She wished Ashley a slow, pain-ridden death. He would probably end up crazed with syphilis anyway.

She had money enough to stay a while at the Red Lion Hotel in Truro. She did not expect to find her brother there; he would believe she'd come after him. No doubt he was already out of the county. If she ever saw her brother again she thought she might plot his end. Her only hope was to snare a rich husband, some old gentlemen who would adore a young attractive wife on his arm. Otherwise, she would have to get herself set up in reasonable luxury as a mistress. No garret living for her. She would treat her new gentleman, be it a husband or lover, with civility, courtesy and affection. She would put his needs first and respect him in all things and demand nothing for herself. That was a surer way to find the security and consideration she craved. How could she have been so supercilious and unfeeling? It was no wonder she was in this terrible situation of her own making.

Panic rose in her stomach and lashed at her heart, making her feel sick and dizzy. She was scared and could hardly breathe. She put her knuckles to her cheeks. 'It will be all right. It will be all right. I must stay calm.' Last night she had sewn her remaining jewellery into the hem of her petticoat. It helped, having something to fall back on. She cheered a little and practised a confident smile. 'We'll do just splendidly, Venetia; by the end of the day our fortune will have changed.' She hoped so but her voice wobbled and sweat pricked at the back of her neck.

Suddenly the carriage gave a sharp lurch and she was thrown to the floor, with Venetia squashed under her and yelping. The horses were whinnying in complaint. 'What...?' It took many difficult moments to get righted. She soothed Venetia and then looked out of the window. And she screamed at the top of her lungs. A footpad was on the verge; he had come out of the woods and had a gun trained on the coachman.

Helen sat back rigid on the seat and clung to Venetia, her heart thumping in fear.

'Get down!' she heard the footpad order the coachman in a coarse drawl.

There was a cry, which made her think the coachman had been felled, and she huddled in terror. What would be her fate?

The carriage door was yanked open. 'Out!

Frozen, she could only stare at the dark figure brandishing a firearm at her.

'Get out! Do it now.' The footpad thrust up an arm and was reaching for her.

A new wave of panic helped lift her off the seat and poke her head through the door. 'Don't hurt me! I have money and you can have my wedding ring. Please don't hurt me.'

'Get out and put that dog down.'

Shaking in fear, Helen made to step out. She was caught in a cruel grip and pulled out roughly and Venetia was snatched from her arms. 'No!' The coachman was sprawled on the ground with blood on his head. She noticed the obstruction in the road, the old fallen tree that had stopped the carriage.

Terror-crazed and in hysterics, she watched as her beloved pet was thrown down to the ground. She screamed and screamed as it was kicked and kicked again. She kept screaming after the dog's howls ceased and Venetia was still, her little body broken and oozing blood. The attacker turned to her. Her hand to her throat, she backed towards the carriage. 'No! Get away from me! Get away!'

He was on her in swift steps. He stared at her, a hate-filled glare glittering out of dead-cold blue eyes.

She petrified. 'Wh-what do you want?' There was something insidiously evil about him. This was more than a violent robbery. It seemed a personal offence against her.

He lifted a hand, large and iron-like in a gauntlet. She followed the movement. He made a fist, waved in front her eyes, then flung it up to his shoulder ready to swing it back at her. He was mocking her. Terror that was fresh and a thousand times multiplied weakened her legs and insides. She was totally helpless. She was his to do with as he wanted. The punch would come and she couldn't move a muscle to avoid the blow.

'Yow!' he cried, half-crazed, and punched her in the mouth. She howled in pain as her bottom lip and the skin on her chin split. Her reticule was snatched from her wrist. Then she was being dragged away into trees. 'No! Not that! Please, someone help me.'

She was hauled off her feet and her shoes were dragged off and her feet were scraped along, becoming bloodied by stones and the cold ground, and then brambles and under-growth of the woodland floor were hurting her and tearing at her clothes. He was so strong and determined that try as she might she couldn't gain a moment to struggle and try to get free. She was being pitched into a living nightmare, a woman's worst fear. This monster was going to rape and murder her.

When they were deep in the woods she was thrown against a tree. 'Bitch,' the attacker seethed in a low, horrible voice.

'No, don't. Please don't, not that,' Helen sobbed in terror. This man was a beast, a savage.

'I don't want your body,' James roared. He needed to soothe his loins every day but not here and now. 'I don't want you, never you, not if you were the last woman on earth. You're just a rich whore. I wouldn't degrade myself. You're nothing; you're filth, worse than the scum in the gutter. Don't talk to me, I hate your voice, I hate everything about you. Give me the ring and the rest of your jewellery.'

The fact he seemed to have a particular grudge against her and saw as her utterly despicable chilled Helen to her soul. He was depraved. She cowered, expecting him to tear her apart with his hands. Her own hands were almost incapable as she tried to peel off her glove. With an impatient growl he grasped her wrist and ripped the glove off, hurting her, then he pulled off her wedding ring, hurting her again. She saw his glowering blue eyes steeped in crazed menace above his disguise. Why did he hate her so? Did she know him? He seemed to know who she was and all about her. He was behaving as if she had at one time practically destroyed his life. Could she have hurt and offended someone that much?

He looked at her ears and tore open her clothes at the throat. 'Where's your earrings, your necklace?'

'I-I don't have one. All my jewellery was stolen from me yesterday. I'm telling the truth, I swear,' she pleaded. If she survived this, the necklace was all she'd have.

James knew she had been robbed but she had been wearing diamonds the day before. He also knew how women protected their valuables. He'd search the clothes she was wearing later. The sale of the earrings and necklace would help fund his new life. He slapped her face hard again and again, and each time she screamed in pain and fear, which excited him like nothing had before.

'You bitch!' he cried, and rained blows on her.

Helen screamed and sobbed. 'Help me! Help!' She tried to fend him off but it was no use. He was madness itself. She had been brought to utter degradation and would be brutally murdered. The beast might torture her for hours. *Oh God, oh God.*

James delivered a particularly savage blow. Helen felt an enormous explosion in her head, heading her towards darkness. She longed for the darkness.

Sweat dripping off him, James was in a sense of fierce elation. He let it take him and he held on to it. He looked down in satisfaction at the felled woman. She wasn't dead, that wasn't his plan for full revenge. He felt about her petticoats and located the shape of the hidden diamonds. Ripping the material, he hid the pouch of jewellery on his own person. He carried his victim to the dog cart, covered her over and drove off at speed.

Half an hour later he was back on the road to Poltraze, in his usual suit of clothes. He grinned; everything was working out well, the carriage and driver had not been discovered. He hurled down Helen Churchfield's trunks and rifled through them, setting aside the things a criminal would take to sell, tearing and soiling her clothes in his mad joy. The incident would be put down to a violent robbery and Lady Churchfield abducted. He leered. He had hidden the witch where he could have more fun with her and in a few days he would move her to where she would be found.

He loaded the unconscious coachman up on the dog cart and drove on to the big house.

Wearing a suitably shocked expression, he was going to derive the greatest pleasure in the drama of raising the alarm.

Seven

Flint Retallack was hiking home after the morning core at the Carn Croft mine. His dark hair was damp and curly after the hot bath supplied on the surface. He was scrubbed clean but dirt stained his big rough hands. With him was his next-door neighbour, Wilf Treneer, a young family man. They were part of an eight-man team, four working the mornings, the others working the afternoons, changing over after a week. It gave them time to supplement their earnings on their own smallholdings or the local farms, a much-needed diversity for if a bid for a set produced a poor bargain, of little or low quality ore underground, the result could be near poverty. It was a precarious, often unforgiving way of life. Injury, perhaps in a rock fall or explosion, or illness gleaned from the cramped, airless conditions underground had brought destitution to many a miner. Times were grim, the winter had been hard and the last harvest poor. The high price of corn had brought much discontent and even riots. Flint was not near dire straits but it could all change in the beat of a heart.

'Good news about another new mine going up 'cross the downs at the end of the year,' Wilf said, always a little breathless. Unlike Flint, striding along energetically, he was a little stooped, pulled down by worries and poor lung health. When both men had reached the grass at the mine surface, they'd been weary and sweating from the tremendous effort of the risky vertical climb up hundreds of wooden and iron ladders. Then the cold air had hit them like a blast of ice, hurting their lungs. Flint recovered quickly but Wilf had a hacking cough that took minutes to die away. They were always the last to walk home, Flint waiting to walk with Wilf.

''Tis said 'twill have a man engine to bring the men up and down; suit me if we get work there.' Wilf banged on his concave chest in an unsuccessful attempt to ease his breathing. 'A longer walk to 'n' fro but will be far better than the ladders.'

'Good news all right,' Flint said, joining Wilf in a conversation they'd had a few times before. Work and food on the table was paramount to the men and their comrades, a proud breed. There was a concern the good ore in the Carn Croft, mined for over four decades, was running out, the depth down to several fathoms. The Wheal Verity meant security and should provide work for at least the next two or three generations, all being well. Flint crossed his fingers.

'You going out again to search for that lady

what went missing when you've had your dinner?' Wilf asked, pressing cheap tobacco into his blackened clay pipe with a nicotine-stained forefinger.

'Might as well, after I've seen to the small-holding. Can't see her being found round here after so many days, but there's nothing to lose by having another try.' Flint scanned the colour-less landscape. Dips and rises, smatterings of high and low rock, banks of bramble, furze and clumps of heather could all be used to hide a body. It was unlikely that Lady Helen Church-field would be found alive. The squire was offering a reward of twenty guineas, a small fortune, for information of her whereabouts and every inch of local land was still being scoured daily by Meryen's inhabitants and people from further abroad. Evidence showed that after the attack she had been taken away from a small clearing in the Poltraze woods by a small cart. Her body could have been dumped anywhere, most likely thrown down one of the old mine shafts.

'Squire will be glad if the lady's found for his wife's sake, but don't s'pose he really cares a toss. He was throwing her out anyway. Wish I could find her, 'tis a struggle bringing up so many young'uns,' Wilf sighed.

'You'll have to stop breeding 'em, Wilf.' Flint grinned.

'What, not take a bit of comfort from the missus?' Wilf answered in the same light-hearted vein. 'It's the only thing I got to look forward to, that and my pipe. Besides, I love my young'uns. If I'm lucky enough to live to a good age they'll be a comfort to me.' A good age usually wasn't old age for a miner, not after the rigours of cramped labour in such airless, dust-laden conditions. 'Time you found the right woman and settled down, Flint. There's still room in your house even with Eva there, and you can always build on. My missus says your mother can't wait to be a grandma. What's taking you so long? The maids are always giving 'ee the eye, good-looking man like you. You keep dipping your feet in the waters but when are you going to take the plunge?'

'All in good time, Wilf, when the right woman comes along.' Flint rolled a smoke.

'There's some right pretty maids in the village. Must be one or two that really takes your fancy.'

Flint was thoughtful. 'I fancy a lot of them, just haven't found one with that special spark.'

'You won't get anyone at all if you're going to be too choosy.'

'I'm in no hurry, Wilf. What's meant to be will be.' Flint felt a strange sensation crawl up his spine, as if some primitive sense was prodding him about something, but what? He scanned the area with keen eyes.

'What's up? Seen something?' Wilf paused with a burning match, his snub nose sniffing like a dog.

'I don't know.' Flint left the path and strode several feet through rough foliage. It was as if

98

something was calling him. This had happened before, when out hunting rabbits or fowl. A nudge deep in his inner self virtually pointed him in the right direction and he would bag a good catch. He had never told anyone; he'd rather people think he was skilled or lucky instead of having a sixth sense.

Wilf reached his side and Flint moved off again. There was a crater-shaped dip just ahead where heather grew. There was something odd at its rim, something small and white. Wilf was there. Flint grabbed his arm. 'Over there! I can just make out what looks like a hand. It could be the missing lady. If so we'll share the reward.'

With Wilf in some excitement, the men hurried to the place and with every step it became more apparent that Flint had discovered a small human hand. Attached to it was a female form in tattered, once fine clothes, her limbs battered and bruised.

Flint flinched at sight of the body. It was badly beaten, its fair hair tangled over its puffy face. He'd heard the description given of Lady Churchfield, and he was in no doubt he was now looking down on her. There were marks on her wrists where she had been tied up and about the mouth where she had been gagged. Her attacker had been careful not to leave clues of what he had bound her with. Flint took off his coat and laid it over the body. 'I'll carry her to the undertaker and then we'll go on to Poltraze.'

He frowned. There was something odd. This was near the regular route taken to and fro by the majority of mine workers so the body could only have been placed here a fairly short time ago. The killer obviously wanted his victim to be found at a certain time. He studied the ground in all directions; it had been greatly tramped over by the search for the lady and thereby gave no clue as to which way the killer had come and gone.

The instinct again took hold of him, drawing his eyes to the woman. He crouched and touched her neck.

'What're you doing?' Wilf asked.

Flint pressed about the cold flesh. He felt nothing; his fingers were rough from constant physical work and lacked some sensitivity. He lifted tangles of hair away from her face and then puckered the split lips and put his cheek close to the open mouth.

'Surely you don't b'lieve she's alive, Flint. She's dead as a door nail.'

Flint concentrated. He drew in a breath. Thank God he had followed that inner call. He could feel the faintest of warm breath. He moved rapidly. 'She's alive, just.'

'Eh?'

'We need to act fast, Wilf, or it will be too late.' He gathered the waxen form up in his arms, walking off. 'The nearest place is Chy-Henver. We'll take her there.'

'Can't believe this, she's alive. Why not the doctor's?'

'He might not be there and his wife would be useless. Chy-Henver is her only hope.'

Half-running and half-walking back to the path, Flint and Wilf took the shortest route to Chy-Henver. They reached the stream and went across its stepping stones. Wilf opened the back gate of the property and the men marched up to the back kitchen door. Wilf didn't bother to knock, he opened the door and Flint followed him through to the kitchen. There was no one there but a hearty fire was burning in the range.

'Hello! Anyone home? Clear the table,' Flint ordered Wilf.

Wilf swept off a sewing box and pairs of rolled-up stockings waiting to be darned. Flint laid the woman, wrapped in his coat, on the table then grabbed some linen airing near the range and placed it over her. It was vital her body was warmed. He went through to the rest of the house. 'Hello! We need help!'

Rachel was already in the hall and coming to investigate. She heard Dora coming out of one the bedrooms where she was cleaning the window. She was worried at finding this man here. 'What is it? Eva?'

'No, me and my neighbour's just found the missing lady from Poltraze. She's in the kitchen, in a very bad way.'

Rachel sped after him to the kitchen. She gasped in horror, rooted to the spot at the dreadful state of Helen Churchfield. It was hard to believe the mauled grey person was the same proud lady who had swept into her sitting room a few weeks ago.

'Will you help her?' Flint asked tersely, unsure of her reaction. They had a mutual dislike and if she chanced to be visiting Eva when he was at home they ignored each other.

'Yes, yes, of course I will; there's no need to take that tone. Carry her upstairs. Your neighbour can run to the workshop and ask my brother to ride and fetch Dr Lockley.' The cheek of the man, why did he believe she'd refuse charity to Lady Churchfield after she had been so willing to help Eva?

She met Dora in the passage. 'Could you make up a hot-water bottle and bring up hot water and towels, and some water to drink. It's Lady Churchfield. She can be put in my room. The fire's lit in there. Then can you make up the main guest room for me, please?'

In her bedroom, Rachel threw back the bed covers then used the sheet laid over the lady as a draw sheet until she was washed and put into a nightgown. Flint laid the victim down, easing away his coat. Rachel wrapped her in the draw sheet then pulled the covers up over her. 'Poor thing.' She grabbed her face cloth and gently wiped some of the dirt off Helen Churchfield's face. 'She's been missing for days. She must have gone through the most unimaginable terror, torture too it seems. Who could have done such a vicious thing? He's a beast. Do you think she'll live?'

Now Flint had had time to sum up the situation he shuddered with the awfulness of it all. 'I can't see it, but if there's the smallest chance...'

Rachel glanced up at him. His broad frame seemed to fill the room. 'I take it she wasn't far from here on the downs. That means the perpetrator hadn't long left her there, doesn't it?'

Flint nodded grimly. 'Points to him being a local man; someone with local knowledge anyway. He's very dangerous. I'd say he'd enjoyed doing what he did to her. He could strike again.'

Chills travelled through Rachel and she shuddered. 'It could be someone known to us. Oh my God. Can you make sure that Eva does not wander off?'

'My mother and I keep her well cared for,' he growled.

'I did not say you didn't!' Rachel was plunged into dread; if a killer was lurking about then Jowan would forbid her to go out alone and she wouldn't be able to meet James if he sent word he was free. Still, James would soon be here. She had still not seen him since Lady Churchfield's first visit. She had received a note from him advising her that there was no point in going to Lowenna because he would be unable to join her there for some time. She worried that he might be avoiding her – he had not kept away from her this long before – but she comforted herself with the fact he had to spend a lot of time at Poltraze and he had other patients too.

Dora struggled into the room laden with a pitcher of steaming water, towels and a glass of water. She went back for the hot-water bottle.

'Can you women manage or do you want me to fetch Frettie Endean?' Flint offered, when she had returned.

Rachel glanced at Dora, who looked doubtful. 'It would be good to have Mrs Endean here, thank you.'

'I'll do that, then make my way over to Poltraze with Wilf. The squire will send a carriage for her, I suppose, if the doctor says she can travel, but that's unlikely. I doubt she'll last the day. Good luck with her.' Flint went to the door.

'We'll do our best for her,' Rachel said. She didn't feel the same way about this lady as she had Eva, but she greatly pitied her.

Flint nodded his thanks and left. Rachel Kivell was a curious mix of moods and ways. She was a dark beauty. She was a loner who spurned all male interest in her. That was a waste. Eva adored her. She would run to her and babble away in her childish talk, eager to see what 'Miss' had brought her each time. His mother liked and respected her, but Flint balked at her haughty manner. He couldn't forget how she had off-loaded Eva into his mother's care. He couldn't stand being in her company for more than a few minutes and assumed she felt the same about him. She'd want rid of Lady Churchfield as soon as possible.

Every few moments, while Rachel and Dora eased the rags off Helen Churchfield's abused body, and washed her and put a nightgown on her, they checked to see if she was still breathing, expecting her to expire at any second. They exclaimed in horror at her injuries. A handful of her hair had been pulled out, the skin of her heels had been scraped off and her left wrist and some ribs were broken. As a widow, Dora insisted that she see to the patient's lower regions.

'Has she been...?' Rachel whispered.

'Well, it doesn't look like it,' Dora said grimly. 'That surprises me. The man who hurt her was a savage. I hope he's caught and hung, although hanging's too good for the brute. She was a stuck-up mare by all accounts, and only come down here to leech off the squire, and she got rightfully booted out for upsetting Mrs Nankervis, but no one deserves this.'

'She's got nothing left now.'

'Nothing at all; he had even destroyed all her clothes on the road. The squire will want to see right by her though, no doubt.'

'I hope so.' Rachel frowned, putting a glass of water to the lady's swollen split lips and tipping drops of water into her mouth then dabbing at the dribbles because none was swallowed. There was no one to take on Lady Churchfield like the Retallacks had taken on dear Eva.

James got there quickly. For once he had been at home. He examined the patient in Rachel, Dora and Frettie Endean's presence. He approved of the many dressings, including cold flannels to reduce the swollen areas of her face that Frettie Endean had put on his patient, and the treatment to her wrist. Frettie Endean was an excellent bone-setter. 'Mrs Endean went ahead in case you were unable to come until much later, Doctor,' Rachel explained. She tried to catch his eye but he was distant and serious.

'Quite so. Lady Churchfield's heart is beating quite strongly and her lungs are clear so she will probably be spared pneumonia. It is my guess she was kept in an old outhouse or something and not left out in the cold or she would surely have perished,' James said gravely, relishing the memories of his subsequent assaults on the lady. He had been careful to keep her alive and not beat her too badly about the head. He wanted her to come round and remember every terrifying moment, to experience her utter degradation, to never know peace for the rest of her life. She might become mentally deranged and end her days in an asylum. She had paid for treating him like dirt. 'It's hard to determine how long she has been unconscious or whether, if she comes round, there will be any damage to her brain. She has taken a massive beating. Infection and dehydration will be her worst threat. She must be given sips of water every few minutes, if necessary force some down by stroking her throat. I'll leave something to help build up her constitution. I shall call back tomorrow. Inform me if you have any sudden worries.' He put a collection of small fluted brown bottles on the chest of drawers and wrote instructions on the labels.

'Can I offer you refreshment before you leave, Dr Lockley?' Rachel put an urgent note in her voice, one he would understand.

'A small glass of port would be nice, thank

you, Miss Kivell.'

Rachel was so relieved. She had feared he would simply go and leave her wondering wretchedly what she had done wrong. Dora sat with the patient for the meantime and Frettie Endean left. Rachel led James downstairs. She was dismayed to see Jowan waiting for news.

'It will be touch and go for a few days,' James explained.

'There's nothing you can do, Jowan,' Rachel said. 'You might as well go back to work.'

'Do you think the squire will take over responsibility for the lady?' Jowan asked the doctor.

'I should imagine so. She is his kin by marriage. But he was particularly angry with Lady Churchfield for causing distress to Mrs Nankervis. She does not know her cousin was abducted. I imagine he will not allow her to be informed of what has happened today. You are happy for the lady to remain here for the time being?'

'I am not happy about it at all. I can't imagine her being the least bit grateful, but there is nothing else for it. I suppose the squire will send word after Flint Retallack has told him the news. Rachel, do not let this overtax you. You have been quiet and listless of late.'

'You are not well, Miss Kivell? Perhaps I should give you a consultation,' James said kindly.

At last Rachel had James's attention all to herself. 'I'm not unwell,' she told him in the sitting room, slipping her hand into his. 'I've been missing you. You haven't even sent me a note.'

'I'm sorry.' He squeezed her hand gently. 'Things have been hard for me these last few weeks. Mr Nankervis is demanding my presence twice daily at Poltraze. And Charlotte is delicate and I cannot forsake her for long.'

'But you can me?' Rachel was hurt. She seemed so far down in his priorities.

'Darling.' He glanced at the door then kissed her hand. 'Very soon we will be together for the rest of our lives. I have also been busy on our account. I am hoping to hear that I have acquired some rooms in Edinburgh.' A lie; it was Charlotte who was hoping to hear good news from her aunt. 'Please be patient a little while longer.'

'Oh James, darling.' She heaved a great sigh of happiness. 'Forgive me; I've been very silly.'

'Actually, darling, I think it would be a good idea if we never meet at Lowenna again. Now we're this close to getting what we want it would be foolish to take risks. My reputation would be ruined and your brother would, very likely, try to break my back. Take your things out of the house. I know you have Lady Churchfield here, but will you do that as soon as you can? The moment we reach Edinburgh you can write to the landlord informing him that Mr and Mrs White no longer require the house.'

'I'll do it the instant I can get away. I love you

108

so much, James.' Her skin glowed and her eyes sparkled. She could hardly contain her joy and excitement.

'You're so beautiful, Rachel.' He listened. No one was about and he took her lips in a fierce kiss. He wanted to make love to her badly and it was hell that it wasn't possible now.

Rachel enjoyed the kiss but she was also glad when it ended. He was quite carried away, squeezing her tight and crushing her lips.

'I'm afraid I must go. I've got patients' notes to write and an appointment in the village at four o'clock. I'll see you tomorrow. You had better get back to your charge.'

'Yes.' Rachel kissed his chin. 'I'll sit with Lady Churchfield for the rest of the day and sleep in the armchair tonight.'

She saw James to the front door, then took her embroidery upstairs. She was in for a long vigil, perhaps a crisis, but she had wonderful thoughts of the future to fill her mind and keep her alert.

Eight

Michael Nankervis was on the way to Chy-Henver. He had just ridden past the two miners who had turned up to report their grim discovery – he had not acknowledged them as they walked home, pleased with their ten guineas each reward. What a damned pity Helen wasn't dead. He could have had her buried quietly and forgotten about her. At least she had been taken to Chy-Henver instead of being brought to his door. He had a proposition for the young Kivells, and if necessary he'd make it plain that if they weren't prepared to nurse Helen until she recovered, or hopefully died, they would no longer get business commissions from his estate. There was no way he was going to re-admit Helen Churchfield into his house. He went straight to the carpentry workshop.

Jowan and Thad came outside to meet him, removing their leather aprons. They did not touch their forelocks; Kivells offered subservience to no one. Jowan ordered one of the boys to take the squire's horse to the stable. 'I take it you've come about Lady Churchfield. Would you care to step inside the house, Mr Nankervis?'

'Indeed, I wish to speak to you both about her.'

Once inside the sitting room, Thad said, 'This also concerns Rachel. I'll call her downstairs.'

'As you wish,' Michael said, with chin up and shoulders back. He took the prominent seat at the hearth and accepted the offer of brandy, appreciating its fine taste.

Rachel came in with Thad, hoping to hear good news about Helen Churchfield's imminent removal. The men all drank brandy and she sipped a sweet sherry.

'I'll get straight to the point, Kivell,' Michael said firmly, looking at Jowan as the leader of the gathering. 'I have no desire to have Lady Churchfield back under my roof. I am sure she is in no fit state to be moved at present anyway. I would not, of course, expect you to bear the expense of nursing and providing for her. I have brought with me the sum of fifty pounds. I am hoping you will agree to take it and to care for her ladyship until she has recovered or, in the event that she does not rally, she dies. If you wish I can engage a nurse to give her twenty-four-hour care. Well?'

'I don't want her here indefinitely. It may be weeks before she is strong enough to move on,' Rachel blurted out. This could clash with the date she and James were to go away. 'And then what?'

Michael turned stony eyes on her. 'I will see to it that Lady Churchfield will go on to suitable accommodation, Miss Kivell.' If only the wretched villain had finished the woman off; this whole business could cost him dear. Adeline would find out about it in due course and out of her good heart would insist that her cousin be set up comfortably with a small staff.

He turned to Jowan and wasn't surprised to see a grave and unyielding gleam in his eyes. 'Keep the lady here and I assure you that no one will be inconvenienced. Understand my situation. My child's birth is not yet due and Mrs Nankervis is not hale. I cannot risk harm to her health or my child's. If you are prepared to spare me these anxieties then Poltraze will be pleased to do business with you for the foreseeable future.'

'And if we do not then we shall get no more work from Poltraze,' Jowan returned, his tone as hard as steel. The estate provided a good deal of business but he wasn't afraid to tell Michael Nankervis to go to hell. However, if Rachel would not be bothered with the nursing workload, and he and Thad did not have to even see the lady, perhaps her presence could be tolerated. If she died it would be soon. She was young and, before the attack, strong and healthy so if she did not succumb the likelihood was that she'd recover quite quickly. 'I suppose the lady could stay if you provide a nurse, but on the strict understanding that she is to leave here the moment she is well enough to travel.'

'Jowan!' Rachel exclaimed crossly. 'Thad, haven't you anything to say?'

'I can't see that it would hurt for the lady to

112

be nursed here. After all, she's been through the most dreadful ordeal.'

Rachel was seething. Thad was too soft and Jowan was only concerned about the business. But it was his business, his and Thad's, and she was soon to forsake them, perhaps forever if they refused to forgive her. She had no right to be selfish. She did not have to nurse the Churchfield woman herself. She had a happy future ahead, and sadly she had just realized how much of a wrench it would be to leave Chy-Henver and her family behind. 'Yes, she has. I shouldn't forget that.'

'So it's agreed?' Michael said, finishing his brandy.

'It's agreed,' Jowan said, suppressing a sigh. He hoped the family weren't about to regret this. One thing was certain: if Lady Churchfield survived he wouldn't allow her to revert to former kind.

Michael held out his hand to shake on it. A Kivell never went back on his word. He handed over the fifty pounds, reminding Rachel of the deal she'd struck with Irene Retallack over Eva. He inquired, 'May I take a look at Lady Churchfield? I would like to see for myself her sad condition.' Rather he wanted to ascertain if she looked about to die.

'I'll show you up,' Rachel said.

She watched the squire's face as he gazed down at the woman wrapped in warm blankets in the darkened room. It struck Rachel how small and vulnerable the lady seemed, but she couldn't tell what he was thinking behind his dour expression.

Michael hid his shock at Helen's deathly pale, bruised and swollen face but was dismayed to find he might be in for a second disappointment. She seemed to be breathing well. Damn it, the woman must have a strong constitution. He shook his head. 'It's terrible to see her like this.' He didn't mean it in the way Rachel took it to be.

'There's one very important thing that hasn't been mentioned,' Rachel said.

'Which is?'

'Who attacked her? He must be a madman. It's thought it's likely he's a local man, a miner even, who did this, although none, apparently, has the type of small conveyance used for the abduction.'

'The coachman could only give a little information about the rogue who stopped the carriage – a young man, he thought, of medium build, rough and hard, in dark clothes. All the whereabouts of the servants at Poltraze during the time have been accounted for. It took a clever, calculating mind to do this, not a simple miner, to my mind.'

Rachel shuddered. 'But it really could be someone living among us in Meryen.'

'The authorities will have something to go on now Lady Churchfield had been found. The downs will be searched thoroughly.' *This crime is something your evil father might have done when alive*, Michael thought, indulging in a lengthy look at the young woman standing across the bed from him. Rachel Kivell was gorgeous, with perfect contours to her face and body. She didn't couch her words; she was as much a rebel and as high-minded as her brother. She would be passionate, a delight to have an affair with.

'We must be on our guard. The villain is very cunning.' One of the first things he had done after the attack was to send his daughters, under armed guard, to their maternal grandparents in Truro. 'I shall gain reports of Lady Helen's progress from Dr Lockley. Now I must go. I'll see myself out. Good afternoon to you, Miss Kivell.'

'Pompous prig,' Rachel muttered, listening to his heavy tread down the stairs.

Putting a towel under Helen Churchfield's chin and lifting her head, she carefully put the glass of water to her lips. This time the woman gave a small cough as the water hit her throat and her swallowing mechanism worked. Rachel was pleased that in her deep unaware state she was able to take a few sips. 'That's it, Helen.' There seemed no point now in formality. 'Fight, get better, don't let that beast steal your life.'

Dabbing Helen's mouth dry, Rachel resumed her seat at the bedside and, unfolding one of her battered hands from the blankets, she held it gently. Pity for the lady had turned to the desire to see her become well. Rachel felt hatred towards the monster responsible for this. No one had the right to treat someone so savagely, to torture and degrade someone so.

'Get well, Helen. I pray this man will be caught and you'll get justice and see him hang.'

Nine

Darkness and pain, it was all Helen knew.

The brutal voice shouting in her ears, 'I hate you, hate you, hate you! Do you hear me? I've made you pay.'

'No, please, please! Not again! What have I done to you?' There was no use in pleading. The beast had no pity, no soul. He gloried in hurting her. He laughed throughout each beating and called her the vilest names.

'You deserve this, bitch. You're no lady. You're dross. You're lower than the gutter. No one will ever look at you with respect again. You deserve this. I hate you. Everybody hates you. Remember that, remember that!'

She had no idea how long she'd been kept prisoner or how many times her jailer had come to torture her. 'You're scum; you're the lowest of the low.' His jeers went on and on. There was a smell on him not unknown to her but one she couldn't place in her horrendous plight.

Cold, she was so cold. She couldn't see. Something was blinding her. She couldn't shout or scream. Something was gagging her and making her choke. She was afraid to move. Mocking words from her tormentor echoed like shards of glass inside her pounding head. 'Don't move; you're next to a pit. The slightest movement and you'll fall in. It's a long, long way down.' At any minute she could plunge deeper into hell.

But wasn't death better than this, almost stripped of her clothes and waiting to be hurt and taunted again or to be left to starve to death and rot? The beast spoke as if he wanted to keep her alive for a while yet, but he would tire of his torture and end her life, slowly and agonizingly.

She listened. There was only a creeping, a scampering – perhaps a mouse or some other small creature? Her tormentor wasn't here – at least she prayed he wasn't. Perhaps he was present and asleep. She was on her back on cold, damp ground, on thick dust that scratched her. Her limbs were sore and ached; she must move to gain some circulation. Could she possibly get away? She had to try, it might awaken the beast and bring him to fury, but she had to try. Somehow she had to fight back.

She edged in one direction. It caused agony in all her limbs. She inched again and again, needing to catch her breath each time. She continued her journey in the enforced darkness, all the while frightened she would pitch herself down the pit. Was it night or day? It didn't matter. She tried not to think how she would stand up and open a door if she felt she had come to one. She hit something hard, a wall of some

117

kind she guessed, so the pit wasn't this way, if there really was one – it might have been part of his way to torment her. Sobbing, wetting the gag, she squirmed and wriggled back the way she had come. Her bare foot nudged something that moved. She didn't have time to hold her breath as a loud rumble broke out and objects fell down and rolled over her legs. Under the restriction of the gag she screamed in pain. The smell of wood filled her nose. What did that mean? She couldn't think. The centre of her being was filled with terror. If the monster was here she had surely wakened him. Or when he next came he would fly into wrath at her bid to escape. There was no way out for her, only at some point a terrible undignified death.

She shook her head franticly. *'No! No!* Help me someone!'

The whole household of Chy-Henver was disturbed by the ghastly shrieks.

Rachel ran to her former room in her night-dress. Helen was thrashing about in the bed, clawing at the nurse, who had been sleeping in a made-up bed in the room, and was now struggling to get her patient still. Rachel ran round the bed and reached for Helen's flailing hands. 'It's all right, Helen, you're safe, you're safe. You're in a warm comfortable bed and you're being looked after.'

For three days Helen had twitched and lurched and groaned in her deep sleep but she always responded to Rachel's soothing voice. Gradually her lashing lessened and she twitched and

118

whimpered, terrifying images still playing out in her stricken mind.

Jowan and Thad were at the doorway. 'Can we do anything?' Jowan asked.

'Lady Churchfield was having a nightmare; she was likely reliving her harrowing ordeal.' The nurse, matronly and plump, wrung out a cloth in the wash bowl to cool her patient's fevered brow. 'It shows she's beginning to come round. She may have more distressing episodes to endure yet. I'll sit up with her. I'm sorry the rest of you were disturbed.'

'There's nothing you men can do,' Rachel said. 'I'll make Nurse Carveth some tea. I'll take over from you in the morning, Nurse, and you can have breakfast and take a rest.'

This became the pattern for the next four days, and Rachel was pleased to take turns with Helen's care.

It was almost time for supper the following day before James arrived for his daily check on the patient.

'I thought that you weren't coming at all,' Rachel said, dismal in spirit for he seemed in an odd mood, seeming not to want to be here at all. She wondered if it was worth asking him her usual question. 'Have you heard about the rooms in Edinburgh?' She did not. James was becoming remote with her. He didn't look to be affectionate or to be alone with her. Had she been making a huge mistake? Could he be trusted?

'I've had a lot to do.' He caught her arm on

top of the stairs and whispered in her ear. 'Rachel, everything is arranged. We'll be leaving here on Friday. Don't pack a lot of things. We'll stop off on the journey and I'll buy you a whole new wardrobe of clothes. On the day be sure you leave a letter for your brother explaining that this is what you really want; I don't want him coming after us and causing trouble. It's really going to happen, darling. I'm so sorry you've had to be so patient.'

'James!' She was gorged with bliss. How could she have doubted him? He had been distracted because he'd had a lot of planning to do, and she must allow that he would find it hard to leave behind the wife he respected. 'This is wonderful, darling! I can hardly believe it. What time shall I leave here? Where will we meet?'

'I'll make the final arrangements in a day or two. I'll have to find out what Charlotte's intentions are to be on the day. Not long now, my darling. Hold fast.' He squeezed her arm and entered the sick room.

'How is Lady Churchfield today, Nurse Carveth?' he asked, polite and officious. She informed him about the disturbed night. He did the usual examination: pulse, heart and lungs. 'All seems well. Are you turning her regularly?'

'Yes, Doctor.'

'Good. We don't want her to develop bed sores. Is she able to take more fluids?'

'Yes, Doctor; she even managed a little

chicken broth today.'

'Excellent. She is emerging from the stupor. It's only her ordeal that is holding her back. Her subconscious is trying to protect her. She is going to be severely traumatized when she does come round. I'll leave some valerian and laudanum.' He packed his bag. 'You and Miss Kivell are doing excellent work here. I shall return the day after tomorrow.'

Before leaving the room he took a long look at his victim. It was a pity he would not be around to witness her suffering when she was cognizant. He was confident he had put her through enough to change her haughty personality forever.

He drank the usual glass of port and kissed Rachel lightly, lingering over her face. 'I love your eyes. They're as beautiful as a tigress's. I love your strong brow and fine nose, the perfection of your cheek bones. I love your fabulous mouth, so soft and wonderful to kiss. To me you are ... No, I shall let you wait until we are away together and I shall tell you exactly all my thoughts about you. Goodbye for now, my sweet Rachel.'

When she closed the door after him she leaned against it, putting a hand to her breast. James was such a romantic man. In a few days she would be his forever. She prayed her family, especially Jowan and Thad, would understand, and then she would wish for nothing more.

Irene Retallack was being helped by Eva to lay

the supper table. 'That's it, my handsome, now you can lift the plates down off the dresser. Be careful.' Eva never put the cutlery in the right formation but Irene and Flint never checked her, happy in her delight at helping as much as she was able. Irene was proud of her protégée. It took a long time for Eva's simple brain to master a task, but if she did it regularly she coped well. Clean and tidy, in a light-blue check dress, half white apron, her thin mousey hair in a top knot, her light brown eyes goggling, she was like a cross between a child and a sweet goblin. On Sundays Irene put ringlets in her hair for chapel, topped off with a rose-bud decorated bonnet, and she was proud of the little soul who sat beside her, so well behaved, and hummed through the hymns and said 'Amen' to the prayers. The worshippers saw Eva as somewhat of a novelty but many had taken her to their hearts and gave her little gifts and spoke to her as one would a dear child.

Eva took the white, green-rimmed plates down one by one, setting them roughly in the right place. Tucked under her arm was the yellow-haired doll Rachel had given her. Eva called it Dolly and rarely put it down. She remembered the salt and pepper pots by herself. It was of some pride to Irene that now, because of Flint's reward money, they could afford condiments on the table. Irene put small dishes of various pickles on the starched white tablecloth to go with the brisket, potatoes and vegetables. A treacle suet pudding was steaming on the slab.

'Now for the bread, my handsome; it's in the larder,' Irene said. She and Eva had been making loaves and splits all afternoon. Eva was heavy-handed and this was perfect for kneading bread. 'Flint always enjoys your bread. When you've done that you can fetch him in from outside. Get him away from those goats.' From the reward money Flint had bought a billy and three nanny goats and had built a goat house. He was proud of them and liked to look them over.

'I'll go, I'll go,' Eva giggled, and went to the larder cupboard.

Irene was hit by a sudden painful headache. 'Ow.' She pressed a hand to her temple. She felt dizzy, very strange. She staggered back and fell on the brass firewood box. Everything blurred. 'E-va, ge-et F-lint.' She felt wet between her legs and was ashamed of it; her right side had become numb and she slumped forward on to the floor.

Eva put the bread on the table. She gazed about, puzzled. Where was Missus? She was there just then. Eva crept round the table and cried out. Missus was sprawled on the floor. What did this mean? She shuffled to her and fell to her knees, clutching Dolly tightly and crying, 'Missus, get up, Missus get up!'

Her foster mother's face was twisted and dribble was running out of her mouth. Eva couldn't make sense of it but knew something was wrong. For a moment she panicked, but then she knew what she had to do. *Miss!* She must run to Miss. Her befuddled mind had forgotten about Flint. She hobbled to the back door, left it open and hurried off as fast as she could on her bowed legs. She had the judgment to hit the road in the right direction and knew if she kept going she would reach the house where Miss lived.

When she left the village lights behind the moonlight prevented her from wandering off the road and getting lost. 'Jesus will help, Missus said so.' She kept muttering to fight her fears as she went along, stumbling in pot holes and over big stones.

A fox let out its eerie call and she screamed in fright and put Dolly in front her eyes. Before she would have dropped down to the ground and curled up in fright but some instinct told her to keep going. 'Got t'get help, got t'get help.'

A soughing wind started up and she whirled round, fearing the bogeyman was behind her and would eat her up. 'No, no!'

She burst into tears and reached out with a feeble hand. There was nothing there to touch and, trembling, she turned round and carried on. The tune of a hymn came into her mind and she hummed it loudly; she had never learned the words but she felt a bit braver. She tucked Dolly into the bodice of her dress and put her hands over her ears to shut out any more bad noises. In this way, ruining her soft slippers, she finally got to the big gate behind which she knew she'd find Miss.

As she had done before, she raised her arm and fumbled with the latch. She had to stretch to her utmost and it hurt her back and her thumb to lift the lever. She pushed the gate open and shuffled up the path lighted by the porch lamp. Taking Dolly out of her bodice, she wrapped her in one arm, and balled her fist and banged on the door and kept banging. She had to get help for Missus.

She heard footsteps on the other side and stepped back out of the porch, afraid now.

Holding up a lamp, Jowan was surprised to see the doorstep empty. 'Hello? Who's there?' He stepped over the threshold. 'Oh!' It was a shock to discover the little bent figure clutching a doll. Recognizing Eva and her fear, he said softly, 'Hello, Eva. Are you in trouble? Have you come to see Rachel?'

Nervous of the big strange man she backed away, nodding.

'All right, Eva, don't worry, stay there.' He knew she would panic if he tried to coax her inside. 'I'll fetch Rachel.'

Flint finished off a roll-up cigarette. It wasn't his goats he had on his mind. He was thinking about a village girl, sixteen-year-old Serenity Treneer, a sister of Wilf's. Now, thanks to the reward, he was a man of some means and felt it was the right time to settle down and start a family. He would carry on as a miner for a year or two while building up the smallholding, then he planned to live entirely off the land. He wouldn't have to suffer the fate of lung disease or crippling arthritis without hope of an income as had been the lot of many a miner before.

Serenity was the younger by eleven years, and worked as a bal-maiden on the mine surface, breaking up the ore. An eye-catching, hard-working girl, her name belied her vivacious disposition. She laughed over just about anything and sang loudly; she was witty and clever and not easily fooled. She was greatly sought after by the youths and single men, some coming from further away on market day to catch a glimpse of her. He needed to be quick or Serenity would be snapped up and hurried down the chapel aisle. Flint decided Serenity Treneer would make the ideal wife for him.

Satisfied, he stretched out his brawny arms. His mother would be pleased. She had pestered him about becoming a husband and giving her grandchildren. Strange, he had been out here a long time and had thought he wouldn't get to finish his smoke before Eva appeared to call him in.

In fact, he realized, all seemed unusually quiet. He found the back kitchen door wide open. He didn't bother to take off his boots or wash his hands at the stone sink. There were no sounds of crockery rattling, no chattering voices. A sensation of alarm hit him. He could smell the supper burning. He rushed through to the kitchen. At first it seemed deserted, then he saw his mother's feet down on the floor, stick-

126

ing out from the table leg.

'Mother!' She was lying on her side. He fell to his knees beside her, his hands hovering above her for a moment, then he shook her gently. 'Mother, what's the matter? Did you take a fall? Oh, my God! Oh no, Mother!' He saw the awful truth in the distortion of her face. His dear mother couldn't move or speak and although her eyes were open he was sure she was aware of nothing. She had suffered a stroke. She would be humiliated if she knew she had wet herself.

Very carefully he gathered her up in his arms. He would need help to open the doors in order to get her upstairs and on to her bed. 'Eva! Eva! Where are you? Missus needs your help.'

There was no answer and no sound. Eva must have been frightened by his mother's collapse and gone into hiding, fearful that it was her fault. Manoeuvring so he could grab his mother's shawl off a chair back, he put it on the settle for her head then laid her down. He went to the kitchen door of the stairs, and shouted up the stairs. 'Eva, sweetheart, it's Flint, can you come down please?'

Receiving no reply, he took the stairs three at a time and entered the smallest bedroom, Eva's room. If she was hiding in here it would have taken time and effort so his mother must have had been lying on the kitchen for a few minutes. 'Eva?' He looked under the bed and behind her clothes, hanging from a rack – a good amount for a working-class girl, thanks to him and his mother and Rachel Kivell. There was no sign of her in the other rooms or downstairs in the small front room. 'Oh, no,' he sighed, his worries escalating. The open door ... Eva must have taken fright and run away. He'd have to look for her but for the moment his mother was his first priority.

Taking the front steps he ran the fifty yards to Wilf Treneer's little cottage, knocked on the misshapen front door and went straight in. The children had all been put to bed and Wilf and his wife, Johanna, and Serenity, joining them at the supper table, met his breathless anxiety. Flint blurted out, 'It's Mother, she's had a stroke, and Eva's run off somewhere.'

A minute later, Flint was back home with Serenity, who had come to help. Wilf had gone to fetch Frettie Endean and Dr Lockley, and to organize a search for Eva. Flint could afford the doctor's fees. He was desperately worried to have left his mother even though he'd had no choice. If she had worsened or died all alone he'd never forgive himself. One glance, however, told him she was exactly as before. 'Help me get her upstairs, Serenity.'

When Irene was placed gently on her bed, noises were heard downstairs, and then outside in the road, the clip-clop and rumble of a horse and trap. Flint and Serenity responded to Frettie Endean clomping up the stairs. 'Help her, Mrs Endean,' Flint implored. 'Will she always be like this? Some people recover from strokes, don't they? What are my mother's chances?'

'It's too early to say yet, Flint. The next forty-eight hours will be critical,' Frettie replied, going on firmly, 'Now, no arguments mind, but this is no place for you. I've got to get your mother undressed ready for the doctor. You get down to the kitchen and do something about that burning food. Serenity, my luvver, fetch up some hot water. I'll sort out a clean nightdress for Mrs Retallack.'

'Missus! Missus!' came the frantic shout from below.

'It's Eva.' Flint hastened downstairs. He was amazed to see his foster sister in the company of Rachel and Jowan Kivell.

'Eva ran to you? I should have guessed,' Flint said, scooping Eva into his arms. 'I was worried when I couldn't find you and Dolly, sweetheart.'

'Fl-int, Missus poorly,' Eva murmured, her eyes darting in fear.

'She didn't know how to articulate it but she came to me for help,' Rachel said, proud of Eva's foresight and concerned about the reason. 'We brought her back straight away. Has Mrs Retallack had an accident?'

'Worse than that.' Flint let out a mighty breath, feeling he could easily crumple as he explained what had happened to his mother.

'We're very sorry,' Jowan said. 'We're here to help. Just tell us what we can do.'

'Doctor is being fetched. You can stay and re-assure Eva and get her something to eat. After she's tucked up in bed, Mother or I always tell

129

her a story. I'd be grateful if you'd do that.' Flint kissed Eva's cheek. 'You're a good girl. Missus will be very pleased. Flint's proud of you, sweetheart. Come and sit at the table. Miss Rachel will give you some bread and cheese.'

Rachel saw to Eva's meal, pouring her a mug of tea from the large brown teapot that Serenity had placed on the table. Settled now, Eva ate and drank, chattering to Dolly on her lap all the while. Rachel was pleased to be able to see James again during this errand of mercy.

Flint felt at a loose end now he was banished from the sick room and Eva was home safely, and there were plenty of women here to do the things women usually did at these times. He wanted to weep but held it in, of course. If he knew Jowan Kivell better he'd ask him to step outside for a smoke while he waited for news. Damn it! Kivell was running his eyes over Serenity. She wasn't taking any notice of him. She exchanged a bit of banter with the mine boys but she warded off any serious interest in her. She wasn't fast and loose and he liked the idea of Serenity becoming his bride all the more. No time for such thoughts now; he paced up and down rubbing the back of his neck. Where were Wilf and the doctor? Serenity poured hot water into a pitcher to carry upstairs.

Rachel held out her hand. 'I'll do that.' She wanted to see Irene's condition for herself.

'Huh,' Serenity muttered under her breath. So, Rachel Kivell sweeps in and takes charge over her, leaving her to clean up the kitchen.

The Kivells thought they could do anything they wished and were above everyone else except the Nankervises. No matter, she was very fond of the kindly Mrs Retallack and dear Eva and, brought up as a good Methodist, Serenity was glad to help for their sakes. The only thought she had about Flint was to feel sorry for him. She poured two large mugs of tea. 'Can I get you men anything to eat?'

Flint shook his head. His gut was too twisted in worry to want food.

'No, thank you.' Jowan smiled and then introduced himself.

Flint grimaced. He should have answered Serenity properly. She'd think he had no manners.

'I'm Serenity Treneer. I was having supper next door at my brother's when Flint rushed round to get help. I'll clear up the burnt food and wash the pots.' Serenity was unused to close male company outside her family and these two men were overly masculine types. Jowan Kivell was well known for flirting and using women for pleasure and she didn't like him giving her the eye.

While Serenity was busy in the back kitchen the two men glanced at each other. Shuffling on his feet, for he did not feel particularly welcome here, Jowan asked, 'Has your mother been unwell lately?'

'No. A bit tired, perhaps, but this is a bolt out of the blue.' A flood of guilt burned inside Flint. He should have urged his mother to take more

131

rest. She was always busy. He had never known her to be still. When she wasn't on her feet she was sewing or knitting. If he had married by now there would have been a daughter-in-law here to help in the house.

'Was looking after Eva too much for her, do you think?'

'No. Eva settled in almost at once. She's like a child but she never throws tizzys and she's not a bit demanding. Mother's found a lot of delight in her – we both have.'

'Mrs Retallack will need a lot of nursing over the next few weeks. It will be hard for you. Eva's not going to understand what's going on. Would it help if we took Eva home with us for a while?'

Flint's reaction was to say no. It didn't sit easy, accepting help from the self-important Kivells. But he had to arrange for someone to sit with his mother while he went to work and tended the smallholding. Eva would be an added burden for a carer, and she might be unsettled by Flint's mother's lack of response to her until, pray God, she got better. 'I'd be grateful for that, but I'd like Eva to be brought here to see us. I'm going to have to get a proper housekeeper.' It hit him then that his life was changed forever. He needed to earn enough to pay someone to take charge of the house and care for his mother and Eva. No new wife would want to do that. His future wasn't going to be one of personal fulfilment as he had been planning only half an hour ago.

'I'm sure Rachel would be glad to do it.' Jowan was keen for this. Rachel seemed happier this evening but she was apt to be downcast. Eva would be a good diversion for her.

'But will she manage? She's got Lady Churchfield to care for.'

'The nurse is responsible for her care. Eva will be fine at Chy-Henver. She can have a little room all to herself.'

'Thanks, Kivell, it will be a lot off my mind.' Flint looked in anguish at the front door. 'Where's Wilf and the doctor?'

Five minutes later Wilf was there, but he had brought the apothecary Henry Cardell, Jowan's uncle by marriage, with him. 'Doctor refused to come,' Wilf said in disgust. 'Said he'd been seeing patients for the last eighteen hours, needs his rest, and has to go over to Poltraze at daybreak. He said Mrs Endean will know what's best to do.'

'Damn him! My mother's life is at risk,' Flint seethed. 'I've never missed my doctor's pence at the mine every month. He must know I can afford to pay for my mother or I wouldn't have sent for him. Thanks for coming, Mr Cardell.'

Serenity had come through to listen. 'Well, that doctor's only really interested in those with money. Shall I show Mr Cardell up?'

'Please, Serenity.'

'And will you go to my sister and tell her there's been a change of plans, Serenity?' Jowan gave her a lingering smile. 'Eva will be spending some time with us at Chy-Henver. Ask her

133

to pack Eva's things. The sooner we leave the easier it will be for Eva to settle in and for the rest of you to tend to Mrs Retallack's needs.'

Rachel was holding Irene's cold, limp hand. 'What are her chances, Mrs Endean?'

'I don't think she'll die. Her heart seems to be beating strong. I've seen many a case like this. Her face has straightened out a bit and her limbs are twitching. She'll make some recovery but it'll take a long time. Hopefully she'll recover enough to be able live a worthwhile life.'

'I hope so; she's a wonderful woman.' Rachel blinked back tears. 'Uncle Henry! Is Dr Lockley here yet?'

'He couldn't be bothered to come,' Serenity said crossly. When she explained the arrangement about Eva, Rachel's heart hit her feet. Would this prevent her going away with James next week? Why did this have to happen now?

Thad slipped up to his bedroom to get the novel he was reading. Lady Churchfield's door was ajar and he saw that Nurse Carveth had nodded off to sleep over some knitting. Curious to see how the lady was faring, he crept to the end of the bed. It was a shock to see her eyes were wide open and staring up at the ceiling. She was completely still. Had she died suddenly? The bruises on her face had faded to a jaundiced yellow and the swollenness had gone.

He tiptoed to her side and his mouth fell open

when she turned her head and gazed back at him. 'Lady Churchfield,' he said softly. 'Can you hear me?'

'Yes.' Her voice surfaced as a dry rasp. She licked her crusty lips. 'Where ... am I?'

Thad knew he should rouse Nurse Carveth but he wanted to talk with the lady. Rachel and Jowan were sympathetic towards her but were eager for her to be out of the house. Thad always looked deeper into people, seeking reasons for their behaviour. From the moment he had glimpsed Lady Churchfield that night down in the hallway he had felt there might be more to her than a self-centred, condescending, high-stepper, although he did admit one would have to dig very deep to find it. Now she had been brought almost to rock bottom, what would be the result?

'You're at Chy-Henver, the carpentry business. You called here one night some weeks ago when your hired carriage went off the road. Do you remember?'

She brought a trembling hand out from the bedcovers and pressed it to her brow, furrowed with aches and bewilderment. What had happened to her? Why was she in this little room? She had come to a few moments ago and had lain in a daze until this man, not a gentleman but well dressed, had spoken to her in this little room. 'No. What name did you call me?'

'Lady Churchfield. You're Helen Churchfield. Is that name familiar to you?'

'No, not at all.'

Thad was impressed by her dignity; she had no idea who she was but she was not giving way to panic. 'You have a cousin, Mrs Adeline Nankervis at Poltraze. You were staying there.'

'Pol-traze.' She rolled the word inside her befuddled mind. 'Is that a big house?'

'Yes, it's owned by Mr Michael Nankervis. I'm Thaddeus Kivell, by the way, known as Thad. My cousin and I jointly own the business here.'

Helen swallowed and licked her lips. Her mouth was parchment dry and felt furred up, but she did not ask the tall man for water. It would never do to favour that sort of help from a man of lower station. Then she saw she was being attended by a nurse and that she was snoring with her head down, but right now she wanted to question this man – nurses were never forthcoming, urging one only to take medication and rest. 'Why am I here? Why not at Poltraze?'

'You were leaving there but sadly you were attacked and robbed. You were abducted and found not far from here on the downs. It was considered ill-advised for you to be taken away.' How would she react if she remembered all or part of the dreadful facts? After what she had been put through she could be affected in just about any distressing way. She would have to be told she wasn't welcome any longer at Poltraze. What reasons could be given her?

Exhausted by the effort to talk and to remember, Helen was drifting into deep sleep, her eyelids closing.

Thinking Nurse Carveth really ought to be told about her patient's wakefulness, Thad went round the bed and gently shook her shoulder.

'Oh! What ... Oh, Mr Kivell, I nodded off. Is something the matter?'

'Lady Churchfield was fully conscious for a few moments. She has no idea who she is.'

'Why didn't you wake me?' the nurse chided, up on her big feet. 'Out of the room, young man, and please don't venture in here again without my permission.'

Thad took no heed of the order. He would seek to talk to Helen Churchfield again. Her progress meant Rachel and Jowan would hope soon to have her out, but Thad wanted to make sure the lady, stripped of her memory, was ready for the next enormous change in her life.

Ten

For Eva's stay at Chy-Henver, Rachel thought it best she shared her room, at the back of the house. Eva had been through a lot of disruption and had clung to Rachel's hand during the journey to the house. She was a little used to Jowan but unsure of Thad, another stranger, even though he spoke softly and kindly.

'You'll sleep with me in this big bed, sweet-heart,' Rachel explained. She smiled as Eva giggled while she helped her change into her nightdress and to brush her teeth with the tooth powder, and into bed. Eva had three missing teeth, luckily not in a prominent position, and her other teeth were in poor condition. Rachel would take her to Uncle Cardell to have them looked at and possibly some pulled. Poor Eva, she would hate it, but it would be better than getting agonizing toothache or an abscess.

Rachel tucked her in, kissed her cheek, now ruddy and just a little spotty, and turned down the lantern light. Holding Dolly to her chest, Eva put her hands together and closed her eyes. 'Dear Jesus, dear Jesus, Amen. Help Missus, Amen.'

'Amen,' Rachel repeated, touched by Eva's trust and learning, and the fact that she had not forgotten Irene. She recited a story remembered from her childhood about fairies and little furry animals – no giants and wicked witches to frighten her – and Eva fell asleep quickly.

Rachel went to the next room. Helen was also sleeping, an alert Nurse Carveth glancing at her while she fed the fire with logs. 'Thad said she had come round and was actually speaking to him. Does this mean she will wake up normally in the morning?' Pleased about Helen's pro-gress, she gazed down on her face. Some of the fineness had re-established itself but she was far from peaceful, grimacing and moaning, her whole body restless. Dreaming of dreadful

138

things, no doubt.

'I should think so, Miss Rachel.' Nurse Car-veth felt her patient's brow then placed a damp cloth there to cool her. 'Mr Thad said she was totally lucid and of a quiet mind, but that was because she remembered nothing, not even who she was. It will probably be a different story when her ordeal comes flooding back.'

'It might not though; that's a possibility, isn't it? She may never remember what's gone before in her life. It would be a blessing and a curse, I suppose.'

'We can only wait and see. I suggest you get to bed, Miss Rachel. There might be a rough ride ahead and you've got the other young woman to look after now.'

'And Mrs Retallack to worry about. Good-night Nurse Carveth.'

Getting into bed with Eva was strange but it was also a comfort to have the innocent soul close by. Rachel felt guilty to be shortly leaving her behind for good. It was hard to dream of her coming happiness when all around her were suffering. She would let her joy wash over her next week, but she knew she would always hold some sorrow at missing her family and friends. By running off with a married man she would cross a line that could never be retraced. She would be a scarlet woman, a trollop, and a home-wrecker. She would be denying an in-nocent woman of her husband, the husband she was devoted to. For the rest of her life she would have Charlotte Lockley's heartbreak and humiliation on her conscience. Could she go through with it? How could she not? She loved James so much it was impossible to live without him.

Flint sat all night with his mother. Frettie Endean in her usual caring way had stayed on. He left the room only when it was necessary for Frettie to see to his mother's personal needs. He kept the fires fed, paced about and prayed, went outside for a smoke and to cry privately. The Methodist minister had called and Flint had stood at the bedside like a helpless child. 'Please don't let my mother die, please make her better,' he'd joined in the prayers. 'I'll do anything, but don't let her go on like this.' His greatest fear was that she would remain paralysed and unheeding, a shell of her former self. She would hate that, but he couldn't bring himself to pray that if this was the case that she be taken up to Heaven.

At first light he tended to the animals and fetched in water and wood. He faced the black iron slab in the kitchen, so empty and bleak without his mother bustling in front of it. How did his mother make tea? Frettie Endean would be gasping for some and she deserved a hot drink after her tireless efforts. He'd never made tea before but he had watched his mother often enough so he should know but his mind was blank.

A tap on the back kitchen door hailed the arrival of Serenity Treneer, on light feet. She pulled off her shawl and placed it over a chair then tied on a full white apron. 'Hello, Flint. I'm here to do what I can before I leave for work. Johanna will take over from me, and I dare say others will be popping in all day. You're not to worry about anything except yourself and the smallholding. Wilf said if you're not going below grass today, he and the others will manage the tribute. I'll start by making tea and some breakfast.'

'Thanks, Serenity.' Her kindly presence brought tears behind Flint's eyes. 'I'm not hungry but I expect Frettie would appreciate some oatmeal. There's plenty of goat's milk. Have some yourself.'

'I'll make up a pot full. You should eat something, Flint. It's what your mother would want, for you to keep up your strength. Has there been any change?'

'No, she's barely moved. I'll leave you to get on and go up and check on her. Thanks for coming, Serenity.'

'It's what we're all put on earth for, to help one another. I wonder how Eva got on last night.'

'Rachel Kivell will take good care of her.' He paused at the stairs. 'But I do miss Eva, it's like she's been my little sister forever. I can't wait to have her back home for good.'

That morning Charlotte Lockley was overseeing the packing of her and James's things. 'I don't like leaving for Bath without saying a

141

proper farewell to the village, James. I haven't even said goodbye to my friends.' Good manners were important to her.

'My dear, your friends here hardly count. The vicar's wife is insipid and Mrs Nankervis is not receiving visitors. Mr Nankervis has agreed we may leave straightaway. He's got a new man attending his wife and has arranged for someone to take over here at the end of the week. We are no longer required,' James said tightly. 'You are in a delicate condition, Charlotte; our child is precious to me, and the sooner I get you away to take a leisurely journey up to your Aunt Eliza's the more at ease I shall be. It is three weeks before I take up my new practice. We shall be able to do some socializing, look for the best clientele.'

James went to the study and packed the last of his books. 'Can't think why I ever came to this damned, God-forsaken place.' He used the worst of language under his breath. He couldn't wait to shake Meryen's dust off his shoes. It had been a trial to hide his fury from Charlotte at the way Michael Nankervis had dropped his services and was totally unconcerned that he was leaving, but it was consolation that he would now better his position and move in the best of circles. It didn't matter that he wouldn't witness the suffering of Helen Churchfield if she regained her senses. It was enough to know he had damned her to a hellish existence forever. He didn't give one single thought to Rachel.

* * *

When Dora arrived for work the following day she didn't even bother to put on her apron before she plunged into the latest gossip. She was throbbing with excitement. 'Miss Rachel! You'll never guess—'

'Shush, Dora.' Rachel frowned crossly, sitting at the breakfast table with Eva. 'Must you always come in like a herd of cattle?' Her mixed feelings of elation and guilt and sorrow were beginning to become a strain and she had a nagging headache.

'Well, if you don't want to hear my news – although it will concern you if Lady Churchfield suddenly needs medical help – I'll keep quiet then.' Dora pursed her lips, set her face like granite and disappeared into the back kitchen.

Medical help? What did that mean? Rachel jumped up and followed the maid. 'What are you talking about? Is Dr Lockley ill?' It would be so disappointing not to see James today for Helen's latest examination, to find out if he had a definite time for them to leave. These last days were worse than she could have imagined. Having Eva trot round after her was a joy and there was so much she would like to do for her, like getting her a kitten. Helen had not woken up properly yet and had just been in the occasional open-eyed daze, but Nurse Carveth had said it was only a matter of time before she returned to full consciousness. Helen would need a lot of understanding. Rachel was curious about how she would be – she might be as

143

unpleasant as before – but Rachel felt guilty to be running out on her too.

'I'm not saying anything.' Dora plunged the plug in the sink. When she took umbrage she could sulk for ages. 'Have you finished with your dishes? I want to get on. I'm a lot busier these days with all these extra people in the house.'

This set Rachel on tenterhooks. Something had happened concerning James and she would have to grovel to discover what it was. It wasn't true that Dora now had an unfair amount of work to do; Rachel made sure she did all the extra jobs herself. 'I'm sorry I snapped at you. I'm not feeling well, but it wasn't fair to take it out on you. Please, Dora, tell me what you were going to say. I have Lady Churchfield's interests to consider. She may need urgent medical help at any moment if she remembers everything.'

'All right.' Dora sucked in her cheeks, clearly displeased she'd been denied telling the tale with relish. 'It's the talk of the village. The Lockleys have just upped and left. Packed up and gone, they have. A new doctor's supposed to be arriving at the end of the week.'

'What?' Rachel felt the breath rushing out of her. She felt numb and unreal. This couldn't be true. She hadn't heard right. 'Say that again?'

'Yes, a bit of a shock, isn't it? Dr Lockley and his wife have left Meryen without as much as a backward glance. That's all they cared about we here. I always thought that man was a snob.'

Rachel felt as if she was shrinking a bit at a time, that she was being compressed by some terrible great weight and would end up ground down flat on the floor. James had run out on her? Gone without an explanation or even a short note? The awful truth dawned on her in a terrible rush. He had lied to her all along. Everything he had promised her was a lie and she had fallen for everything he had said. He had used her. He had never intended to go away with her. He had never loved her. She had been a stupid, blind fool.

'There's more,' Dora went on triumphantly, getting into her stride, washing dishes. 'One of the maids says she knows for a fact that Mrs Lockley is expecting. She always knew when the lady was indisposed and that hasn't happened for at least a couple of months. They've gone up to Bath, the maid believes, where the baby will have a better start.'

Charlotte was pregnant? James had said he hadn't lain with his wife for years, yet all the time he had been calling on his marital rights. Dots danced in front of Rachel's eyes, her stomach churned, she felt sick. All she wanted at that moment was to die.

'Miss Rachel, are you all right? You've gone as pale as pump water. You'd better sit down.' Rachel felt Dora's wet hands on her and she was led back into the kitchen.

Dora eased her down into the armchair at the hearth. 'Lean over and put your head down, my luvver. It will stop you from fainting. Eva! Eva dear, can you fetch the nurse? Get help for Miss. Do you understand?' She pointed to the ceiling. 'Upstairs. Go up and fetch the nurse. Get help for Miss.'

Eva dropped the toast she was chewing on. She looked puzzled then seemed to grasp what was wanted of her. Clutching Dolly, she shuffled out to the hall and, grabbing the banister rail, she made a slow trudge up the stairs. She knew there was someone in one of the rooms and she knocked on them until one was opened.

Nurse Carveth stared down on her. 'Yes, what is it?'

'Help Miss, help Miss,' Eva whispered nervously to the looming stranger, pointing towards the stairs.

The nurse summed up the situation. Just in case, she picked up the smelling salts. 'You stay here. I'll go down and see what's the matter.'

Eva waited for the stranger to clomp down the stairs. 'Miss, Miss,' she whimpered, but she did as she was told. She looked into the room and saw someone in the bed. Not wanting to think frightening thoughts about Miss, she went into the room to see who was there. It could be Missus. Missus was poorly and lying in bed. She shuffled up to where she could see the person's face.

A lady was lying there, with pretty fair hair. 'Dolly see? Dolly see, lady, lady?' She held her doll up to look.

Helen opened her eyes. She blinked. What on earth was that just inches from her? She closed her eyes, opened them again and it was gone. She licked her lips. Her mouth was so dry, her throat so hot and sore. She looked up at the ceiling. She recognized the coving and lighting, and remembered the man who had spoken to her. She had been hurt and brought here to recover. What did he say his name was? What was her name? He had mentioned it but she couldn't remember. She gulped a breath in too deeply in panic.

A small movement caught her eye and the distraction halted the revolting feeling about to overwhelm her. There was someone here, a child, stooped, bow-legged and vacant-looking. No, not a child, an adolescent girl, perhaps a little older than that, but certainly a perpetual child by some cruel act of nature to her brain. She was well dressed with ringlets and ribbons in her mousey-brown hair.

'Hello, who are you? What's your name?'

'Eva.' Eva was used to being asked her name and answering. She put her doll forward. 'Dolly. Eva. Dolly.'

'I'm pleased to meet you, Eva. Dolly is very pretty. I'm ... Helen. Yes, that's it. I think my name is Helen.' It was an enormous comfort to remember part of her identity. 'Who else lives here with you?'

The girl didn't seem to understand and just stared and grinned. Helen saw medicine bottles on the bedside table. She reached for one thinking the label would likely have her full name on it, but lacking movement for so long, her arm wouldn't stretch far enough. She pointed before her arm flopped down on the bed. 'Eva, could you pass me one of those little bottles, please?'

One of Eva's favourite things was to pass and fetch things for others. Lifting one of the tiny bottles very carefully, she put it into Helen's waiting palm. Helen lifted the bottle to her eyes. There was writing on the label: Valerian, Lady Churchfield. She recalled the man telling her he was called Thad Kivell, that this house was Chy-Henver, part of a carpentry business, and she was Helen, Lady Churchfield. For some reason she didn't feel she had the right to the title of Lady, and she knew somehow she hadn't been born a Churchfield. Who was she really? She studied her left hand. There was the faint indentation where a wedding ring had been and healing flesh as if it had been ripped off her finger. What had happened to the ring? Had it been stolen? Had she torn it off because her marriage had ended badly to Sir Somebody Churchfield? What a strange thing not to be able to remember her own husband. What was her subconscious mind protecting her from? What was the story behind her injuries? With a heavy heart she knew she had been beaten brutally and had not been in an accident. There had been a nurse in attendance – where was she?

'Lady poorly,' Eva piped up. Then, taking in the lady's strained expression, she became un-settled and made for the door hugging Dolly tight to her chest. 'Lady poorly ... Missus
148

poorly ... Miss poorly...' She must go down to Miss; she needed Miss.

'Wait, Eva, are they laid up in bed too? Who are you, Thad's sister? I wish you could tell me everything.' Had these two other women been hurt too? This was all so strange and frightening. She tried to sit up a little but her head began to spin. If only she could get out of this bed and make her way downstairs and seek answers.

Then she heard the barking and yapping of dogs outside, dogs at play, but it shot a dark horror all the way through her and she gripped the bedcovers. Venetia! A terrifying flashback of her precious little brown and white dog being kicked to death played out in every sickening detail inside her stricken mind. She was back on the road, cowering beside the carriage while her beloved Venetia was yelping in terror and agony. And now she lay panting against the pillows with her hands clamped to her mouth so she wouldn't frighten Eva. She sobbed into her hands as scalding hot tears seared her eyes and spilled over her fingers. Venetia had died because someone hated her, Helen, and she couldn't bear the thought that it had all been her fault.

Eva saw her crying; she was puzzled but knew in her limited senses that the lady needed help, like the kind Miss and Missus gave to her. She shuffled back to the bed and, after a struggle, got her small self perched up on it and placed a little hand on the lady's shoulder.

Helen grasped her hand. 'Oh Eva, don't go,' she wept. 'Not yet, please stay with me awhile.'

Rachel had rallied to the smelling salts and was sipping a cup of hot sweet tea to stop the nurse and Dora fussing. Inside she was hurt beyond comprehension yet felt strangely anaesthetized, the result of the shock, which might not be an ally in the end, but was so welcome right now in her desperation. Her heart had been shattered into a million pieces, never to be whole again. If the Almighty at that moment gave her the option between life and death she'd choose death because she had no idea how she would go on.

'You've been overdoing it, Miss Rachel,' Dora chided like a bossy mother. 'You've took on too much. Eva's not much trouble and we can manage her between us until Flint can have her back, but take my advice and send word over to the squire that he must take over Lady Churchfield's care. You're not responsible for her; she's had a bad time of it, I know, but she's not worth making yourself ill over.'

Nurse Carveth shot Dora a hostile look. If the maid had her way she'd be out of her job sooner than anticipated or made to endure the upheaval of a move with her patient. It was good to be here with the hospitable Kivells and Miss Rachel helping with the nursing. 'I'll take you upstairs, Miss Rachel. You need a long rest then a nourishing meal. Dora, could you make a pot of chicken broth?'

'Of course,' Dora replied tartly; she knew what to do. 'I'll put plenty of blood-strengthening herbs in it. I'll tell the men Miss Rachel's been took bad.'

As weak as she felt, Rachel couldn't stand the thought of being treated as an invalid or to have Jowan and Thad fussing over her. 'I'm all right, really,' she stressed. 'It's nothing. I get like this occasionally. It's only nature, my monthly. I'll be fine in a minute. Thank you for your concern, both of you, but all I want is to see where Eva is. It's a fine day outside. I'll take her down to the village to see Mrs Retallack. The fresh air will do me good. I'll go on to my Uncle Henry's and get some liquorice; that will build me up. Please let's hear no more about it, I certainly don't want to be embarrassed by having to explain to Jowan and Thad.'

'Well, if you're sure, Miss Rachel,' Nurse Carveth said doubtfully.

Dora said authoritatively, 'Some maids do have a bad time of it. Some aren't right until they're married and had their first baby. That usually sorts nature out for 'em.'

Cold fingers of fear crept into Rachel's stomach. She had lied about having her monthly. *Please God, don't let me be pregnant now.* She just couldn't have a baby. It was the last thing she wanted, a constant reminder of James's betrayal by having his baby. It would ruin her life. There was only one thing that would take her mind off this, one person, and that was Eva. She'd go to her at once and get them both out of the house before she went mad.

She climbed the stairs, her legs like water, with Nurse Carveth close at her side. 'Did Eva go to our room?'

'I don't know, Miss.'

The door to the sick room was ajar and Rachel was astonished at the scene of Eva comforting a weeping Helen. 'Oh, bless her.'

'She's a little treasure.' Nurse Carveth smiled.

They went in to ask Helen why she was crying. She was awake and had obviously remembered at least some of the details of her ordeal. Rachel knew one thing. Eva was more than a treasure and a blessing. She was the only one who could now provide some purpose to her life. Thank God she was here right now or Rachel wouldn't be able to go on. She would speak to Flint Retallack today. There was no way she was going to give Eva up again.

Eleven

'You wish to see me, my dear?' Michael sauntered up to Adeline where she was reclining comfortably on the couch in her room. He was pleased at how she had perked up under the care of the new physician, Dr Manners, who had prescribed a slightly more mobile confinement for her, allowing her to spend short periods out of bed looking over the panoramic view of the parkland. 'A lady cannot be expected to find the necessary strength to endure her labour if she is treated entirely as an invalid and all she is stimulated by is the sight of the ceiling. Mrs Nankervis needs to be kept interested and cheerful,' Dr Manners had stated.

'Yes, dear.' Adeline waved a two-page letter at him. Her expression was serious and her tone peeved. 'I've received this from Mrs Hobden and it has provided me with an unpleasant shock. She is worried that I have forsaken our friendship because I did not answer her previous letters. Also she has detailed the terrible fate that has befallen Helen on the day she left here, and asks what I think about the fact she is being nursed at Chy-Henver. I take it, Michael, that you did not want me to know about Helen's abduction and that you ordered my mail to be kept from me?'

He hid a scowl. Damn the wretched vicar's wife and damn the servant who had passed on the letter. 'I make no apologies, my dear. It was in your best interests. Helen had caused you nothing but distress from her first day here and she was very nearly responsible for the loss of our baby. How could I tell you about Helen without you becoming inconsolable and causing further risk to yourself and the baby's health? Helen was missing for days; every day for you would have been a torment. I daresay Mrs Hobden has dramatized the whole affair. Did she mention I'd offered a reward of twenty

153

guineas for information about Helen when she went missing? Helen was discovered close to death near to Chy-Henver. The two miners who happened upon her did the right thing by taking her there. She would not have lived if they had brought her here. I'm paying well to have Helen cared for with every consideration.'

'I thank you for that, Michael,' Adeline said, soft and pliable again. 'You did very well for Helen. I see that now. I'm sorry if I intimated an unjust accusation. Apparently Helen has passed crisis point and has regained a little strength. As soon as she can travel she must be brought here.'

'No!' Michael linked his hands behind his back and leaned towards his wife. 'Adeline, please understand there are very good reasons for which I cannot possibly have that woman back under our roof.'

'What reasons?'

'I would rather not explain. My dear, trust me that I know what's best.'

'I acknowledge your kindness towards me, Michael, but I would prefer that you tell me everything. One cannot keep secrets anyway. Servant gossip alone will provide me with the facts and they will inevitably be blown out of proportion. I would rather not receive any more disagreeable shocks.'

'Very well, but I wish I'd never had to tell you this, Adeline.' He sighed as if he had a great burden on him and shook his head sadly. Sitting on the edge of the couch, he took Adeline's soft white hands in his. 'This is going to be difficult.' Not really; Helen Churchfield would be further damned by the time he had finished. He wanted her out of his life without having to put his hand any deeper into his pocket. 'Try not to be too upset by this, my dear. After I told Helen she must leave here, the following morning she went into another of her rages. I've never seen a lady behave in such a disgraceful manner. She yelled like a fishwife. She blamed me for everything, even for Ashley stealing her jewels. Even though I offered her a reasonable settlement, she spat and swore. She said I must let her stay here for good. I refused and she screamed that she hoped ... that she hoped our baby would be born dead. I couldn't believe what I was hearing.'

'She actually wished that?' Adeline shuddered, her wan face darkening with affront.

'Try to be brave, but I'm afraid she did.'

'She wished our baby dead?' Adeline's voice rose. 'How could she? The despicable bitch – but then Helen always was utterly selfish and vindictive. If she had approached you in sorrow and with decorum and informed you of Ashley leaving her destitute then you would have been only too glad to offer her indefinite hospitality. I am sorry for her over the loss of her little dog but it in no way compares with the possible loss of our child. Thank God she survived her ordeal. What plans have you for her now?'

'So you forgive me for denying you your post? I promise it won't happen again.' Michael kissed her hands tenderly and she kissed his. What a joyous thing it was to have a compliant wife. 'It's time I went over to Chy-Henver again and arranged to have her removed from the village, then all speculation about her will gradually cease. Will you be happy to allow me to use my own judgment concerning her future?'

'Gladly. I trust you to do what is right and fair. I don't want to think about Helen ever again. Is there any hope her attacker will be apprehended?'

'It seems highly unlikely. The circumstances were most peculiar. The authorities believe the villain may have moved on to new pastures. Let us hope so. Now, my dear, all we need do is to look forward to the birth of our child.'

Rachel drove with Eva in the trap to Three Steps cottage, chatting to her or thinking about Helen to allow her no time to think of her heartbreak. Not far under the surface was a huge outpouring of tears but she was determined not to give way to them, afraid if she wept she would never stop. Helen's plight also made her feel emotional. Rachel had been deeply touched to find Helen trying not to scream and holding back her torment so as not to frighten Eva.

'Take Eva away, Miss Rachel,' Nurse Carveth had ordered firmly.

Rachel had taken Eva to amuse herself with her old doll's house then had returned to the sick room. The nurse had put Helen to lie back and was now preparing a sleeping draught. Helen was crying into a handkerchief, a picture of anguish and dignity.

'I'm sorry about your ordeal, Lady Churchfield,' she had said soothingly, in empathy with her for they had both just been dealt with a terrible truth and faced an empty, torturous future. 'I'm Rachel Kivell, do you remember me?'

'Yes, I think so.' Helen's voice had been watery as she sniffed into the handkerchief. 'You were unwell and I was in some sort of trouble. That was a while ago. Thank you for taking me in again. I heard your dogs barking and remembered my own little dog being kicked to death.'

'I'm so sorry about that. Do you remember anything else?'

'Now, Miss Rachel, it won't be good for her ladyship to dwell on those things yet,' Nurse Carveth had admonished. 'It will be better to allow things to come back to her slowly. Now, your ladyship, drink this and you'll soon be asleep. You've had enough to cope with for one day.'

Helen closed her eyes for a moment then opened them to look up at Rachel. 'There is so much I want to know but sleep would be so good right now.'

'I'll come back later today.' And Rachel had touched Helen's shoulder to convey her support.

Rachel helped Eva down from the trap but

before she could tether the pony to the doorstep railings of the Retallack cottage Eva disappeared round the back. Rachel followed on quick steps, not wanting to be alone for a second.

'Flint! Flint!' She heard Eva's excited squeals.

Rachel rounded the building and went in through the rounded-topped wooden gate incorporated into a low wall of stone. Two more walls and an overgrown hedge at the bottom end enclosed the half-acre smallholding. The ground was well 'teeled', as the locals called it, with rows of cabbages, other greens, onions and more, and a large herb patch and a small flower border. Two pink and grey pigs snuffled in the pen and the goats were grazing near their newly erected house.

Flint was sawing logs by the shed. He ran to Eva and swept her up in his big arms. 'Hello, sweetheart. I've missed you.'

Eva hugged his neck, and although Rachel was glad they shared a close relationship she was wildly jealous, wanting Eva all to herself. Eva giggled as Flint put her down and tugged her doll's woollen plaited hair. 'I see Dolly's got a new bonnet. She's the grandest doll in Meryen.'

He noted how pale and lifeless Rachel was. 'Thanks for bringing her. I'm on the afternoon core and I'm glad I didn't miss her. I hope she's not been too much trouble.'

'None at all; she's been an absolute delight.' There was none of his usual belligerence and Rachel observed the tiredness and measure of helplessness in him. He obviously hadn't had a moment's sleep since his mother's collapse. 'How is Mrs Retallack?'

'Just about the same,' he sighed. 'It could be days before there's an improvement. Frettie Endean's hopeful she'll get some of her movement and speech back. People have been very kind, bringing food and helping out.'

'Well, that's what community life is all about.' Rachel knew this from the frequent times she spent at Burnt Oak, where most of the Kivells still lived. She would take Eva there. She would love playing with all the children.

'Come inside,' Flint said. 'I'll take you both up to Mother. Eva's little voice might rouse her a bit.'

'You seem to have everything under control,' Rachel said to Flint, pleased for him. They were down in the kitchen after leaving Eva upstairs chattering to Irene. Frettie was in the bedroom overseeing things.

'No thanks to that damned doctor!' Flint's strong features grew murky with anger. 'Have you heard he's sneaked off? Good riddance to him.'

Rachel's heart was cut to pieces. How would she cope with her heartbreak and the secret of her shame? She merely nodded.

'Would you like some tea? 'Fraid it's quite stewed.'

'No, thank you. Mr Retallack, I would like to talk to you about Eva.'

'Oh yes?' He responded warily to the serious tenor in her voice.

'I'll come straight to the point—'

'Oh will you?' he interrupted.

'Hear me out, please,' she returned impatiently. 'This will be to your advantage.'

'I doubt it.' He folded his arms. 'Go on.'

'Why do you have to be so defensive?' Rachel narrowed her eyes. Wretched, prickly man, he hadn't heard what she had to say but was intent on making things difficult. Did he believe she was the devil's daughter? 'I want to give Eva a permanent home at Chy-Henver. I could do a lot for her. I—'

'You didn't want Eva before. You couldn't palm her off on my mother fast enough. What's changed?'

The man I love has run out on me, her heart and spirit cried out, threatening to drown her in a pool of despair. She felt she was choking, that the life was being sapped out of her. 'Are you accusing me of contributing to your mother's stroke?'

'No, I didn't say that. What happened to her was inevitable. Why do you want Eva with you all of sudden? It'll be easier for you now, eh? Now she's all cleaned up and learned some manners. Now she's sweet and adorable. She's not some sort of amusement, a pet.'

'I know that!' Rachel cried. 'You've got a nasty mind.' His vilification was too much. She couldn't stand his hostile gaze another moment and ran out of the house. She couldn't stop the tears now, scalding hot and bitter they cascaded down her face, and unable to find her hanky she wiped at them with her sleeves. She halted round the side of the cottage, her body shaking as she was racked with unbearable sorrow. Her legs felt like straw and she threw a hand against the wall or she would have sunk to the ground.

Flint went after her. Puzzled and sorry at upsetting her so much, he was at a loss as to what to do. He wasn't used to this, a woman giving way to inconsolable emotions. 'Miss Kivell...'

Rachel was aware of his presence but she didn't care he was witnessing her at her lowest. She sobbed and blubbered, letting all her desolation spill out. Life could get no darker, what did it matter if the whole world saw her devastation?

Flint inched closer to her. 'Miss Kivell, is there anything I can do? Listen, I'm sorry. I had no right to say those horrible things to you, but it's more than that, isn't it? Something is tearing you apart.'

Using the hem of her mantlet, Rachel mopped her face. She thought of Eva, not wanting her to see her like this. 'I ... I...' she murmured between sobs.

She looked so vulnerable and young and feminine, not the haughty madam of before, and Flint had an overwhelming desire to take her into his arms. 'Has the lady you got staying with you upset you?'

'No, she's no trouble at all,' Rachel took a deep breath to regain some control. 'I feel very sorry for her. She seems to have changed, as if the attack has wiped out all her spirit, and she's grateful now rather than taking things for granted.'

'Seems to me that something's wiped out all your spirit too. Don't take this the wrong way, I know you genuinely care for Eva, but is this why you want her living with you, to take your mind off your troubles?'

How astute of him. She nodded. 'Things have changed for me. I really would like to have her with me. And how are you going to cope with her?'

'There won't be any problem. Frettie Endean's got no family left at home and she's agreed to move in and be our housekeeper, and there's more than enough women ready to offer what help is needed.' It meant he was back in the position of being able to take a wife. When the time was appropriate he would make his intention known to Serenity Treneer. 'I love Eva as my little sister. I'm sorry to disappoint you but she belongs here; she could never be a Kivell. You're welcome to see her as often as you like.'

Oh God. What would she do now? Concentrate on Helen – it was her only hope to get through the dark, empty, meaningless days ahead. 'Wh-when do you want her to move back?'

'Frettie's things are being brought over today. I'll fetch Eva tomorrow morning. It's best she comes back and settles in again before she gets

162

confused.'

'I'll have her things ready.' Rachel was embarrassed now. She had let her defences down in front of this man, shown her weakness, and must be red and puffy in the face. At least Eva wasn't likely to notice.

'Would you like a tot of rum? It's good stuff, better than stewed tea,' Flint asked kindly and winked. 'I keep some in the garden shed. Mother doesn't know about it.'

Rachel could easily drink herself into oblivion. 'That sounds good.' Nothing else in her life would be good from now on.

Twelve

Shown up by Thad, Michael took no care to creep into Helen's room. Helen was asleep, breathing shallowly and far from peaceful. 'I wish to speak to Lady Churchfield.' He demanded the nurse.

Nurse Carveth curtseyed. 'Begging your pardon, sir, her ladyship won't be easy to rouse and it wouldn't be wise. She's not long remembered what happened to her lapdog.'

'I have no time to waste, woman.' Michael was curt. 'Wake her, I say.' It was unthinkable that he should be disobeyed. He would not employ this nurse again or give her a character

163

reference.

Frantic now she had compromised her position, Nurse Carveth shook Helen, none too gently. 'Lady Churchfield, wake up! Mr Nankervis is here to see you. Wake up!'

'This isn't right,' Thad protested. 'Leave her be.'

'If you do not approve, Kivell, then I suggest you leave,' Michael uttered, offended by the carpenter's impudence.

'I have the right to be here. Lady Churchfield's welfare is as much my family's concern as yours,' Thad said, standing his ground. The heartless squire did not take precedence in his house. He gazed in dismay as Helen began to come round fitfully, trying to fight off the hands cruelly disturbing her.

'No, no-o!' Helen groaned.

Leaping forward, Thad pulled the nurse away. He reached for one of Helen's flailing hands. 'It's all right, shush now, no one's going to hurt you.'

Michael was impatient but left Thad to it. He would be better able to speak to Helen if she was quieted.

Sensing the strong rough hand holding hers gently was only meant to give comfort, Helen clung to it. She was in a daze but could smell the manly odour of her comforter and knew it wasn't her attacker. He'd had a scrubbed-clean, foppish smell, hinting of spices – not what one expected in a rough villain.

'Wake up, wake up, Lady Helen,' Thad murmured softly.

Following the mellow voice she allowed herself to be brought through the curtains of grey. Dark smudges under her eyes showed how little rested she was. 'Mmm, who is it?'

'It's Thad Kivell. We spoke the other day. Mr Nankervis, the squire, is here. He wishes to speak to you. Is that all right?'

Michael sighed irritably; the woman had no say in the matter.

'Nurse, help her ladyship to sit up,' Thad said, stepping away. He relinquished Helen's hand, she reluctant to let his go.

When propped up, Helen trembled under the squire's hawk-like stare. 'Why are you here, sir?' She had no recall of this gentleman but she didn't need his harsh expression to tell he loathed her. She sought Thad. He nodded to her encouragingly, which helped. She hardly knew him yet she trusted him; he would not allow anything untoward happen to her.

'I am here because it is I who is maintaining your stay here, paying all your expenses, but now I want the remainder of your recovery to be spent elsewhere and certainly not back in my house.'

'I don't remember your house. I am to leave here?' Helen knew a creeping disquietude.

'Indeed you are, later today. There is a small nursing establishment for gentlefolk at Penzance, overlooking the sea. You will stay there for a week, after which you will be moved to a property of mine in the town. A general maid

165

will see to your needs. How much do you recollect of your last day at Poltraze?'

'Poltraze? Is that your house? Everything is hazy,' Helen said nervously. 'I remember some of the terrible details of the attack on me, the attacker tormenting me many times while holding me prisoner, but I have no idea why I'm here in Cornwall and why I was at your house. I don't know my past and who my family are.'

'Then I shall tell you all.' Without the slightest thought for her feelings, or growing anguish, he told her exactly who she was and expounded each event that had led to him throwing her out of Poltraze. 'Your wilful, disgusting behaviour could so easily have been responsible for causing harm, even death, to Adeline or our child. She will no longer have society with you. On no account are you to get in touch with her. If you do I'll have you tossed out penniless on the streets. I want you out of Meryen forthwith.'

'You had no right to speak to Lady Helen like that,' Thad protested. 'Have you no pity?'

Michael ignored him. 'My decision is made and will not be altered. Nurse, get her things together. A carriage will be here shortly. You may accompany her to Penzance. I will give you money for a few days' lodging.' He ended on a note that would have Nurse Carveth believe he was being bountiful towards her.

'No, please!' Helen cried, wringing the bed sheet between frantic fingers. Her head felt about to explode from all the dreadful facts spat at her. 'I can't travel yet. Have mercy. Mr Kivell?' She lifted an imploring face to Thad.

'Don't worry,' he said, and moved beside her. 'You're not ready to travel and no one is going to make you. Mr Nankervis, I forbid you to upset Lady Helen any more. This is hardly the act of a gentleman.'

'It is the act of a man protecting his family!' Michael snarled.

'Lady Helen cannot possibly hurt your family. I'm sure she will have no desire to go to Poltraze again.'

'If you go against my wishes, Kivell, I won't go on supporting that woman, and nor will I be using your professional services again.'

Thad put a supercilious eye on him. Nankervis knew he could not threaten him or any member of his family with the usual intimidations he dealt out to others. Denying commissions to the business was all he had to call on. 'That's up to you but you will find none better. My cousin and I always have a full order book. Your support to Lady Helen is no longer required.'

'Where does all this leave me?' wailed Nurse Carveth.

'We need full-time live-in staff here. Miss Rachel is rushed off her feet. You may continue here as nurse until Lady Churchfield is well, then if you so wish you may stay on as housekeeper, but you are not to interfere with Dora.'

'Thank you, Mr Kivell, I accept.' The nurse shed a grateful tear then shook herself back into

167

her confident role.

'You have heard my decision, Mr Nankervis. Lady Helen stays here,' Thad said.

Michael thumped his fists down on the footboard of the bed. 'Damn you, Kivell! Be very sure to keep that wretched woman away from Poltraze or I'll have her thrown in gaol for trespass.' He stormed out. Thad Kivell had made him look a fool. The whole village would soon learn about it. There was nothing he could do to hurt or punish the Kivells. He had only the comfort of no longer having to provide for his wife's cousin for the rest of her rotten life. Damn the attacker, why couldn't he have finished off the job and murdered the witch?

Rachel and Eva drew up in the trap while Michael was trotting away from the stables. He did not acknowledge them and his look of fury was evident. Rachel left Eva with Dora. Fortified a little by the rum she had drunk with Flint, but still very much a physical and emotional wreck, she went upstairs to Helen's room.

'What's upset the squire?' she asked Thad, surprised to see him huddled with Nurse Carveth round the bedside. Helen was tear-stained, her green eyes wide with shock. 'Did he upset her ladyship?'

'Please,' Helen moaned. 'No more ladyship or lady anything. I don't deserve the title or aspire to it now I've been brought down so low. I wish to be known as Mrs Churchfield, and Helen to all of you here as my friends. You

168

think of me as a friend, I hope?'

'We do, and we shall do everything we can to protect you,' Thad assured her. In tones of disgust he explained to Rachel the reason behind the squire's visit, then his own decision.

'You find the arrangement agreeable, Rachel?' Helen stared at her avidly, afraid of discord. It was one thing to give her shelter but quite another to offer her a permanent home.

Rachel nodded, numb after the day's events and longing for a few minutes alone in her room. 'I'm sorry you were faced with all that. I was going to suggest that you stay with us.' She had no idea how things would pan out with Helen's foreseeable presence but at least it would help take her mind off her misery and the loss of Eva. 'I'm glad you'll be staying on too, Nurse Carveth.'

'I'll be glad to take the strain off you, Miss Rachel,' she said. 'You're not looking at all well. May I suggest you take a short rest this minute?'

'I will, and then I'll spend some time with Eva. She's going home tomorrow.'

'I shall always be grateful to you, Rachel. What will your brother say about me staying on?' Helen murmured, fearful again.

'He'll agree with us when he learns the facts.'

'But I have nothing – no money, nor anything to sell to pay my way. The attacker stole the last of my jewellery. I'll try to think of some way to repay you all for your kindness. I don't expect to be waited on, and when I'm recovered I shall help in any way I can. All I want is to feel safe.'

'Don't concern yourself about anything; you are safe here,' Thad said, torn with strange feelings about her stricken air. 'You need only to concentrate on getting well again. That goes for you too, Rachel. I'm getting worried about you.'

'No need,' Rachel said with false breeziness.

She went to her room and changed out of her travelling clothes. She would not give way to her great agony now, to dissect and mull over James's ill use and betrayal. That could wait until tonight, when at least she would have the consolation of having Eva with her.

Thirteen

In the boiler house of the Carn Croft mine, Flint and Wilf, with two of their comrades, and other underground workers, men and boys over thirteen years, changed into their working garb. The flannel shirts and drawers, canvas trousers and jackets were all stained a tawny colour but were perfectly clean. Pulling on a white night-cap, the men covered it with a round iron-hard hat for protection against falling stones. They hung two tallow candles from a jacket button-hole and carried another in one hand. By the end of the eight hours all their clothes would be

170

soaked through with sweat.

One of Flint and Wilf's team, Jeb Greep, a young enthusiastic Bible Christian, bowed his head and all except the most ardent atheists and scoffers did likewise. After Jeb Greep had implored the Almighty to deliver them back up safely, Flint added a prayer for his mother's continued recovery. In a slow, flat tone she could manage to say quite a few words now, although her memory was poor, and she could now feed herself and see to her personal needs and do a bit of knitting. She had a pronounced limp in her right foot, but in the main Flint had his mother back. With Frettie Endean in charge of the house, life passed along smoothly.

The workforce went outside. Their ears were blasted by the noise of the mine workings but none flinched, all were hardened to it. Some of the uninitiated likened it to a devil's domain, dark temples in a satanic nightmare. The steam pump hissed and pounded as it raised gallons of water from the mine depths. Chains, giant pipes and conduits stuck out in every direction, clanking, rubbing, grinding and vibrating, ripping up nerves. They were huge beams of timber and heavy coils of cable. The chimney of the engine house, a tapering tower of stone, was crowned with black-stained red brick, belching steam and smoke, ominous to some yet a glorious monument to the skilled stone masons. There were great barrows and wagons, numerous boarded sheds where equipment was kept and the sheds where the bal-maidens, including Serenity Treneer, were hard at their labour breaking up the risen ore, and boys and girls at their various picking and washing stations, and the more significant counting house. All in all it was like some immense living sculpture.

On their way to the trap door, the first vertical ladder and the black depths, Flint and the other single men drew admiring glances from some of the bal-maidens. Flint looked for Serenity. He didn't spot her but suddenly he didn't care. She never showed him any interest. He didn't know whether to be glad or disappointed that the young pretty woman found him easy to overlook. He just somehow knew she wasn't for him.

The morning core was up and the trapdoor, built into a platform over a deep gully, was raised to reveal the opening of the shaft like a chimney. Flint and Wilf went down last to allow for Wilf's slowness. Flint went down before his friend, ready to reach out should he falter or seem about to fall. It struck Flint how much he looked out for Wilf; he was not unlike Rachel Kivell caring for her dear Eva and now her lame-duck lady. Flint was godfather to all of Wilf's brood, and if Wilf should die or become incapacitated, Flint took it for granted that he would see they didn't starve and would be brought up with good values.

They began the long tricky climb down the narrow shaft, their crib bags hung over their shoulders and tools tied to their backs, not talking as concentration was supreme, soon leaving behind the few chinks of light seeping through from the outer rock. Before they reached total darkness they stepped across to a narrow landing place, each lighting a single candle and pushing it into the lump of damp clay stuck on the front of their hats. Down again they went, familiar with each irregular rung and holding on tighter to parts slippery with water or copper ooze. They passed by galleries long worked out and went on down until they reached ninety fathoms, stepping across to another landing place and entering the wide rift of the gallery where they worked. Jeb Greep and the other man would drive at the eastern end of the set. Flint, with Wilf panting noisily, advanced to the western end. They had to stoop in some places and rock pressed in all around them. The flaring light of their candles was above them and pitch darkness beneath and before them. Some boys on their first day down panicked and had to be taken up to grass and sometimes even a man of many years experience succumbed, in this unnatural nether world where every noise, even one's own breathing, was eerie, to moments of claustrophobia and sudden terror of being trapped down in the bowels of the earth forever.

Sweat poured out of their every pore, mixing with the mud, tallow and iron drippings. Reaching the place where the morning team had left off, they didn't pause but got straight to work, breaking into the ore seam with their pickaxes.

Halfway through the shift they stopped for crib, squeezed together on a rock ledge. Wilf unpacked his crib bag. Flint just gazed ahead the shadowy rock.

'Aren't you going to eat nothing?' Wilf chewed on a large bite of food. 'I promise you, Johanna makes a brave pasty.'

'What? Yes, of course, it was kind of her to bake one for me too.'

'You already said that. Things getting to you, are they? You got a lot on your mind. Do you wish you'd let Miss Kivell take Eva after all?'

'No, dear God no, but I was pulled up by how much Rachel Kivell cares about her. I got mazed when she asked to take Eva on for good. Well she was quick enough to fob Eva off on us, so I went for her. She didn't answer back as before but just went to pieces, ran outside and cried like a baby. I found myself feeling sorry for her.'

'And...?'

'And nothing, Wilf,' Flint replied sharply. There was nothing else to read into it. 'It took me by surprise, that's all. She's a puzzling woman.' It pleased him for some reason that Rachel Kivell had a fragile side to her.

'And a mighty pretty one; bet you wouldn't mind claiming a kiss or two off she.'

'Don't be daft.'

'What's daft about it? You're not her sort, I s'pose, but she'd be all right to dally with.'

'I'm hardly her sort, am I? And I couldn't be bothered. Anyway, I like casting my eye round.'

'You need a wife, boy, more 'n ever now.'

'I couldn't ask a woman to take on all my responsibilities.'

'What! They'd line up for it. You're quite well set up now, and the girls have always seen you for a fine-looking fellow.'

'Bloody hell, Wilf, you don't half talk some waffle.'

Johanna Treneer's pasty of cubed beef, potato, onion and turnip in a thick, crimped pastry case was delicious, but Flint didn't taste a single mouthful. If he'd told Wilf he'd once planned to court his sister he'd try to inveigle him and Serenity together. Wilf had hinted that they'd make a good match. Serenity was a nice girl, and she had all a man could want in a wife, but the more he thought about it the more Flint wondered if he really wanted to get tied to one woman. He enjoyed seeing women at his leisure and Lizzie, a serving maid at the Nankervis Arms, was always happy to oblige for a shilling.

Wilf was right, he did have a lot to regard, and it would take time to settle down into a new routine with Eva back home and Frettie Endean as housekeeper. He was better off on his own.

Fourteen

Mid-week, in the early afternoon, the church bells rang a joyous peel throughout Meryen.

'What's that all about then?' the villagers wondered. They had known nothing like it before.

They soon learned the news was to their advantage and were delighted. Mrs Nankervis had delivered a healthy son and heir at Poltraze. On the following Saturday afternoon and evening, when his tenants were most able to attend, the proud squire was throwing a hog roast in the village as part of the celebrations. He would provide beer and potatoes and other fare, and have planks laid down for dancing. Extra food, while starvation and ruin always lurked like a spectre, and a chance for free entertainment and laughter was an eagerly anticipated gift. What was more, every child born that year was to receive a guinea.

''Course, squire himself won't show his face there,' Dora told Nurse Carveth, now using the honorary title of Mrs Carveth, as together they set about a morning's baking, sleeves rolled up above indomitable elbows, flour filling the air, turning out loaves of bread and splits, scones

176

and saffron cake, tarts and flans. They got on well, gossiping like two runaway ponies about local life and the peculiarities and scandals of villagers and past patients. 'Thinks himself too grand to mix with the likes of us.'

'I'm glad to hear it. I hope never to set eyes on him again; got the manners of a hog, probably trained the hog for the roast himself.' Mrs Carveth and Dora joined in some uproarious tittering.

'I hope Miss Rachel goes, she needs some merrymaking. She's so down nowadays.' Dora missed the sparks that used to be the norm between her and Rachel.

'Hasn't she always been quiet and moody then?'

'Not her, she belonged to be headstrong and full of verve. It's like something's sucked the essence out of her. I thought 'twas Miss Helen getting her down, but, well, she barely pokes her nose out of the door, and now Miss Rachel isn't much better. She's stopped going to church and calls less on her relations. The only place she goes to regular is to see little Eva.'

'Well, it's a good thing her family come here and she fetches Eva here sometimes. Funny set-up here; an illegitimate brother and sister and a high-born lady living with them as a sort of companion. And the relations are a mixed bag. That maid Clemency, well I won't go on about her now ... I think Mr Thad has a bit of a thing for Miss Helen, don't you?'

Dora made a thoughtful face. 'I don't know

177

about that. He's not like the other Kivell men. They can be rather wild, stubborn as mules; it don't do to mess with none of them, even Mr Thad, but he's serious and sensitive, sees more in people than all the others. He never flies off the handle. I like un very much, he got manners like a prince.'

'Yes, he have. Mr Jowan's grateful but he takes things like women waiting on him for granted. They're both in their twenties – wonder which one will settle down first. Come to that, I'd have thought Miss Rachel would be looking for a husband, thought she'd have men running after her like buzzing bees. Her background might put off some what like to stick their nose in the air. She'd only like a man tough like her menfolk, I s'pose, but she's got the looks and figure to grace an angel. It could be her ways that's putting suitors off – I mean her melancholy and the way she shuts herself off aren't particularly attractive.'

'But like I said, she wasn't always like that. Can't think what the matter is. Let's make a nice sponge cake for tea to cheer her up. Miss Rachel don't eat enough to keep a sparrow alive these days. Do her and Miss Helen good if they went along to the hog roast. I'll mention it to the men. Think only they who could encourage them to get out of here for a while.'

Rachel and Helen spent the morning in the garden, potting in the greenhouse and sweeping the paths. It was perfectly warm and sunny and in the afternoon they took their sewing out to the little green-painted summerhouse. Like the other two older women, they had gelled, something that would have seemed impossible three months ago. They respected each other's long silences, never probing, but ready to listen if the other had something to say. Neither of them opened up, keeping their miseries under a tight rein.

On one occasion before Helen was well enough to leave her bed she had seized Rachel's embroidery and shown her prowess with needle and silks. So they worked on linen for the household, and Helen, also an expert lacemaker, had thought to make items for sale to help repay for the clothes, as fine as Rachel's, and the other necessities bestowed on her. Rachel said her company was enough recompense and the men wouldn't hear of it; when a Kivell offered hospitality it was not with the notion to gain any benefit.

Rachel leaned on the belief that she was Helen's protector and defence against the depression and madness that might yet loom up after her ordeal, that this was the reason that made it worth her getting out of bed each morning. She tried not to think about her own life and future. Thank God, time had passed and she'd discovered she wasn't pregnant. To have had James's baby inside her would destroy her, and he had already crushed her heart and stolen her spirit. He was a shallow liar. He had ripped out her heart and she had nothing left to give.

She was numb and as cold as winter.

At four o'clock Dora and Mrs Carveth gaily brought them out afternoon tea. 'Look what we've done for you.' Dora beamed like a mother spoiling her offspring. 'It's a vanilla sponge with jam, fresh cream and icing.'

'What's the occasion, is it in honour of young Nathaniel Albert Michael Nankervis?' Rachel said blandly, disappointing the two older women with her total lack of enthusiasm.

'No, it's to tempt your taste buds,' Mrs Carveth said, cutting large slices of cake and handing the plates to Dora to place on the cane table.

'It looks delicious,' Helen said in appreciation. The cake was as good as anything she had been served in a big house. All in all she preferred the less fussy food here.

Jowan and Thad arrived, bringing with them the smell of sawdust and the sense of hearty commotion, an unwelcome addition to the young women. 'Ah, sponge cake, my favourite,' Jowan said and flopped down with his feet up.

'Boots!' Rachel chided.

Jowan laughed and planted his feet on the planked floor.

Thad plonked two large mugs on the tea tray. China teacups wouldn't hold enough Darjeeling for him and Jowan. He parked near Helen at an angle where he could see her face. He enjoyed perusing her fair loveliness; she was like a tragic heroine of ancient Greek fables, but he longed to see her smile.

Helen did not mind Thad's company but she was never sure about Jowan. She had grilled Rachel about whether he objected to her staying on here and all of Rachel's reassurances that Jowan would have reacted in exactly the same way to Michael Nankervis's bullying tactics did not convince her. Jowan took little notice of her and she was careful to keep out of his way. Haunted by ghastly memories and nightmares, some so real it was like experiencing the trauma all over again, knowing the way of life she had wantonly sacrificed, she clung to her position here, taking pains never to do or say anything that might offend these new friends. They were all she had in the world.

The men both wolfed down two slices of cake and Rachel refilled their mugs. With lowered eyes Helen ate and sipped demurely while Rachel nibbled and only got through half a cup of tea.

'We've had an idea,' Jowan said, primed by Dora. 'We're going to take you ladies to the hog roast. There will be lots of our people there and we might as well join in the celebration.'

'If you don't mind I'd rather not go,' Helen said, not meeting Jowan's piercing dark eyes, always an unsettling occurrence.

'But you haven't been past the garden gate yet.' Thad smiled. 'Meryen is your home now and you have the right to wander about it. We need not stay long.'

'I ... Please, there would be too many people

181

for me to contend with.' Helen fought down a feeling of dread. The garden gate was her limit; the world outside seemed a huge dark menacing void to her.

'Helen's right,' Rachel snapped in her defence. 'She doesn't want a lot of nosy people staring at her. Her first outing should be somewhere quiet, a stroll along the road or a short visit to one of the family. I don't want to go to the hog roast either. I've no interest in the squire's baby.'

'Well, that fell flat,' Jowan said in mild complaint, wiping crumbs off his hands. 'You women are a couple of miseries, sticks in the mud. There's no laughter here any more.'

'I'm sorry, it must be my fault,' Helen said, panic taking dominance over her. She jumped up, tense as a coiled spring and ready to run. 'Please, I don't want to go anywhere. *He* might be out there. He might try to abduct me again, I couldn't bear it...'

The others got up to reassure her but Thad got a word in first. 'Don't worry, Helen, don't be frightened. You don't have to go anywhere until you feel ready to'

'And I don't have to go anywhere I don't want to. Leave Helen and me alone.' Rachel moved in front of Helen like a shield. 'Do we complain? If we were too lively and frivolous you would grumble about that. Just let us be; it's all we ask. Can't you understand?' The more she went on the angrier she got. Why couldn't the others, including Dora and Mrs

Carveth, understand they needed no more than their own company, and time to come to terms with things? Then she felt guilty, for they didn't know she had a broken heart.

Jowan was at a loss. Helen he could understand, but what on earth was wrong with Rachel? He made to confront her but Thad pulled him away. 'We had best get on. Thank you for tea,' he added, dragging Jowan outside.

Helen crumpled down in her chair, weeping softly. 'I'm sorry, so sorry.'

'There's no need to be. I understand, we all do.' Rachel sat close and leaned across and rubbed Helen's back.

'I'm not sure Jowan does. He might hate me. The man who did all those terrible things did so for one reason, because he hated me. He kept telling me, *I hate you. I hate you.* And the squire hates me; and my cousin Adeline too. I'm afraid the people out there will hate me,' Helen sobbed. 'I'm such a terrible person that I make people hate me. Oh, Rachel, I'm so afraid.'

Rachel knelt beside her. 'I know, I know. But don't ever forget, Helen, that the people here don't hate you. And nor does Eva. She loves being with you. You never, never have to leave here, I promise.'

Helen leaned down and the two women embraced. To be needed so much made Rachel feel a little better about her own self. This was what she was here on earth for, not to fall in love, to throw her life away on some untrustworthy man, but to help others. She would steer Helen towards the same goal and then she too would feel her life had some meaning.

Fifteen

Eager feet shuffled into Chy-Henver's office. 'Miss! Miss!'

'Eva!' Leaving the boring paperwork, Rachel hugged her. 'It's really good to see you unexpectedly, sweetheart. Did Flint bring you?'

'I did, hope you don't mind us just walking in?' Flint dithered in the doorway, unsure where he stood with Rachel after her breaking down in his presence and then knocking back rum like a true Kivell.

Rachel felt her cheeks pinking up and felt a little awkward. 'Not at all, you're always welcome. I'll call Helen in a minute. She's made some new clothes for Dolly. Is there any particular reason you're here?'

He smiled a friendly smile. 'We've come to ask you a favour.'

'I'm sure I'd be happy to do whatever it is,' she said.

'I'm hoping you'll agree to take Eva to the hog roast this afternoon. She'd love all the sights; there's going to be cheap jacks, sideshows, jugglers and wrestling. Frettie wants to

184

join in the fun and I'll be busy on the small-holding and keeping an eye on Mother, and it would be a shame if Eva missed out.'

'You don't have to beg, Flint.' Rachel clasped Eva round the waist. 'I'd be delighted to spoil her. I'll come and collect her immediately after lunch.'

'Are you sure you won't come with us, Helen?' Rachel popped her nose round the sitting-room door. 'I don't like leaving you alone.'

'I'll be fine honestly; you enjoy yourself with Eva.' Beside the window where she could glance out at the garden, Helen continued her needlepoint, her needle flashing in and out, her hands flying up and under the frame, unfolding a scene of mysticism, of nymphs, unicorns and a crystal stream, all from her imagination, designed to shut out the real world. 'And I won't be completely alone. The men aren't going to attend.'

'Is there anything I can bring back for you? Some treacle toffee?'

'A little delicate white lace, if you would please. Dora's soon to be a grandmother and I'd like some lace to finish off the gown I'm making for the baby.' Rachel was a good friend; she never encouraged her to take a few steps outside the property as Thad often did, telling Helen she believed she should come to it in her own time.

'Dora will be thrilled. Well, the tea tray is all set for you. We'll run along then. Mrs Carveth
185

is walking with us.'

Helen's heart thudded and trembled the instant she heard the door close ... but she would be all right on her own. After all, Rachel had been out of the house many times before. Dora didn't work on a Saturday but that didn't matter. She stabbed the needle into the cloth. If she kept up her usual rate, in an hour she would have the silvery crescent moon, the stars and planets completed. Then she would prepare a tea tray and indulge in a butterscotch biscuit, a pleasant, civilized thing to do.

A knot of pain started in her forehead and spread behind her eyes. She tried to ignore it but gradually and relentlessly pulses pounded inside her skull and a sense of nausea took a debilitating hold on her. Fearing she'd be sick, she covered her mouth with a trembling hand. Why did she have to feel ill now and so fearful? She would have been perfectly happy sewing throughout the quiet afternoon. Now heat pricked at her, all over her body, a strange unpleasant pins-and-needles sensation that set her nerves on edge. It was unbearably stuffy in here. She went to the window and took a few deep breaths of air at the open pane. It didn't help. Would anything? *Stay calm. Concentrate on something.* If she did that she would be fine in a moment. She gazed out at the arch where rambling roses would soon trail, darting her eyes to the camellias and azaleas in full bloom, and the tulips, polyanthus and crocuses in the borders. Some deadheading needed to be done;

she could put on her gardening gloves and go out and attend to it.

She looked at the door and it appeared to lean in towards her. And the walls were closing in, like living things set on merging together and crushing her inside the bricks and plaster. Turning round and round she stared up at the ceiling, her eyes gaping, terror pooling in her every fibre, reducing her to panic and madness. It was impossible, and yet the ceiling was coming down on her fast. She would be trapped and suffocate. Her next breath wouldn't come. She had to get out of this hostile room right this moment or she would die.

Dashing to the door, she thrust it open, sprinting along the passage then through the kitchen to the back kitchen. Chills like sharp dead things sank into her spine and into the very cavities of her bones. Shaking as if in freezing temperatures she reached for the door but recoiled. She couldn't go outside. The downs were out there, where her attacker had dumped her and had probably kept her prisoner. He might not be far away. He might be watching the place, ready to leap out of the shadows and snare her again, eager to heap pain and hate on her again. She hated the far-reaching scenery of the moors outside and tried not to look that way when in the garden. Here in this dull, rather dark back room she felt she was trapped in an early tomb. Wave after wave of fever-pitch dread enveloped her, perspiration trickled out of every pore and her legs felt they would not longer hold her up. She was shrinking. She couldn't breathe. She was losing her mind. She couldn't breathe!

She fled back to the kitchen, throwing her hands on the table for support or she would surely sink to the floor, her breath coming in horrible snaps. She had gone the right way to get help. Thad was only across the backyard. He would help her and be understanding. He'd do something to stop these revolting sensations. She had to get to him. Somehow she must find the courage to leave the house. It was either that or shrivel up here and suffocate to death.

There was a strange noise. *What was that?* It was like a high screech, an unnatural lament. Her desperate mind told her it was a deliberate ruse to torment her. It had to be her attacker. He had come for her. He was going to plunge her into more suffering. She opened her mouth to scream and plead for help but she had petrified and her throat had closed over.

Then she knew what the sound was. It was nothing ominous. It was only someone whistling and it was a cheerful tune. Thad! He was coming inside and he would make everything all right. Making her feet move she staggered to the back kitchen just as he was opening the door. 'Thad,' she cried, and stumbled into his arms.

'Huh,' he gasped.

She had slammed into him, surprising him, but she clung on. 'Oh, Thad, I've been so frightened.'

She felt his arms go about her, then after a moment he eased her away and looked into her face. 'I'm afraid Thad has slipped over to Burnt Oak to see his parents,' Jowan said. 'What on earth's the matter, Helen? You're shaking.'

It felt as if her insides had dropped out of her. Thad wasn't here and she had thrown herself on a man she was wary of. Her face was on fire with embarrassment and disappointment. Jowan would think her a silly female, a nuisance, and wonder why Rachel and Thad were prepared to put up with her.

Jowan had never seen anyone so stricken. Keeping a grip on her, for he was sure she'd drop down from fright and weakness, he went on, 'What's frightened you so badly? Have you seen a stranger? Don't worry, I'll send out the dogs.'

'N-no, it wasn't that.' She was appalled her voice surfaced as a whimper. 'I-I thought I was going to die.' That sounded pathetic.

Jowan summed up the situation. 'I think I know what's happened. The women aren't here and you've been overcome by panic. Come along and sit down, I'll fetch you some water.'

Sitting at the table, shuddering, she dabbed her eyes with her handkerchief, and felt stupid when her hand shook round the glass of water.

'Take a few sips.'

'Thank you, you are very kind.' She coughed as the first sip hit the back of her throat.

Jowan took the glass from her. 'Want some tea now?'

She shook her head, 'No, thank you. I'm sorry to be such a nuisance. When do you think Rachel will be back?'

Jowan chewed the inside of his mouth. Helen relied on Rachel too much, which wasn't good for either of them. 'Its better you don't stay on your own; why not come with me and look over the workshop, see where Thad and I work.'

'I suppose I could.' He was right, she was scared of being alone and she needed something to take her mind off her anxiety. She could make it there in his company. 'Are the other men and boys there? I would feel...' She trailed off, lowering her head.

'They've gone to the festivities. I've been veneering a Bible box for the vicar he's to present as a gift, come and see what you think of it, just for a little while.'

'I will, thank you.' She still wasn't sure about the short trip across the yard but she didn't want to antagonize Jowan, especially while he was being so kind. It was all her years of training to be a lady that enabled her to rise on steady feet. Outside she blinked as the sun hit her eyes. 'My hat...'

'A few seconds of sun won't mar your perfect complexion,' Jowan said, and he took her arm and tucked it into his.

Perfect complexion – he had noticed her that much? She felt shy. Dora had gossiped about Jowan being a dedicated womanizer, but she was also pleased. In the past she had taken great pains to retain a clear white skin and had been conceited about it, so now it was good to know she looked well.

'You've lived and worked here for about six years, after your elder brother and his family emigrated, Rachel told me,' she said to be conversational.

'That's right.'

'It must be good to have so many close family members and all doing well for their selves.'

'It is. Are there many in your family?'

'Just the rotten brother who abandoned and robbed me, and the elder brother who inherited our father's estate, he doesn't want anything to do with me. It was my own fault. I was too indulged and demanding, a despicable person.'

'Well done for changing,' Jowan said simply.

Helen thought this might have been said with some admiration.

'Here we are. Take a look round. I've tidied up so you shouldn't trip over anything. My bench is right in front of you and Thad's is under the long window. The item that's covered up is something he's making in secret, for Rachel I suppose. It's her birthday next month. We want to make it an occasion to cheer her up so the family is planning a secret party at Burnt Oak. We'll arrange for Eva to be brought along too. And you, Helen, if you feel you're up to it by then.'

'I'll try,' she said, not wanting to go at all. Burnt Oak seemed as far away as a distant country and she feared the very thought of mingling with so many people, who could be raucous by all accounts. 'I'm glad I know about Rachel's birthday, I'll sew something for her.'

Gazing from the double doors, Helen took everything in. The pleasant smell of scented woods infiltrated with the stronger pong of lacquer. Work stations for different tasks. Tools of various sizes all neatly arranged, most up on the walls. 'I'm amazed. The Bible box is as perfect as any I have seen. The workshop is so much bigger than I'd thought. Was all the furniture inside the cottage made in here?'

'Yes, most of it. Some we inherited from my brother Sol and his wife Amy, and Amy's father, who owned the business before them. Helen,' he asked carefully, 'do you miss your homes, the one where you grew up and your late husband's?'

'No,' she answered tightly, stepping back and looking out to the road.

'I'm sorry, I shouldn't have mentioned it.'

'It's not that, Jowan.' She gazed up at him and her pale features twisted with regret. 'I thought I had it all, wealth and the best of everything, but there was no love in either home, just a constant shuffling for position, the emphasis on things that seem trivial and even immoral now. I had no love in me, except for my dear Venetia. I was a horrid person. I never gave a single thought to how the servants' lives were, if they were ill or seemed upset I was furious. And if I could put anyone of my own standing down I relished doing so.'

'There was obviously a lot of good under the

192

surface or you wouldn't be the quiet, grateful woman you are now,' he said.

'You know that's not true.' She looked down at her feet, where her heart, soul and spirit were nowadays. 'If I hadn't been abducted and tormented and nearly died I would have attached myself to any rich man, even as his mistress. I was desperate to carry on living a privileged life.'

'That was an honest confession. It shows how much you've changed, Helen. Feel proud of that.'

'I'll never feel proud of myself, but I'm honoured to have you, Rachel and Thad as my friends, and Mrs Carveth and Dora to be happy to treat me on the same level as you.'

'So you prefer your life now to how it was before?'

'I can truthfully say yes. I feel I have more purpose to my life now. I just wish...'

'Go on,' he prompted, pleased she was opening up her feelings. 'You can tell me anything, Helen. You have my word I'll keep it to myself; you can trust me.'

'Well, I do have a lot on my mind, but I haven't told Rachel because I don't want to burden her.' She took a deep breath as the shakes got a grip again. It was hard to bring her fears to light. Her voice grew smaller. 'I wish I wasn't afraid all the time.'

Jowan spread a light hand on her shoulder. 'What are you afraid of? Say it, Helen, I'm here to help and protect you.'

'The downs, the heath out there where I was found, I can't bear to look that way in case *he's* there waiting for me.' At the end she looked fearfully into Jowan's eyes.

She was like a lost and pitiful child and he wanted to reassure her. 'Think about it, Helen, the downs can't hurt you, only if you wander off and get lost in poor weather. As for your attacker, I've a feeling he's long gone.'

'But you don't know that for certain. He could be out there anywhere, watching the house and waiting to pounce on me,' she wailed.

'If anyone was lurking about we'd know about it and so would the dogs. No one meaning ill intent would get past Cally, Iggy and Samson. They're lurchers and can sniff a stranger from miles away. And we won't let anyone hurt you, Helen. You won't ever be left alone. And when you're feeling scared just tell someone, no one will mind. We're here to help you.'

Helen nodded. 'I know, and I'm so grateful.' Her voice broke and tears glittered on her lashes. To have this man, who had been hostile to her very first haughty demands, being kind to her led to a welcome outpour of emotion. The attack had made her feel dirty and obscene, the crazed hatred heaped on her had bore into the deepest part of her being, but now she felt that perhaps she was a worthy person.

'I know what you need.' Jowan was suddenly jolly. 'Come with me.'

'To where, where do you want me to go?' She

194

was unnerved.

'Just to the stables.' He pointed along the yard. 'Do you mind?'

'No.' She was comfortable with that as long as she didn't look towards the downs.

He took her past the stalls and into the tack room. One corner was cordoned off by hay bales, and behind them on the floor of loose straw was the female lurcher Cally with her three-week-old brood of five puppies. Leaning forward, Jowan scooped out a tiny grey and white body. 'Here, hold it. It's a little girl.'

Helen took the puppy and cuddled it in her arms, smiling. 'She's sweet. Rachel mentioned the birth.'

'Would you like to have her, something of your very own?'

Glancing at the largeness of the mother dog, her coat wiry, Helen made up her mind. 'It's a kind thought. I hope you don't mind but a lurcher is very different to Venetia.'

'I understand. You'd prefer a tiny lapdog. Well, we'll keep her anyway. How would you like to name her?'

'Can I?' Helen stroked the little face. 'Let me think, it mustn't be anything too *boudoir*.' She laughed, knowing a happy moment for the first time in ages. 'Star, would that be acceptable?'

'I like that. Star it is. You'll be able to watch her grow up. Perhaps one day you'll go for a little walk with her on the downs.'

'I...'

'Don't worry, I won't push you, but I think it

would be a good idea if you faced the downs a bit at a time. It must be awkward facing away from one direction. When you're ready I'll stand beside you. Now, why don't we go inside for tea?'

Helen was relieved to be back in the safety of the kitchen and pleased and hopeful after the progress she had made. Jowan sat at the table. It would never cross his mind to actually make the tea. Helen put the kettle on the hob then went into the pantry to fetch the biscuit barrel. Turning round, her elbow hit a small crock and it was knocked off the shelf. 'Oh no!' The pleasant smell of mixed spices hit her nose but it made her scream.

Jowan rushed in to her. 'What is it, a mouse?'

She was trembling, her face a mask of horror. 'I've remembered something about the man who attacked me. He smelled of spices.'

The hog roast was held in a field adjacent to the side of the churchyard. Rachel kept Eva on the periphery of the festivities for she was nervous of the crowd and excited noise. It meant not taking advantage of the squire's generosity on the giant spit but even the mouth-watering smell of the roasting pig couldn't tempt Rachel's poor appetite. She enjoyed Eva's delight at the Punch and Judy stall and when buying toys, fudge and 'triggy' apples, and the lace for Helen, off the cheapjacks.

They sat on the grass to eat hevva cake bought from the baker's stall, Eva with Dolly on her

196

lap, murmuring happily between munching and shedding crumbs. Rachel couldn't help herself and glanced in the direction of the doctor's house, its chimneys in sight above the high hedge and between the ash and elder trees. Did James ever think about her, as she did him every day and through the lonely nights? Part of her hoped he'd communicate and when the post boy delivered mail she longed for there to be a letter from him, explaining he'd had no choice to slope away and begging for her forgiveness, that someday he'd come back for her, but as the weeks wore on she knew no such letter would arrive. Other times she didn't want that, to be hanging on to a heartless liar's promises, for that was what James had been. If he had really loved her, even though he couldn't bring himself to leave Charlotte, he would have done something to spare her this humiliation and heartbreak.

After two hours, when Eva got sleepy with the excitement, Rachel took her home. Eva plodded into the kitchen with her eyes almost closed. Flint was sitting at the hearth in a rare quiet moment – he usually liked to keep busy. He sprang up. 'Someone looks like she's had a good time and is ready for a nap. I'll take her up.'

'I'll tuck her in,' Rachel said. She was glad to have at least spent some worthwhile time with her. The only way she was going to get through her aching loneliness was to focus on Eva and Helen. She would never take the risk of giving her heart to another. She saw her future as a fading spinster, Helen as her fading widow companion.

Moments later she and Flint were gazing down on the sleeping Eva, curled up with Dolly under her chin, like two fond parents. 'Dear of her,' Rachel whispered. 'Her face was a picture at the Morris dancing and the performing dogs.'

'If not for you she wouldn't have known such delights,' Flint said gratefully.

Rachel was uncomfortable with his praise. Before the day Eva had turned up cowering in the garden she wouldn't even have noticed her. 'You and Mrs Retallack have done more for her. I must go. Helen is waiting for the lace she asked me to get.'

Flint quietly closed the bedroom door after them. 'Straight home to be with your other involvement – the lady and Eva couldn't be more different but you've gone out of your way to do your best for them both.'

Rachel whirled round to him on the low square landing. 'Don't be nice to me. I preferred it when you loathed me!'

Flint's fawn eyes grew wide. 'Where did that come from?'

Rachel couldn't bear it that he wasn't offended, that he was not provoked to hard words from which she could retaliate and use to storm off and feed on the aggression. This way stole the last of her life force. Leaning back against the bumpy whitewashed wall she slid to the floor and bawled a shower of blistering tears.

She was completely broken and the very fibre of her was disintegrating.

Crouching, Flint reached out to her but she fended off his hands. 'Rachel, what is it? Let me help you.'

'Y-you can't,' she said through great racking sobs. 'N-no one can.'

Determined not to leave her helpless, Flint persevered until he got her to her feet and was bearing her weight.

Rachel needed closeness and comfort and warmth and reassurance and she let her weak body sag against him. She allowed him to take her a short distance. Motionless again, she cried and cried, and he eased the side of her face against his chest and crooned to her. With one arm round her waist he ran his palm up and down over her shoulder. Little by little she yielded to his strength and gentleness. Finally she was all dried out and rested her cheek on his tear-soaked shirt.

At length he said softly, 'My guess is you have a broken heart.'

'Y-yes,' she sniffled.

'I'm sorry.'

He said nothing more and it helped that he offered no platitudes or asked searching questions but just held her a little closer.

By and by he said, 'Would you like a drop of rum?'

She nodded. 'I could drink a whole flagon.' Her voice was husky from weeping. 'Not because I'm hoping to solve a terrible problem.

I'm not in a delicate condition.' There, she had admitted she'd had a lover. Why could she cry and divulge intimate things to this man and not anyone else? She trusted him as one did a close friend, perhaps because of the way he cared for his mother and Eva. Reluctant to leave his warm hold, she glanced about the small room he had taken her to. It had a single bed and reasonable furniture and oval blue and grey mats on the wooden boards. 'Where are we?'

'In my room.'

Before they went down and cut off the moment she wanted to offload some of her crushing burden. She looked up into his face. 'I've been such a fool, but it's my own fault I'm reduced to this. I did wrong, he wasn't free, and now I'll never see him again. I'm glad of that but the hurt cuts so deep. I loved him so much.'

'I'm sure you did or you wouldn't have got so involved. I don't know what your kind of pain is like but I know the loss of someone I'd loved; I lost my father and brother, and then I had fear I might lose my mother.'

'You don't think badly of me.' It was a statement not a question. Many would view her as a fallen woman or used goods.

'No, that's not my way. We're all human, we all make mistakes and we all look for meaning in our lives.'

Rachel smiled her thanks for his understanding; it was no wonder she trusted him, and now she liked him. He was so different to James, who sought social furtherance and was fastidious about his physical presentation. Flint was rugged and had a refreshing hint of wildness about him. He was hard-working, non-judgmental and open-handed. James was low on human kindness; he had only sought to practise his professional services on the well placed and no one from the labouring class had been allowed entrance to his house. He was a superficial prig and a man who did not deserve to be loved. For the first time she experienced a glint of hope that she would get over him. Flint was still holding her.

If Rachel was happy in his arms he was content to hold her; she fitted against him perfectly and smelled beguilingly of some simple perfume. From behind her tear-streaked eyes he saw a glimmer of her old dynamism. Her face had beautiful contours and her figure was young and wonderfully soft. She was vulnerable right now and he didn't want to take advantage of her, especially if she transferred her affections to him for the wrong reasons, but she was stirring his base feelings and he let them invigorate him.

When his eyes dropped to her lips Rachel recognized the signs of desire. She should break away, suggest they have that drink, better still to go swiftly on her way, but she didn't want to relinquish his interest nor put an end to the pleasure she suddenly knew of his closeness. She stared into his eyes. He met the intrusion and returned it with similar infringement. Only it wasn't that. Both were willing to dwell on the other's eyes and mouths. Touch was wanted and then longed for. Rachel shut out all warning that such behaviour was utterly foolish. She ached for affection. To be desirable to Flint filled her with confidence and she refused to reason ahead. Now signs of sensuality were being tested for and freely given over. Lips were parting and breathing quickening. Invitations were sent and accepted. Hunger was acknowledged. They were on a wave of runaway hunger and need. They gave way to it.

Their first kiss was soft and tentative, lasting an instant before passion took over and all reserves were tossed away. They searched and tasted each other while heading straight for the bed. There was no need for preliminaries; it was demand and supply. Rachel felt her back hit the bed but all her concentration centred on preparing to have her need fulfilled. She wriggled and raised her hips to help Flint push up her skirts and remove her pantaloons. They were both in a hurry, frantic that the moment would not be missed, and she pulled his shirt free and helped him get into position.

His entry and their intimate contact exploded into arched, needy union. Their fused driving was fierce but controlled. His consideration for her pleasure swamped her with an ecstasy she had never known before and soon she hit the first terrific rush towards climax. It lasted and lasted, building with strength that robbed her breath. He used skilled hands to intensify the sensations for her and she called on her knowledge to gratify him. He finished but was able to keep on, kissing her in a number of ways and places, changing their position for fresh adventures. Rachel was lost in the rawness and the expertise. She did not have to sham each exquisite moment and she was not shy about her partner knowing she was in the heights of bliss. They arrived at the last climax of their frantic journey and flooded together.

Flint had to catch his breath before he was able to manoeuvre the uncoupling, then he drew Rachel to him, where she rested on his arm and drifted on the incredibly wonderful aftermath. She had given herself to another man but she had also taken from him, something she had not been allowed to do before. She had not let herself down and she would not regret it; Flint wouldn't expect anything more than she cared to allow. This might be their one and only time together and they would walk away and remain friends. She had triumphed this afternoon; she had become her own person and she would never sacrifice that achievement.

For him it was sheer pleasure not to pretend feelings he did not own, to disengage before promises were sought from him. He and Rachel were equal, friends and lovers who knew each other's limits, no more and no less. In a while they would get up and Rachel would go home. Perhaps they would make love again and perhaps they wouldn't, it was fine either way, and right now it was good just to go with the moment.

Sixteen

'The tenth of June, the date jogs my memory somehow,' James murmured in the early hours of the morning to the naked woman on the salon floor with him. The cushions thrown down for the rough play and tumble of an hour or so before were strewn to the four corners of the Persian carpet. 'Is there anything of note on today, Bibi?' It was the pet name for the middle-aged duchess he had spent the night with in her home at Bath.

'Nothing out of the ordinary that I can think of,' she purred, drawing his hand to her well-endowed body, insatiable once again for gratification. She was of a sadistic bent and certain parts of James's anatomy appeared to have passed through a furnace. There were objects lying about that would have to be gathered up and hidden from sensitive eyes. 'I've an "at home" at Highgate this afternoon, and I'll be at the Assembly Rooms tonight. Forget the silly date, James, and concentrate on pleasuring me.'

When he got dressed an hour later, aching and sore, he decided that despite the excitement of the encounter he'd try to avoid intimacy with the duchess from now on if possible – she was too extreme and frankly unsightly. That was unlikely, however; she was of the highest in society and it was she who tired of her lovers and not the other way round. Also, if he pleased her he hoped she would recommend him professionally. He always seemed beholden to women one way or another.

Charlotte's insufferable Aunt Eliza never tired of expressing, when Charlotte was not in earshot, how much he owed her. Otherwise she barely spoke to him. The loathsome termagant kept him at bay as if he had the most foul body odour. She was paying the rent on his surgery rooms for a year and after that he was to support his own practice. He and Charlotte were to remain permanently under her roof. Charlotte loved being back among her people but he found it stifling. Fortunately his profession took him out a lot and afforded him excuses to call on anonymous clientele, as he had lied about last night. Aunt Wellbeloved was as correct and stiff as her whalebone corset, a harridan to all except her godchildren, Charlotte being her favourite. Unfortunately she seemed hale and might eke out another decade but eventually she would die, and James had plans for her estate when it passed to Charlotte. If possible he'd give the old woman something noxious, and take pleasure in watching her expire.

He arrived home in time for breakfast at Aunt Eliza Wellbeloved's house in The Crescent. The butler, as grim as the grave, let him in. 'Good morning, Hopkins. Has Mrs Lockley's tray

205

gone up yet?' James was deliberately jaunty as he passed over his hat and gloves, for his every sense told him something was wrong. His insides went to war with his hopes and confidence. Had the old woman had him followed and knew he had been with the amoral duchess?

'Mrs Wellbeloved requests your presence in the morning room, sir,' Hopkins intoned. 'You are to go in immediately you arrive back.'

The butler's every word was edged in disdain and accusation. As far as everyone here, except Charlotte, was concerned, James was 'back' at the house – he was disallowed the honour and respect of being 'home'. 'Off I go then,' James said and rubbed his hands together. 'Then I will require a hearty breakfast. It was a difficult night.'

Hopkins looked at him with obvious distaste. James knew a deep sinking feeling of apprehension. As he went along the hall he realized everywhere was darkened and black ribbon had been added to the picture frames. Oh God, he sighed, some creaking old Wellbeloved had died and they were all to be plunged into mourning. It meant socializing would be forbidden and his movements restricted. In one large picture bay was the portrait of an eighteenth-century beauty, Lady Cordelia Wellbeloved. The light in her eyes reminded him of Rachel Kivell and he indulged in the delicious memories of coupling with her. Silly young Rachel, she had lapped up every one of his false promises. She was destined only to marry some yokel of little importance. Then he realized why today's date was significant: it was Rachel's twenty-first birthday. He grinned and whispered, 'Happy birthday, Rachel.'

Putting on an appropriately dour expression, he went in to see Eliza Wellbeloved. The morning-room curtains were drawn and the room was dim in a little candlelight. The old lady was clad in voluminous black taffeta and lace, a cap hanging down past her wide formidable chin. A small oval picture was in her black-lace mittened hands. James had intended to issue a quiet 'good morning' but something about the lady's grave persona made him wait on her.

'So you are back at last,' she said, shooting the sentence as a barbed indictment.

'I've been attending Mr Melding,' he said in a cut-glass voice. 'His gout afforded him a most difficult night. I am under the impression there is bad news, Aunt Wellbeloved. Is Charlotte well? I really would like to go up to her.' James hated the way she made him squirm. If only he could treat the old witch the same way he had Helen Churchfield.

Eliza Wellbeloved turned the portrait for him to see. It was of Charlotte as a delicate girl of about twelve, a picture of trust and innocence. 'The bad news *is* Charlotte. My dearest niece is dead. She is laid out in her bed and her coffin awaits her.' She did not spare him in her ice-cold delivery. 'Do not insult me by believing I do not know where you were last night and on the previous nights you abandoned my dear girl

207

with your despicable lies.'

James's heart turned to water and he recoiled in horror. 'Charlotte is dead? It's her? No! I don't believe you.'

'It is true! While you were servicing that noble whore your wife developed a blinding headache and her hands and feet swelled up to twice their size. She admitted to me that she had been feeling unwell for days but did not tell you for she thought it was a normal part of pregnancy. You were too selfish to notice her suffering. I sent for my own physician and by the time he arrived Charlotte was delirious. He diagnosed pre-eclampsia and the only way to save her was to get the baby out. We were prepared for one tragedy with Charlotte at only five months, but she died before the operation could be performed.'

James could barely take it in. 'Oh, my dear Charlotte,' he gasped, falling down in a chair. 'Our poor baby.'

'To your feet at once,' Mrs Wellbeloved barked with her long nose to the ceiling in indignation. 'You never cared for the dear girl. You wooed her with your insincere charm and took her away from her family and rightful place and finally destroyed her. Get yourself out of my house this minute.'

James used the plush arms of the chair for leverage to gain his feet. 'I was devoted to Charlotte, I swear,' he protested. He was in a cold, dark desolation. This was all so unfair. 'I strayed, but it is no other than what many a married man does.'

'How dare you make excuses! You are a shame to this family and a disgrace to your profession. Your belongings have been removed to your practice rooms. Be very sure to be out of them by the end of the week.'

'Very well, if that is what you wish.' He was getting angry now. The old woman had no heart. 'I will go up and spend time alone with Charlotte. I take it from what you've said you have arranged her funeral already.'

'She will be interred next to her parents. You are not welcome to attend and you are not to go up to her body.'

'You have no right! Charlotte was my wife. I take precedence over you and all else. It is you who dares to be in the wrong, madam.' He shook with rage.

'You are beneath Charlotte and in view of your habitual adultery you have forfeited your rights. Get out of my sight! The servants are ready to eject you and men will be posted to prevent you from coming anywhere near the funeral. If you approach any of the Wellbeloveds, dogs will be turned on you.'

'And Charlotte's will? I shall be hearing from the lawyer after the funeral?'

'Ah, I thought that would be your main concern.' Eliza Wellbeloved fixed him in her glacial sight. 'It happens that in the event of Charlotte predeceasing any spouse and without issue all her monies will revert to the Wellbeloved estate. You will receive precisely what you deserve, James Lockley – nothing!' She rang the silver bell on the table at her side.

'Damn you, you vile old bitch!' James spat.

'Escort this individual out of the house,' Mrs Wellbeloved ordered the butler and two footmen.

James strode past the servants then made a break for the stairs. He had loved Charlotte and couldn't bear not to see her one last time. He was grabbed efficiently by the coat and both arms and frogmarched to the door. 'No! Let me see her, let me see her! Charlotte, Charlotte!'

In the morning room, Eliza Wellbeloved looked down at her niece's portrait and wept with dignity and absolute grief.

Thrust out on the doorstep, James hammered on the door. 'Charlotte! Let me see my wife!'

Elegant passers-by viewed him with shock and muttered at the disgraceful exhibition. Finally James descended the steps and trudged off. In just a few minutes he had lost everything, he had no money and would soon be out on the streets. He was scared. Robbed of all his pride, he began to cry. There was no use throwing himself on the mercy of his new lovers; he was now a social outcast. He couldn't start up another practice; he had no funds for the rent and no one to recommend him. What was he to do? What *could* he do?

He trailed to a park and sat on a bench staring out across the pond. Was there no one he could turn to? He mulled over his past associations; some women had been fond of him but none

210

would take him in. Apart from Charlotte there had only been one other who had loved him and been prepared to give up everything for him, including her family. Rachel Kivell. Rachel had some money of her own. His only hope was to return to her. As a grieving widower he could spin a feasible story in a bid to win her back. He just had to.

Seventeen

'Does it feel strange to be doing this?' Rachel asked Helen, who was arranging her hair for her birthday celebration at Burnt Oak.

'Acting like a lady's maid? Not really.' Helen checked her work in the reflection of the dressing-table mirror. 'I would have felt be-littled at one time, but helping someone in any capacity feels an achievement to me now. It reminds me that I'm alive to actually be able to do it. It hurts a little sometimes to know I lost my former life entirely through my own fault, but it's not important; I am content.' She pinned half a dozen red and pink silk rosebuds, of her own making, in Rachel's gleaming black hair as the finishing touch above the ringlets around her ears. 'There, how is that?'

'Perfect, wonderful, thank you very much,' Rachel enthused, angling her head for an all-round view in the hand mirror that Helen held up.

'Now for your jewellery; you are to add to your usual bracelet, the pearl drop earrings from Thad and the necklace from Jowan. They will set your appearance off splendidly.'

Smiling, Rachel handed over the new velvet boxes. The jewellery was so valuable that a certain amount of lawbreaking – not locally; Kivells were too wily for that – must have been involved but she would never question it. All Kivell women had such priceless pieces. She saw for herself that her eyes were sparkling like the diamonds round her throat. That might have something to do with Flint. She had told herself she would treat their mad moments of love-making as a once only occasion, a quest for comfort. But twice when she'd ended up alone with him, very soon they had reached out and enjoyed each other's body. Flint made no demands and gave no promises; he was a passionate, sensitive lover, a kind man under his bluffness, and the perfect distraction to help her forget the humiliation of being dumped by an individual whose name she now couldn't bear to say. Flint was to collect Eva at eight o'clock from the party and Rachel, confident she looked her best in aquamarine taffeta, wanted to show herself off to him. Just about none of her family would consider Flint good enough for her, but they'd approve of him in general if he could hold his drink. To her it was good to flirt with a man who was handsome and available.

Thanking Helen, Rachel got up and took her hands. 'Are you quite sure you won't come to Burnt Oak? You could sit in a quiet room. I'll make sure no one intrudes on you.'

'Then there would be little point in going. I'll be fine here with Mrs Carveth.'

'Well, it would be a long day for you and the party will go on far into the night. The rest of us will be off in a little while and we'll collect Eva on the way. Come downstairs with me, Thad has something for you.'

'Something for me? But it's not my birthday.'

'That doesn't matter. You'll love it; it's just the very thing for you.'

Thad was waiting in the sitting room. He made an appreciative sound between his teeth. 'Cousin, you look like a princess.'

'It's all thanks to Helen.'

Thad thought Helen looked as if she belonged to some mystical royal court. She glided rather than walked and exuded a compelling regal grace, with a hint of beguiling melancholy. He wished he owned an artist's skill and could do justice in capturing her haunting beauty on canvas. He watched her all the time and because his reserve was taken for granted no one had noticed. He cleared his throat, shy now. 'Um, Helen, I have a gift for you.'

'Rachel has just mentioned it. I don't deserve anything and it's very kind of you, Thad. All of you here are so good to me.' She smiled, looking forward to the treat.

Rachel took her to the wine table. A large,

roughly rectangular object was set down and covered with a piece of linen. Thad pulled the cloth away. 'There, I hope you like it.'

Helen took in the item and clasped her hands to her face. 'Like it! It's beautiful. I've never seen such a marvellous sewing box. You must have taken weeks to complete it. Jowan pointed out something you were working on secretly on your workbench but he thought it was to be for Rachel.'

'You've been to the workshop with Jowan?' Thad frowned.

'Yes, a few weeks ago on the day of the hog roast. I got into a panic and Jowan came to my rescue.' She gave a brief version of events. 'Since then I've been gradually facing the downs all on my own. Yesterday I even managed to go outside the back gate and reach the first stepping stone of the stream. I didn't mention my intention before; I was afraid if I did it might put me off trying at all.'

'Well done, Helen.' Rachel threw her arms round her friend in a congratulatory hug. 'You keep on trying at your own pace. One day I'm sure you'll be comfortable enough to go into the village and to Burnt Oak. It doesn't matter if you never go out on the downs; if you're not frightened of them that's all that matters.'

'I hope you enjoy using the sewing box,' Thad thrust in. Damn it, Jowan always stole his thunder, and this time he wasn't even here while it was happening. People thought he was happy to be quiet and thoughtful, and indeed he was, but it irked him that Jowan's louder, more flamboyant personality meant he was sometimes overlooked in a way that made him seem unimportant.

'Oh, I will,' Helen said, carefully running her hands over the fine piece made up of hard and soft woods. The sides opened out from the carrying handles, in three layers sectioned for spools, reels, needles and so on. 'I'll have a wonderful time putting my silks, cottons, lace and scissors and all the rest in it. My first occupation will be to make a lining for the interior. Thank you so much, Thad. I'll never forget this gesture; it's so thoughtful and kind of you.'

She proffered her hand but he would have preferred to receive a kiss on the cheek – an enthusiastic kiss now Jowan was coming in the room. Thad kissed her hand and made it look a possessive gesture.

'Helen has the sewing box then,' Jowan said. He was holding a small cloth bundle close to his body. 'I've also got something for you.' He smiled at her. 'Something to keep you company.'

Helen flashed Rachel a puzzled look and she shook her head at the mystery.

Jowan went up close to Helen and whipped back the cloth. Curled up and engulfed in his arm was a scrap of black and tan fluff. Bright nervous eyes surveyed the company from under long shaggy lashes.

'A puppy!' Helen exclaimed.

'And she's all yours. She's twelve weeks old.

She's got a bit of terrier and goodness knows what else in her. I got her off the travelling knife-grinder. I thought she'd be just right for you, Helen. Her paws are tiny so she won't grow to be very big. You'll be able to carry her around wherever you go.'

Helen stayed in shocked silence for a moment then let out an excited cry and reached for the puppy and gathered it to her chest. The puppy snuggled in and gazed up at her from huge soulful brown eyes. 'She likes me! Oh, she's gorgeous. Jowan, I don't know what to say. What an absolutely wonderful thought. Oh, she's shaking. What's the matter, darling? There's no need to be frightened. You're safe now. I'm your new mistress and I'm going to take good care of you. Oh, Rachel, isn't she absolutely sweet? I'll make her a little bed with blankets. I must run straight along to the kitchen. I bet she is half-starved, poor little thing. Mrs Carveth and I can find her something to eat and a little warm milk.'

'She's not fully housetrained,' Jowan laughed, 'so mind your dress. You'll have to keep popping outside to see if she wants to go then make a fuss of her when she does, to train her. I'll fetch a little collar and lead for her from the stable.'

'Can I keep her in my room? I'd hate to think of her left down here at night all alone and shivering in the dark,' Helen begged.

'Of course you can.' Rachel tickled the puppy's soft brow. 'You'll have to think of a name for her.'

'Nothing sissy.' Jowan rolled his eyes in fun.

'Don't worry; I'll think of something that no one can make fun of. Now you had all better run along. Have a lovely birthday, Rachel.' Helen hurried off to the kitchen and moments later Mrs Carveth could be heard joining in the cooing over the puppy. On slow, heavy feet Thad followed his cousins to the stable. As far as everyone here was concerned he hardly existed and he certainly wouldn't enjoy this birthday party.

'It's a treat to see you in your Sunday best suit and boots,' Frettie Endean said, brushing down the jacket on Flint's broad shoulders. 'A clean shirt, you've had a shave and you smell nice. Going to cast your eye round at the Kivell maids, eh?'

'I don't want to let Eva down.' Flint struggled moodily out of her reach. Why did women get silly when a man made an effort with his appearance?

'Now she's not going to notice, is she?' Frettie eyed him slyly.

'Mother likes me to go out looking smart, don't you, Mother?' He presented himself in front of Irene.

She nodded. 'You look as handsome as your father did the day I married him. I'm proud of you, Flint. But I agree with Frettie, you're after some maid or other and about time too. I want grandchildren to sit on my knee before too long.

It's not likely you'll catch a Kivell maid, but if you do make sure it's not one too feisty.'

'Huh,' Flint muttered, then set off for the mile and a half walk to Burnt Oak to collect Eva.

All the way through the village, then striding along narrow twisting Bell Lane and up Oak Hill, his thoughts centred on Rachel. He knew the reason she fell easily into his arms was a bid to overcome her heartbreak, but he was confident she liked him for himself. She cared about his needs when they made love and he didn't get the impression she wished he were the man who'd spurned her. As well as lovers they were trusted friends, and if either of them turned their attention elsewhere they would always remain friends. Now he was eager to see her and claim a dance with her before taking Eva home. He put his hand in his pocket and took out the gift he had for her, a pincushion on the top of a little china shoe finished with a floral transfer. He'd bought it from a gipsy at the market, nothing special but not cheap-looking. It was ideal to give to a friend.

He had always been curious about Burnt Oak, but like all the villagers had never thought to go there without a purpose or invitation. The Kivells still retained the awe and mystery of their more isolated days and a pack of wary lurchers guarded the property. The pair of heavy iron gates, set in the blackthorn hedge-row, usually shut against the world, were wide open today. He turned off the lane and began the steep valley descent and was met by four of the dogs. His fear that they'd jump up and soil his suit was unfounded for they sniffed round him then bounded off below as if to announce his arrival.

Burnt Oak was a compound of six old stone, thatched and slate-roofed houses and three more recently built dwellings. There were craft shops, a forge and farm buildings enclosed within the protective square of granite walls.

A second pair of matching gates was also flung back and Flint found himself crunching across a stone-chipping courtyard. The party was being held in Morn 'O May, the largest house, of small mansion size and cross-leaded windows. Flint went up to the front door, held open by a painted iron cockerel doorstop. There was no one about and there was little point in knocking to be bidden entry – a loud babble of voices rushed out to him. He went into the huge hall where the staircase parted at the top to many rooms; another staircase led to the attic rooms. He followed a long stone passage laid with woven runners. The passage went off in various directions and Flint headed towards the hum of noise. Feeling something of an intruder, he was glad to spy Thad Kivell, with an older woman, coming out of a room.

'Hello there,' he called to them.

'Ah, Retallack, you've come for Eva,' Thad said. 'This lady is my mother. Eva is in the schoolroom with some of the older girls. She's had lots to eat and a good time being enter-tained. Apparently she's now very sleepy and needs to be taken home.'

'She's been quite happy not being in Rachel's company?' Flint was concerned.

'She stayed with Rachel most of the time but the children have made her feel at home,' Mrs Kivell said, smiling in a matronly way and moving off. 'She's a sweet girl. I'll get her ready for the journey. Someone will drive you back.'

'Will you pass on my thanks to all those taking care of Eva? I'd like to see Rachel. I have a little gift for her,' Flint said, the wrapped pincushion in his hand. Mrs Kivell had seemed friendly enough but he sensed cold vibrations coming from Thad. On the one or two occasions he had seen him at Chy-Henver there had been virtually no communication between them.

'Rachel is getting ready for the dancing which is about to begin. I'll pass on the gift.'

'I'd rather give it to her myself.' Flint moved the gift behind him.

'This is Rachel's special day. It's not fair for her to be disturbed,' Thad replied stubbornly. He didn't often get in a bad mood but when he did, especially when he felt pushed out and in-consequential as earlier today when Helen had preferred the puppy to his sewing box, he was uncompromising and tended to hit out.

'I'm sure she won't mind sparing a minute to see me. Rachel and I are friends.'

'Hardly; your sort can't possibly mean any-thing to my cousin.' Thad scowled. 'I suggest

220

you go on your way. As it is someone will have to miss part of the celebration to take you and the girl home.'

Furious, Flint wanted to say a lot more but the other man's stance was hostile and he didn't want to risk a quarrel and spoil Rachel's birthday. Glaring at Thad, he put the pincushion back in his pocket, turned sharply and stalked off to wait outside for Eva. He was disappointed not to see Rachel but Thad Kivell had not particularly rattled him. He and Rachel were friends no matter what.

Rachel heard about Eva and Flint's departure but her dash to the door was too late, as the trap taking them home was already turning out into the lane. She sought out Thad but he was nowhere in the house. Finally she spied him out in the old graveyard where Kivells had been buried for generations before giving themselves over to the ritual of baptism in favour of the sod in the churchyard.

'Thad, what on earth are you doing here? Why so gloomy? And why did you send Flint away and not give me the chance to say goodbye to Eva? What's the matter with you?'

'Go in and enjoy your celebration, Rachel. I want to be alone.' He wouldn't look at her.

'What's happened to upset you? You were fine this morning. You haven't answered my question about Eva and Flint. Surely he hasn't put you in this mood.'

'What do you want him hanging about you for? He's just a no-good miner. Leave me be,

Rachel.'

'I will; you can sulk all night and the rest of your life for all I care! You had no right to make decisions on my behalf,' Rachel cried, her hands pressed on her hips, hating the thought of Flint being made to feel he wasn't good enough to mix with her family. 'I can't stand it when you suddenly get miserable. If you're going to be like this you might as well go home.'

Minutes later Thad mounted his horse and rode home. He had to see if Helen had as much as glanced at the sewing box he'd taken so much trouble with, or whether she had plied all her attention on her stupid little dog.

'Thad, you've left the party early. Is all well?' Helen asked from where she was sewing in the light of a lamp.

'I developed a headache. It was very noisy so I decided I'd had enough.' He went up to her. She was working from the new sewing box, which she had lined and filled with all her sewing paraphernalia. 'You're finding the box useful then?'

'Oh yes,' she enthused. 'There's plenty of room for everything. Thank you so much, Thad. I couldn't have received anything better.'

His mood swung into reverse. His brooding dark features broke into a smile. 'Have you had a good day?'

'I have. With help, I've bathed Willow and she's now sleeping in her bed. See, she's just down by my feet.'

Thad glanced down at the little hairy bundle

almost obscured by a piece of soft tartan blanket in a small wicker basket. 'You've called her Willow?'

'Yes, do you like it?' She hoped for his approval, for it meant Jowan would like it too. She had spent a happy time coddling the puppy, reflecting on what a kind thought it was of Jowan's to provide her with a new companion. It had occurred to her how good it had felt to be in Jowan's arms the day of her panic, not just as a comforter, but as a man with strong arms and a powerful presence. Her late husband had been of weedy build, and their intimate relations, those couple of times on their honeymoon, had been the briefest of embarrassing contact. In fact she wondered if she was still a virgin. Lawrence Churchfield's fumbling had convinced her the act of love was unsavoury and she had not sought such stirrings, but perhaps with the right man she would enjoy what others seem to seek so freely. Jowan was supremely handsome and overtly masculine – it was no wonder the local women pursued him, and underneath his gruffness he was humorous and chivalrous. Occasionally when he moved past her he'd put a hand on her arm or waist like he did to Rachel, an affectionate and possessive gesture, and one she liked a lot.

'Yes, it suits her. How's she been?'

'A bit nervous, and she hated the bath, but after having more to eat and lots of cuddles she's settled down. Thad, would you like me to fetch a powder for your headache?'

223

He was pleased she was thinking of him, making him a priority. 'That would be kind, Helen. Actually, I'm hungry.'

'That's part of the reason you're not feeling well. Come to the kitchen and I'll prepare something for you. Would you carry Willow in her basket? I don't want her waking up and fretting or having a little accident.'

'I'll be glad to.' He followed her with the puppy and basket, feeling like he was carrying a crown. He had won over Jowan this time. He'd make sure he formed a closer bond to the puppy than his cousin. He wanted Helen, really wanted her. He never did anything quickly and had contemplated his feelings for her and whether a marriage between them was likely to be successful. He didn't want someone subservient and he applauded her genteel ways. He couldn't bear someone noisy, a gossip or a nag. Like him, Helen yearned for a quiet existence in the background. All he wanted was to be her major concern. When the time was right he would propose to her and set them up in a house of their own where he could have her all to himself. Jowan and Rachel would do well not to get in his way.

Eighteen

With Adeline on his arm, Michael paraded to the nursery to inquire about their son's progress. He had taken little notice of the development of his daughters, only pampering the dizzy-headed girls for brief moments, but he lived in delight and satisfaction that he had sired a healthy son and heir.

'And how is Master Nathaniel Michael today, Nanny Johns?' he asked, his straight black eyebrows poised to rise in expectation of another good report.

The nanny of many years' experience in stately homes, competent and of trim figure, nodded in formal abeyance. She articulated in the manner of an adept politician, 'Master Nathaniel settled down for the night in his usual contented manner, sir, madam. He woke for a feed at two o'clock. The wet nurse put him to each breast for ten minutes. The nursery maid changed his soiled napkin and I settled him down again. Master Nathaniel woke at seven o'clock, was fed at fifteen minutes each side. He was bathed and dressed, and after a period of gazing about brightly he drifted off to sleep. He is presently awake in his cradle. I am con-

225

fident the scales will show he has gained well in weight again this week.'

'Splendid, thank you, Nanny Johns.' Michael grinned broadly. At just a few weeks old his son already showed signs of strength and superior intelligence. There would be no shadowy existence for him, as Michael had chosen for himself. Nathaniel would receive the best education and mix with the most influential people. It meant he and Adeline would have to sacrifice their solitude and filter into polite society. When his son was one year old they would spend most of the year in the Truro town house, leading eventually to forays to Bath and London and other big cities. It would also be beneficial for Cecily and Jemima in securing suitable husbands. The girls were still residing at Truro where they had begged to remain for the more diverting company, and had only come home to Poltraze for their brother's christening. The peaceful equilibrium of the house meant Nathaniel had the perfect opportunity to thrive.

The couple spent ten minutes in parental worship over their rosy-cheeked little boy then withdrew for the purposes of the day. Michael was set for the estate office and Adeline to consult with Mrs Benney, the housekeeper.

Hankins, the butler, met them halfway on the way downstairs. 'Dr James Lockley has just arrived, sir, and is asking to see you.'

'Lockley?' Michael tilted his nose. What had brought that insipid medic back to these parts?

The man had gone off on an arrogant note of bettering himself. 'I suppose I will have to see him. Show him into the morning room, Hankins.'

'I did not expect to set eyes on you again, Lockley.' Michael's tone was offhand and layered in suspicion. Lockley was in mourning and seemed not to have slept for days. Thundery shadows tugged under his eyes. He had not taken care with his hygiene and Michael was offended by his stink and the overuse of spiced scent to conceal it. Lockley had hit misfortune. Likely he was here seeking some form of handout.

'I won't tarry in my explanation, Mr Nankervis.' James had difficulty swallowing back a dam of weeping. 'My dear wife Charlotte is dead. Tragically from complications in pregnancy and my child did not survive either. My wife's family informed me that I have no right to her portion and they have altogether disregarded me cruelly. I could not bear to stay on in Bath. Indeed I had no time really to build up a practice there. I have returned here to ask if you, sir, if you would kindly recommend me when I apply for a new post in the county.'

'Ah.' Michael shook his head.

'You are disinclined, sir?' James's face was dragged down. He had stayed in his practice rooms to secretly watch Charlotte's funeral and then linger by the grave in the empty churchyard. Then he had parted with the last of his money for the journey to Meryen, in the hope of regaining Rachel Kivell's affection. First he needed a position; he didn't want to throw himself on Rachel's mercy destitute.

Michael found it amusing to be malicious. 'No, indeed I can do better than that for you, Lockley. The new doctor here thinks the village too lowly for him and is about to move on. You may have your former position back.' It would save him the bother of securing a new doctor for the unpopular post.

Such was his relief, James nearly slumped on his feet in an undignified heap. 'I thank you, Mr Nankervis. It will be some consolation to return to where I spent many contented days with my dear wife.'

'You have my condolences on your loss, Lockley. Poltraze will not require your services so you will have plenty of time to concentrate on the mining community. Wait here, I will write a note to Dr Wills informing him of your regain of the coming vacancy. I am sure he would be pleased to allow you accommodation in the doctor's house until he leaves. Now if you will excuse me I must get on.' He rang to have Lockley showed out.

James followed the butler in utter humiliation, his relief seeping away. He had skipped away from Meryen in the belief he had a consequential future but not only had he lost everything, he was now back in a lower-grade position than before. He would get little respect from the villagers when they realized the squire and the better-off, who followed the squire's example, looked elsewhere for a physician. He might get some sympathy over Charlotte's demise, for she had been well liked and respected. His only hope to get away from here again was in the hope Rachel Kivell was still in love with him and would provide the funds. But Rachel was strong-minded and might not easily be persuaded he'd had a good reason to drop her without a single word.

The morning after her birthday celebration Rachel had rushed to the water closet to be sick. She thought she had drunk too much mead and wines the day before, but the same thing happened the next morning, the next and the next, and in view of her monthly visitation being overdue she feared she knew what the problem was.

She had tried to see Flint to apologize about Thad's rudeness and Flint had tried to see her – she was pleased about that, but they had kept missing each other. Today she resolved to go to the village and wait for him to come home from the mine. Somehow she would tell him it seemed highly likely he had fathered a baby to her. She was sure Flint would stand by her. She had total trust in him, unlike her previous lover. It didn't occur to her that she was in a situation of shame and possible trouble. She had always wanted children and a baby would pull together the last raw edges of her heart, fill the great dark void that James Lockley had created in her once and for all. She now despised Lockley for his callous weakness and for amusing himself at her expense. Thank God she would never see him again. Thank God she had been spared any more of the futile existence of hankering for him.

The times Flint had called at Chy-Henver to give Rachel his birthday gift only to find her out at relatives' or the shops had left him disappointed. He wanted to give her the little china cat pincushion personally and tell her that Thad's antagonistic attitude did not bother him at all. Rachel was his friend and more to him and nothing would ruin that.

He was delighted to find her in the kitchen with his mother and Frettie Endean, dressing Dolly with Eva. 'We've got a guest for dinner, Flint,' Irene said with a proud note. 'Get changed quickly.'

A meal of pigeon pie was eaten and enjoyed. Irene and Frettie passed each other significant glances. 'Why don't you take Miss Rachel outside to look at the garden, Flint?'

'Yes, off you go, I don't want you under my feet while I'm clearing away,' Frettie added stoutly.

Flint and Rachel were amused to glean what was on the older women's minds. Eva went outside with them but they were in effect alone, for she wouldn't understand what they said. Flint had built her a swing and she shuffled over to it and sang to herself as she soared up and down with Dolly.

Rachel started to speak. 'I'm sorry—'

Flint said at the same time, 'I wanted—'

They laughed, and there and then beside the blackcurrant bushes joined in a kiss full of warmth and passion.

'I've missed you,' Flint whispered.

'And I you,' she breathed.

'I got you something for your birthday.'

She held the cat pincushion before her eyes. 'It's lovely; I'll treasure it.'

'Rachel, I...'

'Yes?'

'I don't know really. I just like you being here.'

'Me too.'

'Whee, whee,' Eva sang as she worked the swing.

'Dear of her.' Rachel smiled.

'It's like we've got a child together,' Flint said. His remark made Rachel take a deep breath. 'What?'

'It's just that...'

He thought about it then gazed into her face and raised his brows in question. She nodded.

'You're...?'

'I'm reasonably sure about it.'

'Well, that's not exactly bad news. Is it?'

'No, I don't think so, not really. Do you?'

'No! Not at all, in fact it's ... well it's wonderful. I'll marry you, of course. I mean, if you'll have me? Will you?' The more Flint drank in the revelation, the more he buzzed, excited at the thought of becoming a father.

231

'I will. I think it would be good to be your wife.' She laughed, catching his enthusiasm. 'It will be as if we're giving Eva a little brother or sister.'

They linked arms, happy in the moment. 'A baby,' Flint said. 'It means we'd better get on with things. Mother will be cross with me but pleased as well. I hope your brother and cousin will realize they don't need to point a shotgun at me.'

'It's our lives, ours and our baby's.' Rachel knew there would be ructions ahead but she'd weather the storm. Jowan and Thad wouldn't consider Flint good enough for her but they'd just have to accept it. 'We'll be happy together, Flint.' And as she said the words she was confident of it. She had nothing else to do with her life, so becoming wife to a man she was deeply attracted to and bearing his baby wasn't a bad thing to have ahead of her.

'We will; we come from different backgrounds but we've got a lot in common. There is one thing though – how will you feel about squeezing in here after living in a much bigger house?'

'We could build on. Once Jowan and Thad come round, and they'll have to, they'll want to help out, I'm sure.'

'That's settled then. Mother would prefer a chapel wedding, would that be all right?'

'That's fine by me. I'll get Helen to help me make my dress. We'll have a quiet ceremony and a celebration afterwards at Burnt Oak, would that be all right? Your initiation into the Kivell family.'

'Sounds just fine.' He didn't care what those of Burnt Oak thought of him.

'Yes, it does.'

Before going inside to break the news they indulged in a long kiss, and a few more moments of Eva's childish delight.

Nineteen

'I think you should start speaking to Rachel again,' Helen told Jowan. She was taking Willow for a short walk on her lead in the backyard. Jowan was leaning against the back of the workshop, smoking a roll-up cigarette.

'I will when I'm ready,' he said grimly, his face turned to the downs.

'There's nothing to be gained by continuing in such poor temper. Rachel has been foolish but she has done what many a young woman has when in love. Flint Retallack is going to do the right thing by her; there is no other course and you should wish her well.'

'Rachel's not in love with Retallack. I could break his damned neck! I should have done it yesterday when he was here admitting his crime. He had no right to take advantage of Rachel. It was her goodness to Eva and his mother that led to this. She had no right to give herself to him.' Jowan banged his fist against the thick stone wall.

'She is in love with him. She must be.'

'No she's not!'

'How do you know that? Well anyway, you might as well get used to the situation. Rachel was bound to settle down and start a family one day.'

Jowan tossed the stub away and appealed to her, 'But none of the family wanted it to be with a miner. What if he turns to drink? A lot of them drink their heads off. If he gets killed down the mine she'll end up a young widow. And she won't be living as she's been brought up to. She's let the family down.'

Helen patted his arm and smiled softly to appease him. 'Men of all backgrounds drink too much. Does not your family carouse until all hours? And people of all ages die every year due to many reasons. You've agreed to help extend the Retallack cottage and there is a housekeeper in place. I'm sure Rachel will be quite comfortable. And Eva, who she loves dearly, will be there.'

Jowan shrugged. Helen was right in all she had said. Rachel had shown no interest in any other man so at least she was getting a husband, and her baby would not bear the stigma of illegitimacy as Rachel and himself did. 'What about you, Helen? Will you want to go with Rachel?'

'Rachel has invited me to but it will be a bit

234

crowded. I'm quite happy to stay living here, if
that is all right with you and Thad.' Helen bit
her lip. She didn't rely on Rachel as much as
before and hated the thought of living in a
miner's cottage and in the village. She liked her
anonymous life here.

'Thank goodness for that.' Jowan rubbed her
arm with the backs of his fingers. 'We need a
woman to run the house. It wouldn't be the
same without you and Willow here.' He swept
the puppy up in his hands and the couple
laughed as he received a thorough licking about
the chin.

Thad had come out of the workshop, wondering why Jowan was taking so long. It was as
he'd feared, his cousin was flirting with Helen
again and she was more than happy to be in his
company. He marched up to them and put his
hand out to stroke Willow. 'Hello, little one, are
you being spoiled again?'

'She likes a lot of fuss,' Helen said indulgent-
ly, taking the puppy away, 'but it's time she
went for her walk.'

Thad felt let down that she was leaving
already. She headed down the end of the
garden, went out of the gate and stood near the
stepping stones. 'That's not much of a walk for
the puppy. I'll see if I can coax Helen to go a
little further.'

'Be careful,' Jowan cautioned. 'If she feels
under pressure it might put her back weeks.'

'I'm not stupid,' Thad said and flounced off.

'No, you're not, cousin.' Jowan grinned,

heading back to work. 'Just behaving stupidly because you're in love, jealous fool.' Thad and Helen would probably make a good match, both owning a serious side to their nature. Thad should come out of his shell and make proper advances to Helen.

'Do you think you'd be able to walk a little way along the bank of the stream, Helen?' Thad ventured when he reached her. 'I'll stay close to you. You can turn back the instant you feel you want to.'

The sudden question made Helen's heart pound and inevitably with it came the horrid knot of panic that could spread and overwhelm her so completely. The downs swept off like a voluminous patchwork of muted greens and straw-like grasses, but Helen noted the un-dulating swathes of pink and purple heather and golden gorse. There were pretty dashes of wild flowers. A swallow was soaring high in direct flight, its pointed wing tips and long tail-streamers a sight of majestic freedom. When facing this landscape she found so daunting, Helen concentrated on the pleasant aspects of nature. 'I...' She felt Willow tugging on the lead, eager for more exercise.

'Do you want to go back?' Thad asked. He wanted Helen to transfer her waning depen-dence on Rachel to him, but he didn't want her to be frightened. 'Take my arm.'

She gulped and swallowed. She was not used to being a quaking ninny but had been the first to rise to a challenge, often the instigator of such. Where was the backbone instilled in her from birth? She accepted his arm. 'No, I'll go on a few steps.'

Thad walked on the side next to the stream. He felt like a gallant of olden times. 'It's very brave of you, Helen. If you suddenly want to return just squeeze my arm.'

Helen kept her eyes on the well-trod path as Willow darted about, sniffing out new scents. She was aware of Thad keeping in close proximity, which was a little intrusive but she couldn't do this without his presence.

After twenty yards, Thad said, 'Are you all right?'

Her heart was thundering in her ears, almost blocking out the sighing of the warm breeze. 'I can go a little further.'

'That's good, Helen, you are being very brave.' He pointed a hundred yards ahead. 'There's a large rock there beside the path. Do you think you could make it your goal today? I'll be with you and you'll be perfectly safe. Chy-Henver is still in sight and you can see a long way in each direction if anyone is coming.'

'Thank you, Thad, it's a good idea.' It was thoughtful of him not to push her too hard. It was reassuring to know she could trust him.

They reached the rock and Helen took her arm away. It was roughly the size and height of a garden bench and Helen thought she might sit and linger another time. Willow sniffed about its base. 'She seems to like it here.'

'I think of the downs as a contrary friend,' Thad said. 'In the summer it invites you to wander over it and discover its secrets; in autumn when the foliage begins to die off it starts to turn its back on you; in winter its temperamental and wants to be left alone, and in spring when it shows signs of new life it puts a welcome mat out again.'

'You see it as a living entity. It is, as it supports vegetable, bird and animal life, but I see it as a monster waiting to hurt me.' Helen shivered and looked in the direction of home.

'The downs are only dangerous if you're foolhardy or wander about them in bad weather. The monster is the man who hurt you, Helen, and he's not about here any more.' Thad used a firm expression to persuade her.

'We can't be sure of that.' She shook her head.

'We all agreed, didn't we, that his smell of spices pointed to him probably being a sailor who had unloaded the goods. It's the most likely explanation. I'm sure his ship has long sailed. His crime was so dreadful that if he was still around I'm sure there would have been more incidents of the kind.'

'I suppose you're right,' Helen said, unconvinced; it was only conjecture. The monster could be anywhere, even close by. He was a madman. She would never come to terms with how much he had hated her and couldn't get it out of her head that the attack had been personally aimed at her.

'Don't let it ruin your achievement today,

Helen. How do you feel?'

'Nervous and shaky, but I will try to do this again. I'd like to go back now. I'm going to start on some lace for Rachel's wedding dress.' She was hoping to steel herself to attend the ceremony in the chapel, but she would definitely not go on to Burnt Oak.

Thad recalled the easy friendliness she had been sharing with Jowan. It was unlikely his cousin would form deep feelings for Helen. Jowan was years off settling down, but Helen might come to form an attachment to him. Thad was one to take things slowly, but where risk was involved he was not afraid to present himself. 'I'd like to ask you something first, Helen.'

She looked him in the face and met his earnest expression. 'What is it?

He cleared his throat and his cheeks heated up. 'I've come to care for you very much, Helen. I love you. I would be honoured if you'd agree to become my wife. Will you marry me, Helen?'

'Oh!'

'I'm sorry you didn't hear me come in, Helen,' Rachel said, joining her in the sitting room. She had returned from Burnt Oak after making the arrangements for the wedding reception. It had been an uncomfortable occasion since most of the family shared Jowan's view about her future husband. Rachel hoped they would come to approve of Flint when they got to know him. She had spent most of the time expounding his good points and had enjoyed talking about him and the plans they had already made for their life together.

She had found Helen staring into space over her lace work of linked flowers and ivory beads. 'That's gorgeous. Is it for the bodice of my dress?'

'Yes. I'm afraid I haven't done very much.'

'There's still plenty of time. Have you got something on your mind?' Helen was so serious that Rachel added cautiously, 'If you don't approve of my condition and would rather not be involved in the wedding, I'll understand.' Although it would deflate her.

'It isn't that,' Helen stressed. 'I've no right to judge anyone. I'm delighted you have found someone you feel you can be so close to, Rachel.'

That had been James at one time, Rachel thought, once more regretting her association with him. 'Are you worried about me moving out of the house? I promise I'll visit here regularly.'

'It isn't that either.' Helen braced herself to say what she could hardly believe had happened this afternoon. 'Thad asked me to marry him.'

'What?' Rachel solidified on her way to a chair.

'That was my reaction too. I was taken totally by surprise.'

Rachel sat down. 'What did you say?'

'That I'd think about it; I couldn't say

anything else really. Thad was fully understanding; he said it was a big decision and I was to take my time.'

'It is a big decision for you, Helen. I had no idea Thad had feelings for you. I mean, he never opens up to anyone. How do you feel about it? How do you feel about him?'

On arriving home Helen had tried not to think about the marriage proposal and had started on the lace, but knowing she had to face Thad's proposal sooner or later she had been angry with him for giving her an unwelcome complication. Anxious, she had resolved to move out with Rachel. Then she had mulled over all the implications. Living with Rachel and her new family was not a good option. She would feel out of place and would be in the way. Staying here as the lady of the house would have been the perfect thing. If only Thad had not declared himself. The atmosphere was bound to change if she turned him down. She didn't believe he would be difficult but she would always feel awkward. She saw now something she had missed before, that recently he had become jealous of her friendship with Jowan, even sniping uncharacteristically at his cousin. Did she prefer Jowan to Thad? She liked them both very much, but in different ways. Did she favour Jowan more? It might seem so to Thad because Jowan made her laugh. The men shared similar dark looks although Jowan was the more sensual, but that didn't matter. Thad was the more constant; he didn't seem to share

241

Jowan's roving eye.

It had not crossed her mind since the attack to marry again. There was no denying there were lots of advantages as a married woman – security and status – and it would be good to be rid of the Churchfield name. To be a Kivell would offer her ultimate protection and she would have some standing again; she would no longer be a charity case, not so much a curiosity. It was tempting to accept Thad's offer. But would she be happy having to share her life, not just the physical intimacy – and she didn't really want children – but she would have to sacrifice her privacy, the sweet moments when she was alone in her room feeling secure with strong people around her.

'I like Thad, he's been very good to me,' she replied at last.

'Many a good marriage has been built on mutual respect,' Rachel said, as if a wise old woman.

'Is that what you share with Flint?'

Rachel didn't have to think about it. 'That and more.' She enjoyed being in Flint's arms and looked forward to seeing him when they were apart. He was so different to the heartless, social-climbing James Lockley. Flint would never use her and spurn her like the other had. 'Thad's declaration has been a great shock to you. I'm sure you'll learn more how you really feel about him in the next few days. I would say he'd make any woman a fine husband – and, Helen, you could do a lot worse.'

Dora appeared. 'Miss Rachel, your cousin Clemency's here. She brought this note for you. She's outside playing with the dogs, waiting to see if there's a reply. I'm glad of that; I don't care for her cheeky tomboy ways. Looks as if she hasn't put a comb to her hair in days. Anyone would think she was a gipsy.'

'An enquiry about the wedding I should think.' The instant Rachel saw the firm script on the note spelling out her name her insides iced up and she missed a breath. It was James's writing. He had waited all this time to get in touch with her. It seemed he was even in Meryen, as the letter had not come via the post. 'Excuse me, please. It's a private matter.' Faint and shivery, she left the room.

'Hope it's not trouble.' Dora pushed out her lips. 'Miss Rachel seemed to be all in lerrups.'

'I hope so too,' Helen said, worried the letter might be of a poisonous nature in view of Rachel's pregnancy. Something had greatly disturbed her even before she had read it.

Stumbling into the office, her hands shaking, Rachel peeled away the red wax seal on the folded paper. She glanced up to the ceiling, not knowing how she felt about James right at that moment and dreading what she would read. He couldn't have picked a worse time for this. She was expecting Flint's baby and planning to marry him. She wished she could go out far on the downs to brace herself for James's words and to be able to take her time reflecting on them.

My Dear Rachel,

I have returned to Meryen to explain to you the reason for my sudden departure and subsequent silence. I beg you to believe me that the decision to leave in that way was not taken lightly and I am pleading with you to allow me the opportunity to give you a full explanation. Tragically Charlotte is dead and I am now a free man. My immediate action after the funeral was to return to you in the fervent hope to reclaim your love. I love you so very much, darling Rachel, and always will. Please, please find it in your heart to suggest a time and place where we can meet.

Yours, as ever, James.

No resurgence of love welled up in Rachel. Instead, into every dot and dash of the letter she interpreted deceit and desperation. For some reason James Lockley had lost his wife, and from what Rachel knew from before, Charlotte's family must now have forsaken him. Now he knew how she had felt when he had abandoned her. He probably had little money and few prospects. She would not be cast aside and taken up again merely as a selfish man's refuge. She was second best to no one. A Kivell did not settle for that. James Lockley had no pride and self-respect, but she did. He would have to leech off some other poor unfortunate.

Ripping the letter to tiny shreds, she went outside to her young cousin. Clemency, tall for a fourteen-year-old, was one of the few Kivells who had light-coloured hair, in her case a sort of amber, thick and of wayward ripples and curls. She was from a branch of the family that lived resolutely at Burnt Oak and were as belligerent and lawless as their ancestors. She was smoking a roll-up while throwing sticks for the lurchers. Taking her time aiming the last stick, she gazed at Rachel with questions in her indolent brown eyes. She was a scruff, her dress worn carelessly and leather ankle boots badly scuffed, but she was as sharp as a sword edge and her voice was clear and velvet. 'The doctor didn't recognize me as a Kivell. He paid me not to reveal his presence in the village. I struck a good bargain to do his bidding. He had no choice if he wanted to remain a secret. He could hardly ask someone else. I've a fancy I took most of his money. He's pale and thin. He's trouble in person. Be very careful in any reply to him, Rachel. He's waiting for me in the churchyard.'

Rachel nodded in compliance, discomfited that the girl, intellectual and knowledgeable beyond her years, had summed up the connection between her and James. 'So he's not staying at one of the inns?'

'He's definitely keeping his head down.'

'Tell Dr Lockley there is no reply and that I'm busy with my wedding arrangements.' This way Rachel would get her revenge. 'If he doesn't leave the village, Clemency, will you report back to me?'

'I'll do that. I'll keep on his tail,' Clemency said with relish. She was a skilled poacher and could steal about as silently as a cat.

'Thank you.' Rachel was serious. 'Would you also keep this between the three of us? I don't want anything ruining my future.'

'It won't get past my lips.'

Clemency strode off, her shoulders working in the pride and arrogance of her breed.

Rachel went inside with a satisfied smile. Clemency could be trusted. Her obstinacy ensured no threat on earth would induce her to break her word. And no doubt James Lockley would be wretchedly disappointed with the outcome. Too bad; he shouldn't have abandoned her so callously. His earlier silence was unforgivable. He should have known it would have plunged her into uncertainty and heartbreak. Well, that heartbreak hadn't lasted and she was getting on with her life. He could take himself off and start another new life without her.

Twenty

'There was no reply at all, girl?' James snapped at Clemency. 'Not even a word by mouth?'

'All the lady said was she's too busy getting ready for her wedding.' Clemency enjoyed his shock. Now she would make him squirm. 'What do you want with her anyway? It's all very strange.'

'It's none of your business,' James bawled. 'Wedding? Did I hear right?' After his anxious journey down from Bath, his humiliation under the acid tongue of the pompous squire, the agitated wait in the churchyard, where he'd been forced to hide from the vicar, the verger and mourners at a farmer's funeral, he was being told Rachel was getting married? Damn it! She had taken up with someone else on the rebound. He had not considered that.

Clemency went off on a swaggering step. The doctor could wallow in his own perplexity. Rachel's short time of dejection had been explained and Clemency would take her secret to the grave. What had Rachel seen in that milksop? She was now marrying beneath her but the miner Retallack was a better prospect. The doctor had better leave Meryen without causing

247

trouble. Clemency was as capable of giving him a dipping into a horse trough as any of her kinsmen.

'Wait! I'll give you more money,' James called after her. 'I need to know the details.'

Clemency stopped and half turned round, exuding condescension. 'I don't know any more.'

Damnable brat! There was no point in bargaining with her. She had already taken him for two guineas; she wasn't a miner's whelp – a shilling or two more wouldn't make any difference to her. He shouldn't have raised his voice, he was frantic not to be discovered skulking about. He strode out of the churchyard by the back gate. The lane branched off to the doctor's house but he avoided his former home. With his hat pulled down and scarf wrapped over his chin, he skirted Meryen by way of fields and lonely tracks, unaware the girl was shadowing him.

On a scrap of common land, near a place called Pixie Cross, an itinerant knife-grinder by the name of Dewy had set up camp with his covered wagon. Earlier James had paid Dewy to hold his luggage in safekeeping.

The weasel-like old man was perched on a four-legged stool near his mobile home by his fire, smoking a knobbly painted wooden pipe. A pot of stew was simmering over the steady flames. He watched James's approach from inscrutable rheumy eyes. Next to him sat a quiet old black mutt, tongue out, anticipating something from the stew pot. 'Finished your business then? You don't seem at all content. I've a feeling you won't be staying on in Meryen.'

'I came to catch up with some old friends,' James ground out, 'but there's nothing for me here. I've been told an acquaintance is to marry – Miss Rachel Kivell. Do you happen to know who to?'

'Ais, I do. I know what all of Meryen's up to. She's to marry Flint Retallack, he's a miner and he's got her in a certain condition.' Dewy showed black teeth while he made the actions of a mound in front of his middle.

'Are you sure?' James felt his throat constrict.

'Ais, the wedding's happening quick.' Dewy had a suspicion why the doctor had returned. Rachel Kivell was a fine piece of womanhood, enough to bring any hopeful widower back on a long journey to seek his chance. For drama and because he had a mean streak, he rattled off a ball of lies, 'All the Kivells went after him with guns and knives. Miss Rachel had to plead on her knees for Retallack's life, said she loved him and if they killed him she'd kill herself. They didn't kill him but they beat him black and blue, there was blood everywhere. Best fun I've seen in the village for a long time.' Noting the doctor wasn't fully convinced, Dewy shrugged, 'Wedding's to be in the chapel, ask anyone.'

'How big is she with child?' It could be his child and she was marrying some yokel to give it a name and save herself from lasting disgrace.

There could be a chance of him coming between them.

'Can't be far along; she's not showing.'

James's vision blurred with fury. That meant
the child had to be the miner's. The moment he
had left here Rachel had turned to someone
else. The unfaithful bitch! The whore! She had
not really cared for him. She had used him for
excitement, the opportunity to get away from
this backwater and become a proper lady. He
had come all this way and all he had achieved
was to be treated with disdain at Poltraze and to
be rejected by the woman who had professed to
love him.

'You said you were leaving the area tonight,'
James said curtly. 'I'll pay to be taken to Redruth. I don't want to talk any more.'

'Fair enough.' The knife-grinder stirred his
stew and whispered something to the cur.

Clemency stole away in the cover of natural
banks and willow bushes. The doctor had been
told the whole truth, with embellishments. He'd
realize Rachel was lost to him for good and
soon he would be gone for good.

James went off a long distance. He kicked at
a large stone and kicked it again. He locked his
fists and spat on the ground. *Rachel was pregnant and getting married.* She had played him
for a fool. He'd had to listen to her trying to
inveigle to tie him down and give up all he had.
If he had actually left Charlotte for her she
would have made a faithless mistress. He had
no power to pay back the powerful Well-

beloveds for throwing him out like he was something they scraped off their shoe, but even though Rachel came from a somewhat fierce protective clan, he would find a way to make her pay for shunning him so quickly. His immediate concern was a lack of funds. He needed to make a lot of money, fast. He brooded for half an hour and then he had the perfect idea.

He returned to the knife-grinder, leaned forward to his seated level. 'Dewy, would you be at all interested in lining your pockets in a manner that was unlawful?'

Dewy spooned in a mouthful of stew and slurped it down, thumping his wiry chest to belch. 'I've done many such a thing afore now.'

'Is there anything you'd consider too dangerous or too wrong?'

Dewy drew a long thin blade from the region of his ankle. 'Let's say I'm willing to do anything if the price is right.'

James looked all about. 'This place is a bit too public. Let's talk inside the wagon, and then I'd like you to take me somewhere.'

Twenty-One

Three-month-old Nathaniel Nankervis was being taken for an airing in his new carriage-built perambulator, the hood up to protect him from the sun, insects and disease. Her hands tightly on the bone handle, the nursemaid was proudly pushing him along the paved paths, staying close to the house as strictly ordered by Nanny Johns. She was to take no longer than an hour. She rounded the front of the house and pushed the baby between avenues of rhododendrons, the petals of the beautiful big blooms of red, yellow, peach and white turning rusty with age. It was sheltered and peaceful, birds were trilling, the sun was warm and not too bright. It was a perfect day.

Young Beattie Rowe sang softly to the awake and alert Nathaniel. She had a good life, a cosy little room all to herself, attached to the nursery. Nanny Johns was teaching her the trade of childcare to the gentry and she was impressed with Beattie's aptitude. Mrs Nankervis was also pleased with her progress. From being a farmer's daughter up to her knees in muck and labouring for long hours in all weathers, Beattie looked forward to each day with clean hands and pleasant smells. Changing Master Nathaniel's napkins was a mere trifle.

Alongside the next wide path was towering laurel. There was a rustle among the speckled green and yellowy leaves, a squirrel or one of the pet spaniels, she presumed. Beattie looked about warily – a dog rushing out and making a fuss about the perambulator might scare Master Nathaniel. She'd hate that; she was secretly fiercely protective, loving her exalted charge. There was silence. Beattie carried on, singing gaily again.

Next instant she was consumed by suffocating darkness, her world plummeted from being safe into a black hell. Something was thrown over her head, imprisoning her down to her waist, and before she could utter a scream a blow on the head plunged her into nothingness.

Nanny Johns checked the grandfather clock near a door at the side of the house, wringing her hands. Where was the girl? She had trusted Beattie to bring Master Nathaniel back on time. She was ten minutes late. If the squire knew he would be furious. She prayed that neither he, nor Mrs Nankervis, would happen this way. She went outside and gazed in all directions. There was no sign of Beattie and the perambulator. There was nothing for it but to go and search for the wretched girl. Beattie would be in trouble for this; if she was a long way from the house it might mean her dismissal and the return to filthy work back on the farm.

She had ordered Beattie's route, and once out

of sight of the house ran along between the rhododendrons calling softly, 'Beattie, where are you?'

There was no sight of her, no sound of springy wheels returning this way. Surely the girl couldn't have got lost in the grounds? Nanny Johns made the laurel walk. Soon she shrieked in horror. Up ahead was the perambulator and it was pitched on its side. 'Master Nathaniel!' There was no sign of Beattie. Somehow the stupid girl had caused an accident with the carriage and had run off rather than report her negligence. Pray God the baby wasn't hurt. Nanny Johns tore up to the scene, knelt down and looked for Nathaniel. He wasn't there; all his covers had gone.

Cold fear clenched her heart. She could lose her job over this, the squire's fury ensuring she never got another. Fearing a downward existence, clutching her breast, the nanny ran on. Where had Beattie taken the baby? Had he been killed or so badly hurt that she had absconded with his little body? The tall bushes cleared to open ground and trees.

What she saw sent her into a fit of screaming.

She ran into the house, screaming out of her lungs. 'Help! Help! Mr Nankervis! Madam!'

Michael and Adeline were in the library, their favourite room, and came out to the hall. 'What is all this commotion?' Michael demanded, fear icing his bowels when he saw who was the culprit. 'What's happened? Where's my son? Speak, woman!'

'Oh, sir.' Nanny Johns threw up her hands, on the verge of collapse. She had something in her hand.

Michael went forward and grasped her cruelly tight by the shoulders. 'Calm yourself, woman! Where is my son?'

Her senses and the light in her heart retreating, Adeline stared numbly into the nanny's stricken face. 'Has something happened to Nathaniel? Tell us!'

'B-Beattie took M-Master Nathaniel outside for a walk. When she was late coming back I went out to look for them. I-I found the perambulator overturned with no sign of Master Nathaniel or Beattie. Then I found her tied to a tree! A sack over her head, p-poor girl, she's still there. I left her like that, not knowing if she's alive or dead b-because...' Inside the squire's hold she managed to raise a trembling hand. 'This was pinned to the sack.'

Letting her go to totter on unsteady feet, Michael snatched away what was a piece of shabby paper. He put his long nose to it. 'Oh my God,' he groaned, his high colour drained in a second.

'What is it?' Adeline whispered in dread.

Michael looked as if he had been cut down to half his size. 'Nathaniel's been abducted.'

Rachel was in Three-Steps cottage, up in what would soon be her nuptial bedroom. Flint, Thad and Jowan had carried up the double guest bed from Chy-Henver and a few small pieces for comfort. It left Flint's room with barely any room to walk round the bed or open drawers, but this was only temporary. Plans had been drawn up for the extension of four rooms, two upstairs and two down, which would be completed before the baby's birth.

She laid out the embroidered runners and trinket mats she had stitched for the future she'd hoped to have with James. She had never thought they would end up in a miner's cottage. At least all the time she had spent alone waiting for him had not been for nothing. Was she sad, did she feel cheated about the life she had lost, or rather had never been destined to have? Did she regret not replying to James's letter, which had sent him away immediately and forever? Sometimes she felt these things but then the anger at being used and presumed upon took precedence. She would soon forget James existed. She would have a new family to concentrate on.

Should she tell Flint about her affair with James? He did not seem bothered about her having a previous lover but he might not be impressed that she had been set on taking a married man away from his wife. Flint asked no questions so she decided there was no point in a confession.

In a few days she would become Mrs Flint Retallack and be more incorporated into the village. It would take a lot of getting used to, as would not living with her brother and cousin, but she had adapted to living at Chy-Henver after spending most of her life enclosed at Burnt Oak. She would miss Helen, Dora and Mrs Carveth but they seemed to have already settled into a new routine, Helen stepping up to take her place while she had been busy preparing for her wedding. The best thing about living here was she would see Eva every day.

She was about to share the matriarchal leadership of a house with another woman – not a daunting thing since her mother-in-law-to-be doted on her and overlooked the disgrace of her 'delicate condition'. Mrs Retallack employed her clumsy hands in knitting baby clothes. The main challenge in Rachel's life was to be a wife to Flint. The image of him suddenly stuck out before her like a giant obstacle. She had replaced him as her lover but in other circumstances would she ever have contemplated marrying him? Why had she just fallen into these wedding plans? The Kivells easily bred illegitimate children. She wouldn't have been shunned by her own kind and could have kept her child. She could have gone to a branch of the family further away, given birth, relinquished the child to a relative willing to rear it, and return as if nothing had happened. It hadn't occurred to her for a moment to give her baby away, or not to marry Flint. But was it the right decision to spend the rest of her life with him?

Fingers of uncertainty crawled up her back as she looked out of the window. The back of the cottage and the smallholding was below, Flint's market garden, his poultry, pigs and goats. It

257

was this on which she would look out until her new bedroom was built. Could she stand this more basic way of life? Would the mining community accept her? She was going to have to fit in with two new walks of life.

'Rachel.' Flint was there behind her, home from the morning core; she had not heard him come into the room. 'You're trembling. Is something wrong?'

She heard the note of concern in his voice. Flint truly cared about her. He didn't exist under a façade, he was who he was, and he was ... a good man, he was rather wonderful, and he was hers if it was what she wanted. All she had to do was reach out to him and he would always be there. She turned and put herself in his arms, which as always were ready to enfold her. 'Just excited, that's all.'

'Me too; it's a big step we're taking. You won't regret it, darling.' He kissed the top of her head and placed his face there.

'Nor will you. It will be strange for us both but we'll work it all through. Have Jowan and Thad left?'

'Just now, went off as usual without a word.'

'I'm sorry they're like that to you.'

'Don't worry, it's understandable. They'll come round when I've proved I will give you a good life.'

Before, when they had embraced, their powerful sexual attraction had taken the fore and they had made love; this time they rested in a moment of affection and bonding.

Twenty-Two

Michael was in a lonely glade in Poltraze woods. As directed in the abductors' message he had brought the ransom money of five thousand pounds in a leather satchel. He had used this sheltered place as a boy, for solitude and privacy, keeping books and diaries in a deep dry rot hole of a great beech. He had met women here. Now he was to use the rot hole to place the ransom money. He pushed the satchel through the callus formed round the opening, the cavity on the other side wide and deep. He cried in horror as his hand was covered in beetles and centipedes and shook it clear. His guts were an agony of knots, as they had been for the last two days while he'd raised the money, praying every sleepless moment that Nathaniel was alive and being cared for.

He gazed all around, trying to see round trees and through leaf-laden branches, listening for feet crunching over the woodland floor. He stared upwards in case someone was up on a bough. There was the coo of a wood pigeon, the sound of the light wind swaying the heavy branches, but otherwise it was silent.

He put his hands to his mouth and called,

'I've done exactly what you wanted. The money is there in full. The authorities have not been notified and I've brought no one with me. I believed what you wrote about the whole estate being watched. I shall go back to the house and return for my son in exactly one hour. Please, I beg you to keep your end of the bargain.'

He retreated on heavy feet, reaching a bridle path after a few minutes and galloping home, hating to leave the kidnappers in charge of his son's fate. Tears streamed down his face. Had they been hiding with Nathaniel close by the glade? The abductors were clever and cunning, slipping away with his son and evading the dogs and men sent out immediately in a search. It indicated they might be pitiless and do the worst to cover their tracks. *Please God don't let those monsters hurt my precious son.* Michael sobbed aloud at the thought of Nathaniel being frightened, hungry and soiled. If he got his son back unharmed he would keep armed guards all around the house and never rest until the vile perpetrators were hunted down.

Once again Rachel was walking home from Three-Steps in the late afternoon, leaving Flint after a warm embrace. She was growing closer to Flint by the moment, hopeful he was the best thing ever for her. Her wedding dress was nearly finished, a gorgeous affair of ivory and bronze satin and tulle, with the traditional silk red rosebuds trailing along the skirt and train.

Helen's lace made the perfect finishing touch. She would be the envy of every young woman in the village and her fall from grace would be disregarded for the day. Flint was popular and that should help her be welcomed into his community.

Soon she would tread this familiar path in reverse as a visitor, the downs and mine to her left and the other usual features, like the crop of high granite she was now passing to her right. She went on in a daydream of wedding day expectations, enjoying each detail as any other bride would.

Some instinct tapping on her shoulder told her something was wrong. She whirled round and her world was plunged into danger and panic. A figure in black, face covered, was coming right at her and it had a sack in its hands. 'No!'

She broke into a run. She could hear the figure catching up with her and she made her lungs work harder and legs go faster. She screamed and screamed, hoping someone would hear and come to her aid.

She felt a hand grasp her shoulder forcing her to falter. 'Bitch!' the attacker yelled, wrenching her round.

She kicked out, clawing at the attacker's hands to get them off her, the stones beneath her feet scattering in all directions, but the attempt to overpower her was crazed. A blow was delivered to the side of her head and another hard into her stomach. She howled and doubled over, fearing for her baby, and then was horrified to

feel the sack going over her head. She screamed, trying to wrestle free. Then her head seem to
explode and she was pitched into darkness.

'Rachel should be on her way home by now,'
Thad said, joining Helen at the rose bushes in
the front garden.

She was studying the blooms and buds of
pink and red, deciding which would be the best
on the day to decorate the chapel for the wedding. 'Did the work on the cottage go well
today?' He and Jowan had left Three-Steps
cottage an hour before Rachel.

'It did. Rachel is going to have to live in a
terrible crush before it's finished.' His reply
was tainted with sourness. 'There's not enough
room for a spider to catch a fly in that place.'

Helen gave him a certain look, the same as
she did to Jowan whenever they vented dis-
approval about Rachel's future husband. 'You
gave me a chance when everyone else despised
me. Can you not find it in yourself to grant Flint
the same consideration? I rather like him; so do
Mrs Carveth and Dora.' She strolled along the
path and he went with her, putting his hands
casually behind his back.

'Very well, I'll soften my attitude towards
him.'

'Why the sudden change of heart?' She smiled
to herself, his hardened Kivell surface did not
run as deeply as his kinfolk.

'I don't want you to think badly of me.'

'I don't.' She bent her head and sniffed a

262

crimson bloom, pleased she was able to flirt a little with him.

'Helen...'

'Yes?'

'You know what I'm about to say. I haven't pressed you before, but have you come to a decision yet about my proposal?' He crossed his hidden fingers. *Say yes, say yes.* If she did not he'd step up his campaign, for he was determined to have her. No other woman would do for him. Whatever background they came from they seemed much alike to him. Helen was unique. Her dreadful experience had honed her into the woman she now was and he was fiercely drawn to every part of her.

Helen faced him squarely. 'I've thought it all through very seriously.' It was on her mind every minute. 'Thad, do you really want to marry a woman who might never bring herself to step beyond the front gate? Who couldn't stand being among your large family? I'll be honest with you – I don't really want children. I don't know if that's because I'm selfish or a personal preference. Children, I have noticed, are important to the Kivells. I can't in truth offer you much at all.'

'Thank you, Helen, for telling me how you feel. What if I say that I don't care if you never change a single thing? I love you for who you are, not for what you might be. I can't deny that I'd like to have children but I'd rather not have any at all than have them with another woman. It wouldn't be fair to ask someone else to be my wife when she would only be second best. No one can promise there won't be children in a marriage; could we not agree to leave it to fate? If it happened there would be Mrs Carveth and Dora to support you, and me of course.'

Helen kept her face blank as she thought it through. It was a selfless offer, and a genuine one she was in no doubt. It made her feel small, for her reason to accept his proposal was a selfish one. If or when Thad or Jowan married she would be no more than a lodger, a charity case, and lower-deck to a mistress who might resent her presence. For her own peace of mind she really had no choice about becoming Thad's wife, but she was fond of him, she admired him, and she could endure having a child or two, whom she might care about.

Thad watched as her bare expression gave way to a smile. He took a chance and reached for her hand. She did not pull it away; she did not mind his touch. 'You'll always be safe in my love, Helen.'

'I know,' she said softly.

He initiated new ground and bent his head to kiss her hand. 'Say yes, Helen.'

'I will say yes, Thad. I'd be honoured to be your wife.'

'I'm the one who will be honoured.' His spirit sang out. He dropped a light kiss on her lips. He didn't expect a response and was elated to get a firm one, so he took her into his arms and kissed her with eagerness.

Helen was surprised to have enjoyed the

264

sensual contact. She laid her face against his strong chest and gloried in a secure future.

Riders were heard coming up fast. 'Someone's having a race or there's trouble,' Thad said, reluctant to have the romantic moment ended. He relinquished Helen and went to the front gate. It was the squire and his steward, both clearly bothered, and they pulled up their mounts in a hurry and jumped down.

'Kivell,' Michael said, his face streaky red. 'Is your cousin Jowan about?'

'He's in the house. Why?' Thad wasn't about to cooperate with the man who now shunned their business. Nankervis had better not be rude to Helen.

'Please, I need your help.' Michael was bereft of all pride and rank didn't matter. 'Let us forget past hurts. I need to talk to you both urgently.'

Helen had come to the gate, keeping wary. 'Is Adeline well?'

'No, she's not.' Michael even turned pleadingly to her. 'Our son has been abducted! Please let us enter and explain.'

'Dear God!' Helen gasped, the spectre of her old terrors rising. Evil was again abroad in the area. The perpetrator could even be the monster that had attacked her.

In the sitting room, with Jowan and Mrs Carveth, all listened grimly as Michael recounted the dreadful facts and the growing dread as he'd waited vainly in the glade for his son to be returned. 'Part of me fears the worst

265

for Nathaniel but I can't help hoping that he may be found alive. I have men scouring the woods and all my properties, asking everyone if they've seen strangers or anyone acting suspiciously of late. I've sent someone to Burnt Oak to ask if your kinsmen will join in the search. The vicar is setting up the same in the village. I will pay a handsome reward for information and the return of my son. I know it's an outside chance, but after Lady Churchfield was abducted and now my son, it seems someone may be targeting Poltraze. You know where she was found that day. Would you search that spot and the downs for any clues where she may have been incarcerated? My dear son may be there now. If he has been abandoned alive he may yet be found in time ... Lady Churchfield, I know we parted on bad terms and I have since scorned you, but I implore you to think back over your ordeal. Is there anything you can tell us? Even the smallest thing might be important.'

Helen's insides were coiled into an acidic knot and panic hung over her, but she took a deep breath. 'I bear Adeline and your son no ill will. All I can remember is a rough man, not very big. He was wholly menacing and full of hate. And there was his smell. It reminded me of spices. We think it's possible he was a sailor.'

Michael nodded in gratitude. 'Have you any idea what sort of place he kept you in?'

'I can only think it was a woodshed; there were particles of bark and wood splinters in my

266

clothes. I was blindfolded all the time. The floor was hard earth.'

'I'm not joining a search, for I will not leave Helen, who by the way is soon to be my bride,' Thad said firmly, not pausing to respond to raised brows. 'If the monster responsible for hurting her is the same one who took your son I won't take the risk that he'll come here.'

'I'll set out straight away,' Jowan said, doubtful of finding anything of help but prepared to search for Nathaniel Nankervis as he would anyone else's baby. 'The miners who found Helen could tell you more than us about where Helen was found. Rachel, my sister, is soon to marry one of those men, Flint Retallack. Mr Nankervis, did you happen to see Rachel walking home on your way here?' Jowan was uneasy that his sister was not home yet.

'We saw no one.' Michael glanced at his steward, a small, pale-skinned young man, who nodded in confirmation.

'I'll ride to the village and meet her. I don't want her on the road alone.' Jowan made for the door. 'Retallack should be home. I'll ask him and his neighbour to search the downs with me.'

'We'll ride with you,' Michael said, fighting the weakness in the body with faint hope.

'It's him, I know it is,' Helen declared. Anxiety for Rachel made her angry and indignant towards her attacker. It gave her the strength of will she had thought she would never possess again. She picked Willow up in her arms and held her close.

'I won't leave you for a moment, Helen.' Thad went to her. 'I'll secure the house and keep the dogs in the yard and front garden. I'll prepare the guns, just in case.'

'I can cope, Thad. I'm praying my cousin's baby will be found alive, but I hope it's him, that vile creature who stole my peace, and that he'll be caught and hung. Then I won't have to spend the rest of my days scared that he might suddenly step out of the shadows.'

The three men on horseback rode hard until they came to a spot near the outcrop of boulders where the ground was newly disturbed.

'It wasn't like this when we passed here a little earlier,' Michael said.

'Rachel...' Jowan whispered, his eyes shooting in all directions. A terrible ache in his soul told him that when he reached Three-Steps cottage, Rachel would not be there but had already left for home. He jumped down from his horse and saw something glinting amid the scattered stones. He was wrought with despair. It was Rachel's gold bracelet.

Twenty-Three

In the darkness, her head hurt so much that Rachel kept her eyes shut, careful to lie still on the bed. She couldn't remember how she had got home. Had she met with an accident after leaving Flint or had she been taken ill? Her baby! A throbbing pain in her middle now registered and with a cry of alarm she put her hands there.

'Rachel.' The voice came in a husky whisper as if travelling to her from some mystic region.

'Jowan?'

'I'm not he. Open your eyes, Rachel. It's wakey-wakey time.' The voice now had a sing-song quality, hinting at mockery.

Rachel lifted her eyelids. Images swam before her. She was in a room darkened by the drawn curtains; it was still light outside. This was not her bedroom at Chy-Henver. A man was sitting cross-legged on the end of the bed, his jacket off and his collarless white shirt was spotted with blood. He leaned forward, looming over her, his mouth etched in a peculiar grin.

'James? James!' She tried to sit up but was too feeble and light-headed. 'What's happened? Where are we?'

'We're in Edinburgh, my dear, just like we'd always wanted. Don't you remember the long journey?'

This didn't make sense. She was to marry Flint. If only the confusion fluttering in her head would clear and she could remember exactly what had happened. 'You mean we've actually gone away together?'

'No! Wrong!' he bawled, mocking her and leaping astride her on all fours. 'Don't you recognize this place, this bed, Rachel? We took many a glorious tumble in it. We're in Lowenna, our own little paradise.'

The assault on her on the way home slammed into her mind, like being hit by a hammer. She felt again every fearful agony as the fists smashed into her head and stomach, and the sack being thrown over her to take her prisoner. 'You're the one who hurt me? Who put my baby in danger? For God's sake, why? Get away from me!' she screamed, pushing her hands against his chest with all her might.

His eyes blazing like a madman's, James grabbed her wrists and thrust her arms up above her head. He lowered his leering face just a breath away. 'Yes, I hurt you, you bitch, and you deserved it and more. I'd only just cleared my heels for Bath and you'd gone and laid down for a filthy miner. You're a whore, Rachel Kivell. You treated me with contempt and I allow no one to get away with that.'

Something vital filtered into her consciousness – the smell of his spicy cologne. She

270

was engulfed by horror, revulsion and outrage. 'It was you who abducted Helen! You who did all those terrible things to her – why? You're crazed, evil!'

'I'm not in the wrong,' he spat indignantly, squeezing on her wrists until she cried out. 'That bitch tormented me. She treated me like dross in a sewer. I made her pay, that's all.'

Rachel saw him for the unstable man he was, and that her life was at stake. She must proceed with care and cunning.

'I returned here to request the squire's help in finding me a new post after my wife's hateful family disowned me immediately on her death. Nankervis mocked me. He made me feel as small as a speck of dirt. He said I could take over again as doctor in Meryen but he didn't want me anywhere near his precious family. He didn't care that I'd just lost my wife and child.' James threw back his head and howled like a grieving animal.

'I'm sorry about Charlotte and your child, James. What happened to them?'

He told her with a terrible sob in his throat. Then he raged, 'The Wellbeloveds didn't have the humanity to tell me she was ill and a physician had been sent for. They didn't want me there when she died.' He was racked with more despairing sobs, his knees digging into Rachel's legs and his hands still squeezing hers painfully tight. 'They kept me away from her funeral. They hate me. I'm nothing to them. One minute I had everything and then it was all gone.'

His hot salty tears splattered on to Rachel's face. 'I came back here to you, Rachel, only to be told you'd been unfaithful to me.'

'I'm so sorry, James.' She was appalled at his whining self-pity, but she must be clever and turn his fixated anguish to her advantage or this would be the end of her. 'Listen to me, James. Flint Retallack means nothing to me. I was distraught when you left without a word, but now I understand you had no choice as Charlotte was carrying your baby. I turned to Flint out of heartbreak. It happened only one foolish time with him and I immediately regretted it. When I discovered I was with child I only agreed to marry him to be closer to Eva, the poor girl I rescued. But everything could be different now, James. We could go away together as we'd originally planned. I've got enough money for us to go anywhere we'd like.'

He stopped snivelling and stared down at her.

'James, release my hands and let me hold you.'

He nodded. A bit at a time he eased the cruel pressure on her wrists.

'That's right, my love,' she cooed, which made her feel sick. 'Lie down beside me and let me give you my devotion again.'

He smiled and Rachel was hopeful. Then he curled his lips and his whole face metamorphosed, like a gargoyle. 'Heave-ho!' He sat down heavily on her stomach.

'Arrgh! Please, my baby!' Rachel fought to

push off his dreadful weight.

'Too late.' He laughed uproariously, beating the air above his head with his fists like some savage. 'I've beaten the brat out of your guts. Remember that blow I gave you on the roadside, Rachel? That did the trick.' He pointed to the blood on his shirt, 'See? And look at this.' He reached to the floor and brought up a tiny bundle of cloth. Rachel saw it had been ripped off her petticoat. The bundle was heavily bloodstained. 'This is where your child is, the beginnings of it, not much there, just a foetus of miner's dross.'

'No!' Rachel screamed, lashing out and striking his face, struggling to get him off her, horribly conscious of warm stickiness between her thighs. 'Murderer!'

Storming off the bed, hurting her more in the stunt, he snatched up more tatters of her petticoats and began tying her hands to the bedstead. 'If I couldn't have my child then neither could you and nor that bastard squire have his!' He pulled at her legs and tied her ankles to the footboard. 'I don't need your money, Rachel Kivell! I've got a princely sum off the squire.'

'What do you mean?'

'Of course, you don't know,' he mocked. 'I took the squire's brat and I've got the ransom money. I'm off to start my new life as a gentleman with means to start a good medical practice anywhere I like. No one knows you're here, Rachel. They don't know about our love nest. You'll rot here and die. You'll die the death you

273

deserve, that of a betrayer. You never loved me and I as sure as hell never loved you.'

'You're insane,' Rachel shouted as he came at her with a gag for her mouth. 'You'll get what you deserve one day, James Lockley.'

'People take me for a fool but I'm too clever for the lot of you,' was his parting shot. He pulled off his shirt and put on a clean one. While shrugging into his coat he left, shutting her in the room.

As he clumped down the stairs Rachel struggled to loosen the restraints. She listened for the bang of the front door, leaving her imprisoned all alone and facing an agonizing death, both physically and emotionally. But it seemed the killer of her baby and the Nankervis's son wasn't ready to leave just yet. She heard a mumble of voices. He was talking to an accomplice.

Her baby was not far from her and she ached to hold the tiny mite in her arms. Probably somewhere in the house was the little body of Nathaniel Nankervis. If only she could cradle them both.

She cried, not so much because she was to lose her life but for the hurt it would cause her family, to Flint and Helen when her body and her baby's was eventually discovered, and for never being able to see Eva again. And Flint – she cared a great deal about him. A real and honest love had been springing up between them. The good and happy life they were to have had together would never be fulfilled.

Twenty-four

Flint stared at the squire and his steward in disbelief. What on earth were they doing on his doorstep? The squire looked as if he was about to shatter into little pieces.

'Retallack, we've come with very bad news,' Michael blurted out, his voice burning with tears, his legs barely holding him up. After the abduction of the Kivell girl he had lost hope for his son and his presence here was merely clutching at straws.

'No, that can't be right.' Flint rapidly shook his head. 'Rachel couldn't have come to any harm. She can look after herself.' But this had to be true, otherwise Michael Nankervis wouldn't lower himself to bring such news. He thought his son's abduction and ransom had some connection with Rachel's disappearance. But who would do this? It didn't make sense. It could only be through some madness, a great evil. He pressed at his forehead. Rachel abducted? His Rachel? He couldn't stand the thought of any harm being done to her. Not to his precious Rachel; she was everything to him. 'I heard all the commotion in the village. More people about, people calling to neighbours, but

275

I thought, well, I have been busy and didn't think much about it really. Who the hell could have done this?' Flint wanted to run to the place of Rachel's struggle but first he had to tell his mother what had happened.

A crowd of swarthy Kivells were riding their way. They reined in behind Seth Kivell, father of Clemency. A man of giant size, grizzled, with a full black beard, paid no heed to Flint, disapproving of his kinsman-to-be. He bawled to Michael. 'We're on the lookout for your little boy, squire. Your men asked if we'd seen any strangers lurking about. My daughter met someone acting strangely only three days ago.' He thumbed towards Clemency, who kneed her grey pony forward.

'Who? Speak up, girl.' Michael leaned over the iron railing and stared down on her.

Before she could speak Flint got in first. 'Rachel's been abducted, just a while ago, while walking home from here. Jowan's taken the dogs, hoping to pick up her scent. Who did you see?'

A murmur of shock went round the Kivells.

'It was that Dr Lockley.' Clemency eyed Flint. To offset him or the others drawing the same conclusion as she had, that Rachel and Lockley had been involved, she said, 'He asked me to take a letter to Rachel. I think he'd been keen on her.'

'Lockley! Three days ago, you say?' Michael cut in. 'It's the same day he came to Poltraze informing me his wife was dead and begging

276

me to help him find a new position. I said he could resume as Meryen's doctor after the new man had moved on and to take up immediate residence at the doctor's house. He did not take up my proposition. Go on, girl, go on.'

Clemency glared at him for wasting time – it would be getting dark in a couple of hours. 'He asked me to wait for a reply from Rachel. I could see she wasn't at all pleased to hear from him. She said to tell him there was no reply. Lockley didn't want anyone to see him. I met him again in the churchyard. He seemed furious when I told him Rachel was getting married. He stalked off through the back gate but I followed him. He slunk off to the common land near Pixie Cross and met up with Dewy, the knife-grinder. I heard him ask to be taken to Redruth. I went back a bit later and they had gone.'

'Lockley could have taken Rachel. He came back to try to win her,' Flint muttered, glad there was a lead. 'If he's carrying a torch for Rachel he might not harm her. Let's hope he's hiding out locally.'

'He might also be behind my son's abduction,' Michael cried. 'If Rachel is found then just perhaps...' He turned to the steward. 'Organize a search at Redruth at all the hotels and likely places Lockley might go.'

'Everyone be careful,' Clemency warned. 'Lockley seemed cunning and desperate. He was dishevelled and stank of stale biscuits.'

'Biscuits? Could you mean spice?' Michael breathed, grasping the rail, about to crumple.

'The one thing Lady Churchfield remembers about her attacker is that he smelled of spices. If Lockley was behind her ordeal too it means he's a very dangerous man and my poor son must be dead.'

'Ah.' James took another satisfied swig from the bottle of rum he was sharing with Dewy in the kitchen. Dewy had just arrived back after returning the horse he had hired for James to perform both abductions and pick up the ransom money. Ten minutes had passed since James had shut Rachel in upstairs and the two men had cleared all evidence of them ever being there. They had shared out the ransom money into two old leather bags from Dewy's wagon. 'Well, my friend, we've done good business together. The bodies won't be found for months until the owner of this place turns up when the rent is overdue. Now it's time we were on our way. After we part at Portreath, I'm sure you'll be as glad as I am that we'll never set eyes on each other again.' Dewy had got him a berth on a cargo vessel shipping copper ore.

But Dewy wasn't about to go anywhere. James wasn't about to share all the money.

'Ais, we've got enough to do what we've always wanted.' Dewy kept his crusty eyes rooted on the doctor. It wasn't wise to trust a madman ruthless enough to kill a baby and leave the lovely young woman he'd boasted of an affair with to die, and to have tortured the

278

titled lady, another of his boasts.

'Let us take up our reward off to the wagon then,' James said. Slipping his bag of money over his shoulder, he slid his hand into his pocket and put his fist around a wad of cloth soaked with ether. Once Dewy was unconscious he'd finish him off by smothering him. The authorities would probably believe he died of natural causes and he would go down in local infamy as the abductor and killer.

He motioned for Dewy to step outside first. When he was behind Dewy at the door he drew out the cloth and swung it up and around to cover his nose and mouth. To James's surprise Dewy was suddenly facing him and he felt a thud in his chest. Dewy roughly yanked off James's bag and pushed him away. James looked down and cried in horror to see blood gushing down his shirt. 'W-what have you done?'

Dewy went at him and tore the wad of anaesthetic away. He flashed a bloodied blade in front of James's eyes. 'Took me for a fool, did you, Doc? That was your one big mistake. I knew your game. Well, it's me who's going to enjoy the ransom all to meself and people will know you for what you are, a rotten crazed murderer.' He pushed on James again and he fell to the floor, his back against a cupboard. 'You'll also know what it's like to die slowly.'

James pressed his hands hard against his chest, blood trickling through his fingers, too shocked at the betrayal and his own stupidity to feel afraid. Dewy opened the door then took a moment to grin down at James.

There was a small flash and a bang and Dewy's eyes widened in horror as something slammed into his heart. He was dead before he hit the floor.

'That was your mistake; you should have just gone.' James gasped in pain, letting the small hand gun he had pulled out fall from his hand. He had been stabbed near the breastbone, his heart and lungs missed by a fraction. There was a very good chance he would live if he treated himself. He crawled across to his medical bag.

Rachel's heart leapt at the sound of the gunshot. Something dreadful had happened downstairs, probably a double-cross, but she had to concentrate on getting free. Any second now James or his accomplice might come hurtling into the room and put an end to her life.

She had been tugging desperately to free her right hand but rather than loosen the cloth it had tightened and was impossible to budge. Now stretching to reach the other side, making her body sear with pain, she was just able to work at the cloth with her teeth. Biting hard, sweating with the tremendous effort, the first knot started to part excruciatingly slowly, the wet from her mouth making the cloth harder to shift. The knot gave way and she fell back in exhaustion. She listened. All was quiet. Had the men gone? She had not heard the sound of their departure. She couldn't take the risk of pausing to catch her breath. Flinging herself again to the left, clenching her jaw to prevent herself crying out, she sank her teeth into the next knot.

Working and working, her jaw in agony, her teeth feeling about to disintegrate, she gradually untied the cloth. Her hand was free. It was still quiet downstairs. Surely the men had crept away? The right-hand knot was vice tight and she wasn't going to waste time pulling on it. She reached for the bedside lamp and to lessen any noise laid it on the bed, put the sheet over it and, using a bronze ornament, she smashed the glass. She chose a large sharp fragment and cut through the bond. Then ignoring her aches and the heartbreaking pain in her abdomen she cut through the cloth tying her ankles.

Overcome with nausea and dizziness she was forced to lay down, a hand over her brow, panting and sobbing. A minute later she sat up and eased her legs over the side of the bed. She sank down to her knees and picked up the tiny bundle that was the remains of her baby. She hugged it to her body and keened and wept. 'I'm so sorry. Your father and I would have loved you so much.'

Using the bed to lever herself up she laid the bundle down gently by the footboard. She was bleeding from the miscarriage. The nearest dwelling was about half a mile away, the small quiet farm owned by Lowenna's landlord. If the way were safe and clear she would walk there for help. If she got through this at least her baby would receive a decent burial.

Picking up the poker from the fireplace, she

crept to the window. Dewy the knife-grinder's wagon was below. So he was James's accomplice. He or James had been shot, both might have been hurt, why else had there been no getaway? She tiptoed to the door. She needed to get away from here before darkness fell but her actions must be slow and silent. She must not panic or hasten and give herself away. Danger likely lurked below. Tense and fearful she got through the door and halted and listened on the small landing.

'Huh.'

The sound from downstairs made the air lock in her lungs. Should she hide in another room and wait for whomever it was to go?

'Damn and blast!'

It was James's voice. It sounded as if he was in the kitchen. There were no sounds of Dewy. Had he been killed? There had been no strength in James's voice. He might be hurt and no danger to her. If she could steal down the stairs and get out of the front door unseen she would take Dewy's wagon and make her way to safety. The kitchen door was at the end of a short passage and if the door was open she would be in full view at the foot of the stairs. She might have to make a run for it.

Clutching the narrow banister, the poker tight in her other hand, she descended the stairs, bringing each foot together, praying there would be no tell-tale creak. One step, two, three, down she went. Unidentifiable sounds issued from the kitchen and panting and muttering and swearing. It seemed James really was hurt. Thank God; it gave her the best chance.

She reached the last stair and alighted on the passage runner. Rachel's heart lurched the next beat. The kitchen door was flung back and she could see Dewy's body stretched out by the back door, blood on his chest. James was sitting at the table, facing the passage, his front and hands covered in blood, attending to himself. He was so absorbed that even if she had thumped down the stairs and waved her arms at him he would not have heard her.

The men had harmed each other and they greatly deserved it. A terrible rage at what James had done to her and her baby hit her and became her life force. She had done nothing bad to him but he had treated her like a commodity to be used, and he had killed the most precious thing in her life. Putting the poker behind her back she strode into the kitchen. The air smelled pungently of antiseptic but Rachel thought it also should stink of his villainy and her fury.

'Hello, James.' Her voice was unnaturally calm. 'How bad is it?'

He looked up from stitching the edges of the wound together, having calculated he was not bleeding internally. 'Rachel.' His eyes were drawn in pain, but as they wandered over her face, rather than registering surprise or perhaps alarm, they smiled. His whole face was smiling, an absurd kind of smile. He was thinking,

283

scheming; he had the nerve and logic of a clever lunatic. 'Will you help me?'

'Help you, James?' She stepped closer, her heart beating with pure hatred. 'Why should I do that?'

'Because you loved me once, Rachel. You did, didn't you?'

How dare he throw that at her? Did he really believe he could resurrect those feelings in her? 'I wish only to leave and get on with my life. What have you done with the squire's baby? Is he in the woodshed where you kept Helen?'

'He can't be found at Lowenna, Rachel.'

'What did you do with him? Is he alive? Could you really bring yourself to murder a defenceless baby? Are you that wicked?' With each word she closed in on him.

'Now do I seem like the sort of man who would leave evidence behind? Dewy disposed of him. I didn't bother to ask where.' James dropped his hands, the needle dangling from the catgut.

'Put your hands on the table,' Rachel ordered, just inches from him.

'Now why should I do that?' He smirked.

Rachel brought the poker into view. 'If you don't I'll beat your brains out!'

She saw his hand shuffle towards his coat pocket. Swinging the poker wide she drove it fiercely against his arm. He howled like an animal as his bones broke with a gut-turning crunch. 'Do you think I'd let you hurt me again? To be free to hurt others?' She brought the poker back in a wide arc.

'No, Rachel, for pity's sake!'

'You never heeded anyone's distress,' she screamed, smashing into his other arm. He screamed and fell off the chair, splayed out helplessly on the floor, his head hitting Dewy's boots. Crouching, she searched in his pocket and pulled out the gun. Then she stood over him with it pointed at the middle of his head.

'You bitch!' He lashed out with his feet.

She stepped out of his reach. 'The words I could use to describe you haven't yet been heard on this earth.'

James eyes were like shattered glass, then the madness went out of him and panic tunnelled. 'Are you going to finish me off?'

'How I want to, but I won't deny the hangman his fun or revenge for me and Helen and the squire.' She turned and walked away.

'Rachel, please! Don't leave me. Rachel!'

His screams echoed her steps to the wagon. Hiding the gun in her bodice, she made the painful climb on board. Picking up the horse-whip, she goaded the pony to walk on. The pony was stubborn without its master and she had to persist, but finally she was leaving Lowenna behind.

Twenty-Five

The lurchers quickly established that Rachel had not been hauled away by road. They lost trace of her scent after a short distance across country but recent disturbance of grasses and horseshoe marks helped show the way the abductor had gone. After a mile or so, then passing through fields, with lanes and tracks feeding off in varying directions, the men and dogs were unsure which way to go. Rachel could have been taken anywhere and time was passing. It seemed the abductor had knowledge of the area and he'd got a good start.

Jowan couldn't think of anyone who would commit such a crime. It chilled him to think some evil, calculating mind might have been living in or near Meryen all this time, but he reckoned someone travelling the roads for a living was more likely to be responsible. The knife-grinder had been about recently and he was a shifty character, but it could just as easily have been gipsies, tinkers or even one of the numerous cart carriers that passed through Meryen regularly. It could be anyone. God help the fiend or fiends who had dragged Rachel off. It didn't make sense, unless it was for a ransom, as with the Nankervis child – but in his case a ransom note had been left at the time of his abduction. Thad was home to receive a demand for money if it was the case, but Jowan didn't believe that would happen.

His kinsmen would be scouring the village bounds and far beyond. Like him they would question all road users and stop at farms and wayside cottages and search empty dwellings – anywhere that could be used as a hideaway. He had brought a lantern and he would continue searching all night, keeping to the lanes and firm tracks after dark.

Rachel would rather drive Dewy's wagon all the way home but she was feeling ill and faint and knew she couldn't even make it as far as Meadowbank. She'd go to Tretolgan Farm for help. The buildings could just be seen from upstairs at the front of the house, away across the fields. Hopefully the farm tenants were kindly and someone would ride over to Chy-Henver and fetch Jowan to take her home.

Frustration was her next ordeal. It was going to be very slow progress to the farm; the pony kept stopping every few yards, obviously trained to avoid being stolen. Rachel snapped the whip across its back and tried coaxing sounds, growing ever more anxious as the creature tossed its head, all teeth and temper. The jolting towards the lane jarred and hurt her tender insides and she cried out often. The sun burned down with suffocating dry heat, perspiration ran into her eyes, wetting her tangled hair. A fever was now ravaging her.

It took many wretched, juddering minutes to reach the exit of Lowenna. Then the pony refused to shift one more step. 'Walk on, you stupid creature!' Her screech echoed all around her and seemed to hurtle back and slap her in the face. There was nothing for it but to clamber down and walk. She groaned in pain as her abused body was stretched, nerve clashing on nerve. A mile wasn't far at all, but now with hills to climb it felt she had a mountainous trek ahead.

She tried one more time to coax the pony to walk on, but it threw back its scruffy head and stamped its hooves and displayed worn-down yellow teeth. It was getting ready to kick or bite so she nipped out of its way, which caused her further throbbing and soreness and she clutched her middle. She wouldn't waste precious energy shouting violence at the pony. No doubt the damned beast would back up and wait for its owner. Sighing wearily, gritting her teeth, she trudged out into the lane, a narrow dirt road.

She walked as fast as she was able but almost at once the ascent of the first steep winding hill began. Soon she was battling for breath and slowed to a feeble pace. At this rate she'd take over an hour to reach the farm. At least there would be enough daylight. Her mind turned to her home. They must know by now that she was missing. The whole Kivell community would be out searching for her. She prayed she would meet a member of the family on this road. It would be such a relief, almost wonderful. She hoped someone had informed Flint. He would be anxious for her and their baby, but when he eventually knew – and after her horrendous experience she felt she owed him the whole truth – how would he feel about her having had James as her lover and that she would have willingly helped wreck his marriage? It was that irresponsible situation that had led to her finding comfort in Flint's arms, to the pregnancy and then the loss of Flint's baby. He might view her affair with James as sordid. She certainly did.

Dragging her feet, she went on, step by step, the top of the hill intent on eluding her. Her throat was raw and dry. She was so thirsty. Blood was trickling from her lower regions and she was in danger of becoming dehydrated. If only she'd had the forethought to take a drink of water at Lowenna's well. Each time she thought she had a few more steps to reach the summit of the hill she was agonizingly wrong. When she finally got to the top she leaned against the hedgerow, panting and trying to clear her muggy head.

It was easier going down the other side of the hill but nevertheless it was a trial. The route was so narrow in parts that the wild growth – gorse, cow parsley, brambles – clawed at her clothes. She came to a field gate and sidetracked to look over its top. She sighted the farmstead nestled away between its few fields.

It cried out sanctuary to her, and help and a greater freedom. It would be quicker to go on through the fields but it would involve climbing hedges and probably other obstacles. It was safer to stay in the lane. If she collapsed unseen she could languish and die of infection or exposure, lay undiscovered for days or weeks. If it happened in a really obscure place she might never be found and she couldn't put her family and Flint through that.

She went on, telling herself that each step took her closer to help and safety. A wave of sickness swamped her and her head spun and she had to rest her back against the hedge until it passed, wasting who knew how many precious minutes, in which she feared she wouldn't be able to continue. She felt fresh blood and hoped it was no more than what a miscarriage naturally brought on. Biting her lip hard, she pushed against the foliage and lumbered on again.

She was wheezing up the ascent of the next hill, a second cruel great mountain. Every slow step was wrought by tremendous effort and seemed to take a full minute. The ground rose and twisted and then turned back on itself, a route first stamped out in ancient times to avoid huge puddles. She had to close her eyes to ward off dizziness, peeping out now to prevent crashing into the hedge or stumbling into a hole or against a large stone.

The top of the hill seemed to stretch further and further away. The farm was now out of sight behind a small wooded area and she panicked, thinking she had lost her way. 'Don't be silly,' she whispered, 'there's only one way you can go.'

She grew aware of nothing but the pains in her body, her whole self being jolted and strained each time she lowered a foot to the merciless gradient. A loud whoosh filled her ears and hammers thumped inside her head. Her chest was tight, fighting for breath, her heart pulsing against her ribs, her body at odds in each limb, nerve, sinew, organ and cell. She feared she wouldn't reach the peak before dark and would be left stumbling, prey to the night, prey to time.

She groaned. She was about to be sick. Turning to the hedge she spilled out her stomach, crying and moaning as her insides convulsed and acid burned all the way up to her throat. She longed for an end to her misery. She craved for it. Cried for it. Cried to be home in her bed between her own linen, cleaned up and out of pain, being looked after by her family and Helen. It was the only thing on her mind. At that dreadful moment she couldn't care what Flint thought of her or if she never saw him again.

She didn't know how long she had been bent over, her arms stretched against the prickly hedge for support. With a whining groan she pulled her arms away. They felt like lead weights. Her legs felt like iced water. She felt numb and strange all over. She was floating.

She was sinking. A strange sensation, heavy and lightweight, was spreading through her, turning her into stone and mist. Her eyes no longer opened at her command. The light was fading, now grey, now black. She was drifting. She was being consumed and then she was nothing.

Twenty-Six

Seth Kivell and his kin arrived at the hamlet of Meadowbank and spread out among the few dwellings in the search for information about Rachel, James Lockley and Dewy, the knife-grinder. Seth had five sons and they were all with him. Clemency was there also; she was Seth's only daughter, his youngest child, and apart from forbidding her to carouse in the inns or ever to behave like a trollop, he more or less treated her as another son.

Meadowbank was largely a place of cottage industry. At the first cottage, the female weaver informed Seth that no one had passed through the hamlet that day. 'And Dewy's not been seen here for months.'

Seth asked the details of the locality and sent his sons off in various directions. 'Clemency, ride down there. There's a small farm, and a house rented by a genteel couple who're hardly seen. If you see anything suspicious, come straight back. Don't do anything by yourself. Those men are too much for a girl.'

Clemency rode off at a gallop, a reckless speed for such a narrow thoroughfare but she was fearless. Like all her menfolk she had a gun with her and she was a good markswoman. Within seconds she sighted the small farm not far in the distance and, further along, the chimney tops of the solitary house.

It took a few short minutes to reach the farm entrance. 'Tretolgan Farm' was scrawled on a scrap of wood, which jutted out crookedly on its low post in the hedge. She turned on to the heavily rutted, cattle-soiled track. Patchy hedges and banks of blackberry bushes flanked either side. Keeping good speed, Clemency rode into the front yard, sending a few hens scattering and squawking. Two rough collies were barking ferociously inside the house, rearing up to a window on their big paws. In all the stead was basic and well maintained, but it didn't fit that the dogs were not out in the yard.

Jumping down, she battered on the stable door of the house, which was shut, indicating there were no women in residence, at least not at this moment. The dogs went wild, barking like hounds from hell and scrabbling at the glass as if wanting to rip her apart. 'Mutts,' she uttered under her breath. She gazed about. 'Hello! Anyone here?'

No one came to the door. If someone were home they would investigate the reason for the collies' uproar. At the top of some uneven stone steps washing swayed on the line – a family lived here. She looked through the windows. The rooms were tidy, with clumpy furniture. No sign of anyone, just the slavering dogs. She trawled the outhouses and barn but the only life was the livestock. The place was deserted, yet she had a feeling...

Stepping back, she gazed up at an upstairs window. She saw a movement and would swear that a woman's face had ducked out of sight. It wasn't unheard of to be wary of strangers, wise even when living in isolation, but most people were hospitable. Clemency determined not to leave until she had spoken to the person inside. 'Hello! I'd like to speak to you a moment. Will you lift the window and talk to me, please? I only want to ask a few questions. Please, I don't want anything else.'

She waited. No response. If the person inside wouldn't come out then she would go in. *If* it had been Rachel she'd seen, she might have been pulled back out of sight. The farming people could be allowing Lockley the use of their house. It was a bit fanciful but every possibility must be looked into. The dogs probably had the run of the ground floor. Trying to get inside through a downstairs window was out of the question. Running to the barn, she crept round its side with a ladder and skirted round to the front of the house and placed it against the wall. She hitched her skirts in her waistband and placed her foot on the first tread to climb up to a bedroom window.

Her heart jolted. The barking had taken on a different sound, louder and clearer; the dogs had been let out and were haring round to her. She had to get up the ladder quick.

'Don't move,' a woman's voice hissed.

On the fifth rung, Clemency twisted her head and saw a woman aged about thirty pointing a shotgun at her. She had the dogs under control.

'I'm not a thief. I wish you no harm,' Clemency said rapidly, ready to scale the ladder if the dogs lunged at her. 'I'm looking for my cousin who was abducted earlier today. She's called Rachel. She's pretty and dark and would be well dressed. My family, the Kivells of Meryen, are out searching for her. We believe a doctor might have taken her. All I want is to ask if anyone here has seen anyone like them, or a knife-grinder called Dewy, we believe he's involved. When you didn't come to the door and I saw you hide from me I had to see who it was. Rachel could be hidden anywhere. Please understand.'

The woman was stocky, with a red, weathered face. She made the shotgun safe. Grim, obdurate, she said, 'That's quite a tale, missy. I've heard of the Kivells. Don't reckon any of you lot would mess about, so I'll give you the benefit of the doubt that you're not up to no good. I'm cautious because there was a robbery here before and my husband's at market. Can't help you, haven't seen anyone hereabouts like you describe. If my husband had, he'd have

295

mentioned it. 'Tis rare for people to come down this way, don't lead to anywhere much. I hope you find your cousin.'

'Thank you, Mrs...?' Clemency said, down on the ground again.

The woman just nodded, her stiff expression making it plain she wanted Clemency gone.

'I'm sorry I disturbed you. Goodbye.'

The woman followed Clemency up close and watched her mount the pony. Clemency felt the woman's hard eyes stabbing into her back as she rode away, sure if she glanced back the shotgun would be aimed at her again.

She would go on to the house. The farmer's wife said no one had been seen about lately but she'd go there anyway. She went on down the lane at a canter, first riding downhill then along a fairly straight stretch. There was another downward slope, steeper this time. She raised herself up in the saddle. Most of the house was in view, but there was no sign of life. She would be there in a few minutes.

Rounding a bend she saw a figure in the road and cried, 'Rachel!'

It was Rachel, lying like a piece of rubbish on the wayside, and she was still and in a bad way. It was obvious she had lost her baby. Spurring the pony on, she raced to her cousin. Rachel was facing the hedge, her face pressed against a patch of nettles. Clemency put her fingers to her neck. She was alive, thank God. Clemency pushed the nettles back. Rachel had either escaped her abductor or had been dumped here.

She couldn't have been imprisoned at the farm. If the farmer's wife had been involved, the suspicious woman wouldn't have allowed Clemency to leave so easily.

Calling her pony up close, trying to be gentle – but it took a mighty heave and some struggle – she managed to seat Rachel up on the pony and lay her front down over the pony's neck. Clemency climbed up behind Rachel and pulled her up and held on to her.

'It won't take long to get you to the hamlet. My father's there; we'll soon have you home, Rachel, just hang on, don't die.'

The Kivells often thought of themselves as infallible but no one could forecast the outcome of serious injury and illness, and Clemency's youth and lack of worldly experiences made her fear for them both. Rachel had escaped the clutches of James Lockley, a man as mad as moon blood and as dangerous as a ravenous wolf. He could be coming after them.

Riding as fast as she dared while keeping Rachel safely aboard the pony with her, Clemency made for the hamlet.

Twenty-Seven

Dewy's wagon! Figuring Rachel had been taken along little or rarely used paths, using little more than instinct, Jowan rode and scanned landscape. He stopped to scour a couple of abandoned dwellings and other likely places – a small cave, large rock formations, dells, vast banks of fern, copses. The lurchers detected nothing. Habitations were few; he drew a blank at the empty ones and the residents in the others sympathized with him but could not help.

Where had the wretched doctor taken Rachel? Jowan's fear for his sister, his frustration and anger sped through his veins with ferocity. He prayed to find them soon and Rachel unharmed. Lockley might be trying to persuade Rachel to go away with him, but the lovelorn man might do something rash or malicious if rejected. In any event Lockley would be his. And then he'd be a dead man.

Suddenly the dogs got excited. They were entering the bottom of a meadow where the grass had recently been disturbed, near Meadowbank. He clenched his jaw in confidence that the dogs had picked up Lockley's route. Sitting up sharp on his horse, he scanned the area and his doggedness was rewarded. Away below, at the back of a solitary house, was the knife-grinder's wagon, the pony harnessed to it. Dewy might be about his business for the residents, but Jowan doubted it. He was in on Rachel's abduction for money; the squire's son too. He was amoral and could be paid to change loyalty.

Dismounting to keep out of sight, ordering the dogs to stay, he made the final approach behind a high hedge at the side of the house, then made a stealthy entrance into the garden. There was an eerie silence; something was very wrong, and he was filled with a creeping disquietude. He had brought a firearm and had it ready to fire.

The back door was open. He paused and listened. No one stepped outside and no sounds came from within. The pony was sweating, and whinnied and stamped its hoof. The creature was on edge, guarding its master's property, further proof to fuel Jowan's unease. It was unlikely Rachel was loaded inside the wagon; Lockley and Dewy would have made off with her by now. She must be a prisoner inside the house.

Hunched over, every nerve burning and spring-tight, his need aided his animal instinct and hunter's sureness. Rapidly he padded up to the house wall. There was no point in trying to peep through a window; the curtains were drawn. Rooting his eyes to the back door, aiming the gun out straight in case someone came out, he stalked to the entrance, listening and highly alert. All was silent.

He peeked inside the doorway and his jaw dropped. Dewy was sprawled on the floor, a small flower of blood on his chest, his eyes agog in shock and horror. A knife was lying loose on his fingertips. He must have been about to throw it, but at whom? Jowan's breath clenched his lungs. Rachel? Had she tried to flee and also met violence?

The grip of fear tightened in his chest, then more so as he heard a low moan. Someone was hurt. The open door hid who it was. In one swift step he was at the door and peered round it. Down near the table Lockley lay in a bloodied state, both arms limp and broken. The villains had doubled-crossed each other. Poetic justice, but where was his sister?

'Rachel! Where are you? It's Jowan.' Putting away the gun, he left Lockley and searched the downstairs rooms. They were empty and he ran up the stairs, throwing open the first bedroom door. Nothing. The next door was open. He rushed in. 'No!' There was a lot of blood on the bed. Had that beast downstairs butchered her? Or Dewy? What the hell had they done with her?

'Rachel? Rachel?' She was not in the other rooms. He tore back down to the kitchen. 'Lockley!' He hunkered down to the doctor. Lockley's eyes were closed, his lips colourless from loss of blood, and twitching. He emitted another pathetic moan. Jowan smacked his cheeks, making his head swing side to side. 'Speak to me, you bastard! What have you done to my sister? Where's Rachel?'

The doctor's eyes fluttered open. He was in the most excruciating agony but he recognized his tormentor. 'H-help me, get me away and I'll t-tell you.'

'Like hell!' Jowan wanted to shout, but said in hard tones, 'I'd rather you died a thousand agonizing deaths but I've no choice. I'll get you to a doctor. Is Rachel somewhere safe? Is she alive?'

'Give me your word you won't let me hang for killing Dewy?'

'You have it. Well?'

The glimmer of hope James thought he'd won for himself vanished as suddenly as he'd obtained it. His last piece of cleverness wouldn't work in the end. Jowan Kivell might intend to keep his word but he wouldn't be safe from the rest of his bastard clan. They would hunt him down wherever he went, for however long it would take. Dying on the gallows was preferable, and before that he'd make himself an infamous folk hero and drag Rachel's name through the mire. Hatred surged through him against the face, so like Rachel's, above him. His mouth felt desiccated but he managed to work up a little sour spittle. Gasping and gagging, with a painful crazed breath, he spat. It was a poor elevation and the spittle sprayed back down on him.

Blinking, Jowan pulled back, ripped into fury.

301

'You bastard!'

'You should keep that label for yourself, Kivell, rightly so,' Lockley hissed. 'You and your bitch of a sister. She's dead. I tortured her. I tore her bastard out of her belly then I killed her very slowly. I enjoyed every one of her screams and pleas. She begged like a bitch. You wouldn't have known her in the end. Dewy and I dumped her body far away from here.'

Jowan was consumed with hatred but couldn't scream out the curses on this monster to hound him in the flames of Hell.

'Ah,' Lockley laughed. 'You know what it feels like, the bite of detestation and revulsion. You hate me, Kivell, and can't wait to see me hanging from the gallows. I'm not afraid. You won't have the satisfaction of seeing me in terror. I shall step forward to the trapdoor with pride.'

Like a worm of gall tunnelling out from him Jowan found his voice; it sounded as if it carried the tormenting echoes of Hell. 'Think that, do you, Lockley? Do you think I'm going to let you live to boast to the world how much you made my sister suffer?' Raising his fist, he thumped it down on the bullet wound in Lockley's chest and hot blood wet his hand.

Lockley howled like some heinous beast. Fear flashed through him, driving out all the years of bitter malcontent and the inferno of his insanity. Jowan Kivell was rupturing his wounded flesh. His body couldn't take it again. 'No! W-wait, I—'

302

'Shut up! Shut your vile mouth!' All reason fled from Jowan and he slammed his fist down again and again. 'Die! Die before I rip you apart!'

He was so fanatical he didn't hear James Lockley wail his last words. 'I lied...'

Something made Jowan hold the next blow. Blood seeped from Lockley's mouth and a guttural gasp escaped his thrown open mouth. The beast was dead.

Jowan got up as if in a trance and stared down at the body. His moments of madness left him and he was overcome with grief for Rachel. He slammed his fists on the table, wanting, needing pain. Deserving pain. He had got here too late.

On heavy feet he staggered outside and put his face helplessly to the sky, tears cascading down his twisted face. 'No! Rachel!'

Twenty-Eight

Seth Kivell and his men gathered at the top of the lane waiting for Clemency's return, all sure from their search that Rachel had not been taken hereabouts. The few dwellers of the hamlet had joined the mounted huddle to await the news.

'I'm troubled,' Seth confessed. 'I shouldn't have told the girl to go off on her own. We're dealing with two dangerous men. I'll go on and see where she's got to.'

He urged his horse forward a couple of steps then heard the slow beat of hooves. 'Ah, here she is.' Clemency appeared a few beats later. 'My God, she's got Rachel with her!'

The woman Seth had spoken to earlier offered the use of her home. Rachel was laid out on the horsehair couch in the front room. In privacy from the men, Mrs Tate – a grey-haired widow, deft-handed and capable – and Clemency made Rachel comfortable. A Kivell son rode to Gwennap to fetch its doctor. Other Kivells branched off to tell their kinsmen the search was over, and that fate and God willing, Rachel would live.

Seth ordered Clemency to stay with Rachel. Not a man to deal out affection, he shook her shoulder. 'You did well.' Then, as did everyone else, assuming Rachel had been held at the house below Tretolgan Farm, Seth and his remaining sons ventured off to scout it out.

They discovered the two dead bodies and the ransom paid for the Nankervis baby, and assumed they were the first to reach the grisly scene.

Jowan had set out to recover his tracks and return home to tell Thad and Helen the dreadful facts, and to call a search of the surrounding area of the house to retrieve Rachel's body. He didn't believe all of Lockley's malicious tale. The doctor would have been too keen to make his getaway to take Rachel's body far. Jowan reached his horse but couldn't bring himself to leave the vicinity just yet. Someone must have seen something. He'd ask up at the farm and the hamlet. He rode up across the fields, emerging further up the lane, missing the band on their way to the house.

He called at the farm and received a different response than Clemency had. The farmer's wife met him on the doorstep, keeping the collies inside. Introducing herself as Nell Gundry, she explained that a young female cousin of his had already made inquires, and sympathized over his anxiety – Jowan couldn't bring himself to inform her Rachel was dead. Nell Gundry repeated that she had seen no doctor or the knife-grinder.

Going on to Meadowbank, he saw people gathered outside one particular cottage. What was going on here? A sharp-eyed old man called to him. 'Got good news for 'ee, boy. Your maid's been found by another maid in your family, and brought here. She's hurt and out of it but the doctor's been sent for.'

'What?' Hardly daring to breathe in case he'd heard wrong, Jowan leapt off his horse and pushed through the little crowd. Without bothering to knock, he entered the cottage and there was Clemency with the householder, and a form under a blanket on the couch.

'Jowan!'

'Is it her, Clemency? Is it really Rachel?' He froze, afraid to be told otherwise.

'Yes, I came across her in the lane.'

'Her heartbeat's strong,' Mrs Tate said. 'She's been attended to. She came round for a moment and we managed to get her to sip some water. I'm hoping you'll not have too much to worry about.'

'I thought she was dead.' Jowan let out the mightiest sigh of relief, kneeling beside his sister, who was pale and pinched and seemed to be deeply asleep. He rubbed gently on her wrist. 'Lockley told me he'd murdered her and dumped her body.' What a relief also that he hadn't gone straight home and delivered false news.

The cousins exchanged stories. Jowan left out that he had killed Lockley. It was something he would never regret, even though Rachel had lived to make an escape. Lockley had made Rachel suffer terribly. He was being tormented in Hell now, never to mock Rachel's name.

'You say the farmer's wife was friendly to you?' Clemency asked.

'Yes. Why?'

'Oh, nothing,' Clemency shrugged. 'It doesn't matter now. We've got Rachel back and hopefully she'll come through. My father and brothers will find what you did at the house. They'll come straight back. My father was going to arrange to have Rachel taken home if the doctor says she's well enough to travel.'

'I'll do that. I can never thank you enough for bringing her here.' He thanked Mrs Tate for her hospitality. 'To think she was lying in the hedge and I wasn't far away from her.' He shuddered. 'Without you, Clemency, God knows how long she might have languished there.'

Jowan didn't utter the thought that would be on every Kivell mind – that Rachel would be severely traumatized, especially about the loss of her baby – but at least now she wouldn't have to marry a lowly miner.

It was two hours later when news reached Poltraze that Rachel Kivell had been found alive and had just been brought home. Michael rode at once to Chy-Henver, his heart like a ton of bricks dropped to his gut.

He barged into Chy-Henver and confronted Jowan. 'Does your sister know anything at all about my son? Can I see her?' he begged. He was a man brought down to the lowest depth.

'She's awake but she must sleep soon. Keep it to a few minutes,' Jowan said, feeling for him. The family had got Rachel back but there was no hope for the squire. He led the way upstairs, where Helen and Mrs Carveth were sitting at Rachel's bedside.

'Rachel, it's Mr Nankervis. Do you feel up to speaking to him?' he said softly.

Feeling her whole body was made of lead, Rachel nodded weakly. It was an indescribably strange joy, fed with sorrow, to at last be back in her own bed, but she yearned to sleep and stay so forever, where pain and terrible memories could never reach her.

'Can you tell me anything, Miss Kivell?'

Michael strode close to her, as ashy pale as she was. 'Did Lockley mention anything about my son?'

'He did, Mr Nankervis,' Rachel croaked, wanting to shake off the memory, but she had to do this or heartlessness would damn her. 'I'm so sorry, he told me that Dewy the knife-grinder had disposed of your son, that he couldn't be found at the house where he took me.'

It was the final crushing blow for Michael. He had been besieged by fear and emotion for so many appalling long hours that he couldn't bring himself to cry. Nathaniel was dead and had probably been murdered on the day of his abduction. His little body could be anywhere. Now the search for him must turn to the most dreadful kind. He could do no more than nod. He left the room, the once proud man who had thought he had everything, totally broken.

The next day Clemency was at Chy-Henver. Jowan was in no mood to work and was sitting idly in the office. 'Rachel's asleep,' he told her, 'and is likely to stay that way for some time.'

'I'm pleased she's resting,' Clemency replied. 'What does Flint Retallack say about it all? Does he still want to marry Rachel?'

'He was here last night, angry he hadn't been told before others. I refused to let him see Rachel. He's got no right now and I don't care what he thinks. I want Rachel to see less of that family.'

'Surely that's her decision, Jowan. Rachel is

attached to Eva. You can't demand she gives her up. It will make her loss and ordeal even worse.'

Jowan was struck at how grown-up his cousin was in speech and manner. She took the other chair and, despite her tomboy manner, sat down in soft, feminine movements. Her amber hair, as usual, rippled in untamed waves. She wasn't really a tomboy but a free spirit, proud and comfortable of who she was, a girl turning rapidly into a woman. She was going to be a stunning creature. When Seth realized this he was going to be fiercely protective of her where men were concerned.

'I suppose not,' he said moodily.

'At least Flint Retallack genuinely cares for her, unlike that mad doctor who was crazily infatuated with her.' Clemency examined him to read his thoughts. He nodded reluctantly. Good, he hadn't grasped the truth of Rachel and Lockley's association. If no one else did, Rachel would be brought to no more disgrace than a young woman who had succumbed to a handsome man's charms. People were expressing sympathy over the loss of her baby.

Clemency waited half an hour. Rachel did not stir so she left to return another time. Passing the Retallack cottage, with the work on the extension halted, she was curious about Flint and rode to the side of the place and looked over the wall at the smallholding. He was there, on the narrow path between rows of healthy vegetables, head down while smoking, a bag over his shoulder, ready to go on the afternoon core at the Carn Croft.

Sensing he was being watched, Flint glanced to the side. Shuddering with alarm at seeing a Kivell actually there staring at him – Kivells had been thin on the ground where he was concerned – he hurried to the wall. 'What is it? Has Rachel taken a turn for the worse?'

'No,' Clemency said. 'She's resting.' It was evident he really cared about Rachel, and Clemency, already used to sizing up the masculine and sensual attributes of a man, distinguished why Rachel had been attracted to this sinewy, muscular rough hulk. He had eyes that were both strong and soulful, and firm lines and contours to his face and body.

'And you're here like other members of your family to tell me to stay away from her,' Flint challenged. He was sick to his guts after worrying for hours that he'd lose Rachel and the frustration at finding no sign of her during his own search on the downs. His immediate joy at learning from Wilf, who'd gleaned it from circulating gossip, that Rachel was alive and home had been quickly sullied by the fact that she'd been found some hours earlier. Then he'd suffered the blow of his child being dead. To further crush him, Jowan Kivell had kept him on Chy-Henver's doorstep and as good as told him to disappear from Rachel's life. Of course, the wedding wouldn't go ahead. It would take a long while for Rachel to recover, but their betrothal need not necessarily come to an abrupt

310

end. They had planned a life together, for Eva's sake as much as their baby's. They had deep feelings for each other, he was sure of it. He longed to know what was on Rachel's mind.

'No,' Clemency said, wondering herself now why she was bothering with this miner.

The girl across the wall, up on her well-bred pony, was as haughty as any of her breed, haughty like Rachel had been on his first meeting with her. Flint struggled with anger and offence while hoping somehow that she could yet offer him a little hope. 'Thanks for finding Rachel. Thank God that madman and the knife-grinder killed each other, both greedy to get all the ransom money, no doubt, and she was able to get away.' He dipped his head, ashamed it was not he who had rescued Rachel. He had been of no help to the squire either.

The girl just continued to gaze at him. He asked, 'Was there something else about what happened to Rachel?'

'I don't know,' Clemency said. There was something that refused to leave her mind. She had not slept all last night, thinking it over.

'Can we talk about it? If there's anything I can do to help ease Rachel's pain,' Flint beseeched with his hands, 'anything, no matter how insignificant it might seem. I'll forego my shift at the mine.'

'It doesn't concern Rachel.' Clemency was pleased the miner's interest didn't wane – he wasn't a selfish man – so she went on, 'Do you know that feeling you get, like a sixth sense?

When your mind won't let something drop and you have to follow it through?'

'Yes. It's what led me to discover the Churchfield woman. What are you saying?'

Clemency asked herself why she was telling this to Flint and not her father. She knew why: her father was entirely satisfied with yesterday's outcome and would say he had no intention of wasting his time. Flint was desperate to do something to prove his worth. He had courage. The rest of her family seemed to have forgotten that he had already saved Rachel's life from a murderous miner, Eva's brother.

Moments later Flint was on his way to the Nankervis Arms to hire a pony. Then, for secrecy, he followed after Clemency, who had already left Meryen.

Twenty-Nine

'Wh-where ... am I?'

'You're home, in your bed,' Helen said softly, having barely distinguished Rachel's puttering breath. She feathered Rachel's feverish cheek with a gentle finger, her heart saddened over her friend's great suffering. Angry too at the injustice meted out to her by the same monster who had violated her – and yet if James Lockley, that beast, had not tortured her beyond endurance, she would not be living here among real friends, about to marry Thad, whom she was deeply fond of. Rachel had twitched and groaned in her unholy sleep, murmuring in horror, reliving the fear and atrocity, her mind likely conjuring up ghastliness she had not experienced. 'You're safe. Jowan, Thad and I are looking after you. Nothing can hurt you any more.'

Her eyes squinting, blinking in the trial to hear Helen's voice, to concentrate long enough to absorb her words, Rachel murmured, 'My ... baby.'

'I'm so sorry, Rachel.' Helen could weep for days for her. Rachel was like a child, uncomprehending the blow fate had hammered on her. She seemed so small, lying there with a cold damp cloth on her forehead to ease her fever. Michael Nankervis had crept away from Chy-Henver a pitiful figure of desolation, but he had thoughtfully scribbled and sent a note thanking God for Rachel's rescue and arranged for his personal physician to attend her. With Henry Cardell's specific prescriptions, the doctor had deliberated that favour was on the patient's side to make a full recovery physically – of her mental state he couldn't be sure. Despite the cruel employment of his wanton fists, James Lockley's ego about his professional ability had endured to perform a thorough removal of all of the tiny lost life.

'Eva?' Rachel wheezed. Many of the horrifying images of her nightmares had included Eva undergoing all sorts of humiliation, scourging and wretchedness. She cared more for Eva's peace and well-being than her own.

Helen blessed her for that, and knew the reason behind the question. 'Eva does very well with Mrs Retallack. Flint was here yesterday. He hoped to see you.' She had seen the bond between the couple. To her the men's standpoint over Flint was misguided, thoughtless and wrong. Flint was devoted to Rachel; he was the most likely one to bring her through the days ahead.

Rachel turned her head, just a fraction. It was so painful to move. 'I just ... want to sleep.' Already her tentative wakefulness was failing her.

Helen pulled in her lips. Such a shame, Rachel dismissing the miner, but after her tribulation it was understandable that her emotions were raw and crushed. 'Sleep then, my dear, sleep.'

Clemency and Flint paid a call at Meadowbank, to thank Mrs Tate for her kindness and to glean some information. They then rode to the entrance of Tretolgan Farm.

'It still seems a long shot to me, despite what that woman just told us,' Flint said, set for disappointment, wondering how he could have allowed a mere girl to talk him into this scheme. 'Although the Gundry woman was compliant with Jowan she put a shotgun on you and those dogs sound savage.' If Clemency were hurt the

314

Kivells would kill him for being responsible, and he would be. He was the adult here. He was in no doubt that Clemency would have come here alone; at least he was here to protect her.

'Do you want to go back?' Clemency glared at him. If this man lacked the backbone her family possessed then he certainly didn't deserve ever to become a member of it.

'No, of course not; I'm concerned about you. You're just a girl.'

'I'm not *just* anything. Kivell women are in no way weak.'

'I know that, but you have a tendency to rush in without due thought.' He recalled the first time he'd seen Rachel, almost throttled to death by Eva's brother, Silas Bowden.

'Don't worry,' Clemency muttered, as if speaking to an irritating child needing reassurance. 'I won't do anything silly. The more I think about it the more I'm convinced Nell Gundry has something to hide. Facts are facts. She could just have easily come straight to the door yesterday with the gun to see what I wanted. And why were the collies in the house? Farm dogs are usually put to work. Mrs Tate said the farmer and his wife have two daughters, aged eight and ten. I definitely saw a baby's clothes on the washing line yesterday. Mrs Gundry may have let go of caution there. It could be she's looking after a baby for a relative or something but it might just be the squire's son. And the farm is just a stone's throw away from the house where Lockley and Dewy were holed up. I find it unlikely the Gundrys didn't see them. Lockley might have paid them to look after the baby.'

'I don't think Lockley would have risked that; he was so crazed, fully capable of murdering a baby.'

'He left it to Dewy to dispose of the boy. If he couldn't bring himself to kill him, Dewy might have brought him to the farm.'

'He's never struck me as having much of a conscience, and both men would want to cover their tracks. If there is a baby boy there and we get to see him, how will we know if it's the squire's son?' Flint hoped with all his heart it would be the case. If he was to help get little Nathaniel Nankervis back to his parents, perhaps the Kivells would think a little of better of him. They admired courage and enterprise.

'Apparently he's got a mop of black hair and resembles the squire. I'm sure we'll know.'

'How are we going to take a peek at the baby?'

'Nell Gundry will probably come to the door today. She'll risk too much suspicion if she doesn't. You just follow my lead. I will know how to play my part perfectly.' Determined intention bled from Clemency's every pore. 'You will too, I'm sure.'

Flint was pleased she trusted him, but he was shocked and amused at her eyeing him pertly. It was hard to believe this girl was only fourteen. She was wise beyond her years and radiated a mature beauty. She was like an untamed thoroughbred. She was dazzling. Her enthusiasm was infectious. She had the gift of convincing, of making another want to follow her. Flint was sure that in a couple of years she was going to be a whole lot of trouble to men.

They pursued the farm track at a comfortable trot to create the illusion that they were easygoing. Flint didn't tell the girl to be careful; he trusted her to make the ideal approach in the coming encounter. He felt a bit superfluous. He was just her companion. The farmer's wife could make up her own mind how he was connected to the Kivell girl. The more they gained the dirt track the more he hated being away from Meryen, far from Rachel. If she had roused and hoped to see him, if she needed him, she would be hurt and devastated that he had not been to Chy-Henver today, at least on his way to work. It would fuel her brother's and cousin's opinion that he was too common ever to be welcomed into Kivell ranks. God knows he would have to become more of a Kivell than his own man if Rachel went ahead and married him, but he wouldn't mind too much. He loved her. He hadn't really known until now. He was consumed with ardent, mature and everlasting love for Rachel. He didn't want to go on without her. He wanted the extension on Three-Steps completed and Rachel living there as his wife. He would give himself to her on any terms.

As if aware that something utterly profound had just happened to him, Clemency gave him a long, piercing look. Flint ignored her. Anything on his mind was none of her business.

About halfway to the farmstead the collie pair came hounding towards them on swift thundering paws, barking lustily. Not so much a hostile reception but a raucous one, as if they were under some kind of canine intoxication – the result of their freedom after being kept in at the farmhouse? Clemency reined in and passed Flint a pleased look. He frowned – what was good about the same two awesome big dogs she had been fearful of yesterday?

Confident there was nothing to fear while the dogs were not under their owners' command, that they were enacting their normal wary welcome to strangers, Clemency sang out to them, 'Hello, hello you two.' She kept up the cooing patter when the dogs reached her pony. Flint was amazed the pony stayed quietly resolute. He bated his breath when Clemency slid to the ground, holding out her hands to the dogs. The dogs sniffed at Clemency and in a second she was crouching beside them and they were licking her hands, fussing about her as if she was a treasured friend. So she had a way with animals, but what a risk to take.

'There,' Clemency said proudly, when she had remounted. 'That should do us well. We're far less likely to be seen as a threat now.'

The dogs led the way to the farmyard. Clemency appreciated the peaceful scene, a marked contrast to her first visit here. Animals and fowls were feeding, snuffling, or snoozing, and a large number of cats were either sauntering about or sunning themselves. More importantly two little girls, in calico aprons, cotton bonnets and boots, were busy on the cobbles, one with a besom sweeping away straw and dirt to clear the pathway to the door; the other, taller and older, was struggling with a bucket of water from the well. They stopped dead, putting down besom and bucket, and stared at the newcomers with distrustful curiosity. 'Mother! Mother!' the elder shouted.

Nell Gundry appeared on her granite doorstep, wiping floury hands on her apron. She shut the door and came forward. Clemency and Flint were sure she had been watching them long before her daughter had called. Perhaps the shotgun was in easy reach, primed for use.

'Good afternoon, Mrs Gundry.' Clemency was politeness itself.

'And to you, Miss Kivell. I heard your cousin was found but was hurt. How is she?' She glanced at Flint and nodded in greeting.

'It's kind of you to ask. That's why we're here. This is Flint, another of my cousins. Rachel is resting quite comfortably. We are on our way to the house. Rachel had something she valued with her when she was snatched. No doubt the police are still there. We're hoping they may have found it. We're sorry you've had all this commotion practically on your doorstep. It must be very disquieting for you.'

'I'm just pleased it's all turned out all right in the end for your family. The culprits are both dead, justice done. Now I really ought to go in, I've got loaves to put in the oven.'

'We'll take our leave.' Clemency made to go. Flint didn't like being shut out of a say, like he was redundant, just there as fist and muscle if needed, with a girl in charge. But Clemency turned back at once. 'Oh, your baby is crying. We're sorry if we've disturbed its sleep.'

'Baby?' Nell Gundry's whole set changed to stiffened shoulders, tense hands and darting eyes. 'There's no baby here.'

'But I definitely heard a baby.'

'So did I.' Flint joined in the girl's clever scheme. He pressed his nag forward in a predatory and no-nonsense manner. He and Clemency dismounted.

Nell Gundry beckoned to her daughters, her big rough hands flapping urgently. 'It must have been the cats you heard. They're always fighting and howling. Inside girls, inside now.'

'You do have a baby in your house, Mrs Gundry. We're convinced you have and we want to see it,' Flint said, ready to spring forward if Nell Gundry reached inside for the shotgun. 'You might as well tell us the truth. You do have something to hide, don't you?'

The mother shepherded her young ones inside, shut the door, rose up on her doorstep and folded her arms, but her intention to appear firm and defiant failed her. She fell limp and stooped, stuttering, 'What right have you to question me like this? To frighten my children? Get off this property!'

Clemency allowed Flint to take the principal role owing to his greater age and gender. He squared on Nell Gundry. 'Did you know that the son of Squire Nankervis of Meryen was abducted a few days ago by the dead doctor and Dewy, the knife-grinder? He was just three months old. Does the baby you have match that description? If it turns out he's the Nankervis baby, then you and your husband could hang as partners in the crime and your daughters could end up in the workhouse.'

'Dewy said the child wasn't wanted!' A terrified wail broke from Nell Gundry's throat. 'Dewy said he'd belonged to a woman who already had a large brood and she couldn't cope with yet another. She was glad to let him go to a good home. Dewy knew my husband and I longed for a son to take over the farm one day. I've lost three babies, all girls, since I had my daughters. I'd mentioned to Dewy that I'd do anything to have a son. Dewy sold the boy to us for three pounds and ten shillings, all the savings we had. He brought the boy here naked, inside an old coat, so there was no way of knowing where he came from. He said the boy had lived a long way away but we must keep him hidden until he'd left the area. In view of what you've said, it seems little Albert, that's what we called him, must be the missing baby. Oh my God, we didn't mean any harm. We thought we were doing a good thing for us, the baby's real parents and specially for the baby.'

'Let us take a look at him,' Clemency soothed, not wanting the woman to panic. 'We just want to see the child returned to its rightful parents. If he doesn't appear to be the squire's son then you may keep him and good luck to you.'

Minutes later, Clemency and Flint were on the way back to Meryen.

Thirty

Ravage-eyed, Adeline Nankervis glanced across the room at her husband, curled up in the foetal position on the bed. She was sitting in a corner on the bedroom floor, her back against the cold wall, knees drawn up under her chin, shoulders drooping. She had been there for some hours, insensitive to the discomfort, having ignored pleas from her personal maid to lie down somewhere in comfort. The last thing she wanted was comfort while her precious little baby, the light of her soul, was dead and dumped like waste, after suffering unknown terrors and some beyond-belief horrendous end.

Michael was beyond uttering a syllable. He had hauled himself up here, one grief-laden, lumbering step at a time, had climbed up on the bed as if it were a huge flat coffin, and stayed, prone and blinkless, in self-imposed exile from life.

Her breast impacted with searing grief, Adeline had followed silently in his wake, without the strength or the desire to reach out to him. She didn't want to be touched, wanted no empathy. If Michael had taken any other course, even weeping and wailing like a tempest of winds, she felt she would have hated him irrevocably. She had done all her crying before the moment she had been dreading for days, of grasping from her husband's shattered face their son's fate. Better this sinking into despair.

How long they would stay like this she didn't know. She didn't care. They could remain and simply die. The house, this cold, brooding, haunted house, could run of its own accord. Its mistress didn't care if it was razed to the ground with her inside it. She'd do nothing to save Michael. He'd loathe her to Hell if she did.

Suddenly Hankins burst into the room, face aflame and almost imbecilic, animated as if some inebriated puppet master was pulling strings on his head and limbs. 'It's him! Sir, Madam! Mr Nankervis, stir yourselves! See? See! It's him.'

Michael remained a man of little breath and no feeling.

Adeline looked. 'Michael!' As quick as her unmalleable bones and muscles allowed she was up on her feet, rushing towards the door, arms outstretched. Michael was beyond listening and giving response.

'Give him to me!' Adeline screamed at the

girl stood an inch behind the butler, prepared to claw and rip apart the young saviour, and the guardian miner, of her precious son if he was not handed over at once. 'Nathaniel! My baby!'

Clemency held out Nathaniel Nankervis to his advancing mother. She wanted to ease the baby over but he was snatched away and, alarmed, he started to bawl.

Every minuscule part of Adeline was taken over with maternal joy and nature's need to protect her young. She'd never let Nathaniel out of her sight again. She would not stay in this damned house. If Michael didn't see things her way she'd take Nathaniel and leave him, never to return. Her legs fell away, but Clemency and Flint caught her before she buckled. In foresight, Hankins had brought up a chair. The rescuers eased mother and child down into it. Adeline rocked Nathaniel in her arms, so wonderfully no longer empty, crying with uncontrollable emotion and bliss.

No one had noticed Michael rising like a sleepwalker from the bed. He was at the chair now, watching with eyes like glaring lanterns. 'A-am I dreaming?'

Chy-Henver was dozing away the afternoon in silence – the only way Rachel liked it now. She had the house to herself, except for Helen, who had promised reluctantly to let her be. Jowan and Thad were at Burnt Oak for the celebration Seth was throwing proudly for his courageous and ingenious daughter. Clemency was the toast of the family, and a heroine in the village. The daring rescue of Nathaniel Nankervis had done more for the Kivells to gain acceptance and respect from the village and wider community than anything else. Mrs Carveth and Dora were taking time off for a second hog roast, much grander and more generous than before, given by the relieved and grateful squire for his son's safe return.

Before taking almost immediate leave of Poltraze for his Truro town house, the squire's gratitude to Clemency and Flint had been unbounded. He had flooded them with gifts and a generous monetary reward. Both now had the means to reconsider their future. Clemency need not necessarily bow to her father's wishes, and Flint, if he desired, could leave behind the hard and dangerous life of a miner before age or infirmity forbade it.

Rachel was dressed but in her bedroom, which she had not left for the preceding five days. Slumped in an armchair, she was staring ahead at nothing. She was pleased for the Nankervises, but too numb to grieve any more over her own baby. She felt blank, empty and unreal. She didn't want to think or feel, nor did she care about the conjecture over mad James Lockley's reason for abducting her. Yet she couldn't prevent her fragile mind from straying and accusing her of being defiled, used and dirty. Her own deceit and shamelessness had led to her downfall. She was unworthy of her family, unworthy of Flint, who, she had been told, was desperate to speak to her and did not comprehend why she was shutting him out. Flint deserved an explanation, perhaps a few words in a letter. It wasn't fair to keep him bewildered, but she couldn't bring herself to communicate with him. She deserved her suffering and did not deserve any form of happiness. Flint would soon see she wasn't worth bothering with.

Sluggishly she stood up and shuffled to the window.

It was the first time she had looked out since being brought home. The lonely downs seemed her only ally. Suddenly she wanted to be out there, all alone on the ground that held no feelings, no hopes, no dreams, and no recriminations. She wanted to be absorbed into it. She wanted to run away from everything and lose herself for good. She crept downstairs.

From the sitting room Helen heard the back door opening and closing. She frowned down at Willow curled up on her lap. 'Someone's come in.'

She waited. There was no call or sounds from a home-comer. Strange. She got the awful feeling something was wrong. She was up off the chair, sweeping Willow on to the vacated seat. 'Rachel!'

Through the kitchen window she saw Rachel leaping madly across the stepping stones then taking a straight route out across the downs. 'Rachel!'

Helen ran to the bottom of the garden. 'Rachel, wait!' Her friend did not slow down or turn round; either Rachel did not hear or she wasn't going to heed her.

Without considering her usual fear Helen went after her, taking the stepping stones with more care then pounding over springy and rough ground in her soft slippers, awkwardly making passage through the unevenness, the tall grasses and heather snatching at her ankles. 'Rachel, wait for me. I'll come with you!'

Rachel wasn't going to stop. She had reached some dreadful stage of torment. She certainly did not want any company. Helen came to a halt. If Rachel went on and on and she continued to follow her, perhaps losing sight of her despite the open expanses, they could both end up getting lost. It was sensible instead to go for help.

Back over the stream she went, through the backyard and towards the gate. Panic now decided to play its cruel hand, forbidding her to step beyond Chy-Henver boundaries in this direction. Her heartbeat and breathing flew out of control. Her nerves were minced. The way to Meryen and the surrounding landscape became slightly blurred. She grasped the top of the gate with both hands, closing her eyes, her head and shoulders hunched. She took deep breaths but for moments only. Rachel was in danger and that overrode everything. Anyway, Helen thought as she lifted her head, there was no monster to hurt her any more, and therefore nothing to fear. She set off, harnessing the release of adrenalin to give her uncanny speed.

Once in control she felt a sense of exhilaration at the freedom from restraint.

Her slippers were in ruins and the hems of her skirts coated in dirt when she reached the village. She was almost out of breath having torn along as if a raging fire was on her heels. The few people who were about called to her, asking if she wanted any help, but she ignored them, wasting no time. Her destination was the Retallacks' cottage and it was easy to pick out with its distinctive three steps and the abandoned building work. She was soon up those three steps as if on wings and banging on the door.

'What on earth...?' a woman's voice, worried and annoyed, uttered from within.

'Open up!' Helen gasped with her former edge of command. 'I need to speak to Flint urgently.'

Flint had only to follow the indentations in the high summer growth to see where Rachel had fled, in a fairly straight line. After about a mile he spied her, flung down in a deep stony barren hollow, a small sobbing figure, her ebony hair spread about her shoulders. A picture of utter dejection. To be here in a stretch of wasteland like this meant despair or self-loathing. It splintered his heart and wiped him out. He loved her so much and she couldn't reach out to him for comfort, to ease her unbearable thoughts and feelings. He yearned to hurl himself down beside her and hold her close, to cry out the agony together.

He dropped to his knees and stroked her hair tenderly. 'Rachel, it's me. I'm here for you if you'd let me.' *Please let me help you.*

There was no response and he couldn't tell if she had heard him or felt his touch. 'Rachel, darling, please don't stay like this.' He couldn't bear her being so alone, so wretched and in such discomfort. Hoping she wouldn't fight him off, he lifted her until she was partly up and facing him, thanking God she gave no resistance. She was weak and felt light as air. She kept on weeping in pain-racked, pitiful gulps, her head hung and her hair a wind-tangled curtain obscuring her face. Flint eased her into his arms, cradling her, sheltering her, loving her without intruding on her. She lay against his body, limp and lifeless, eyes almost closed. He couldn't tell if she knew it was he who was holding her.

He gently lifted the tresses away from her precious face. 'Rachel, darling, I'm here for you, now and forever, if you still want me.'

The tears just dried up in her, those already shed crystallizing on their downward path. Her eyelids flickered open. She did not, could not, look into his eyes. 'You should leave me here, Flint.' Her voice came in a raw, husky groan. 'Go on with your life and forget about me.'

'I couldn't do that if I wanted to, and why should I? There couldn't be one single good reason, Rachel.'

'You won't want me when you know the truth. People think the mad doctor did what he did to me out of some kind of obsession. That's not true. He and I were—'

'Shush now.' He gathered her in closer. 'You don't have to explain. I think I know the truth, Rachel. He was the man you'd loved, the one who broke your heart. When he was left with nothing, he returned in the hope of taking advantage of you. In his wickedness he decided to punish you when he learned you were to marry me – that you were,' Flint's voice dropped, 'carrying my baby. You're not to blame for what happened. I don't blame you for the loss of our baby, if that's what's making you feel so bad. Please, darling, you've been through a terrible time, don't keep punishing yourself. Don't punish me.'

She took in his gaze, then implored him. 'I don't want to hurt you, Flint. Don't you see I'm not good enough for you? I believed all Lockley's lies. I thought we were going to run away together. I was fully capable of denying a good woman her husband and bringing her to heartbreak and shame. It was my shameless actions that eventually led to the death of our baby – your baby, Flint. You should hate me. I hate myself.'

'Don't say that. And don't feel ashamed. I could never hate you, Rachel. You fell in love. You couldn't help those feelings. None of us can help whom we fall in love with, no matter how unsuitable the other person. Love is too strong to be easily denied. Yes, it wouldn't have been a right or fair thing to do to Charlotte

330

Lockley if it had come to that, but we all do wrong things, weak things, things we come bitterly to regret. I'm a weak and useless man, Rachel. It's me who's not good enough for you.'

His frank, downcast statement shot some life into her, renewing the deadened part that had numbed her to others' feelings. She was consumed with more sense of discredit; she had been luxuriating in self-pity. Particles of light filtered into her eyes. She stirred in his arms. 'How can you say that, Flint? You saved my life, and Eva's. You care for her and your mother with love and patience. You're loyal to your friends and the mining community. You're a good man, a wonderful man.'

'I'm not, Rachel. I'm seen as some kind of hero for playing a part in bringing home the squire's son. In truth it was Clemency's notion that he might be at that farm. She's just a girl yet she fully intended to go there alone. It was her idea how to approach the farmer's wife. I'd have blundered in and probably ended up at the end of a shotgun with no happy result. Worst of all, Rachel, I didn't find you. Again it was Clemency, your family. Your people are right. I'm not deserving of you. You shouldn't be out here like this. I'll take you home and I won't stay. I promise I won't bother you again. Please don't go on thinking badly of yourself. Rest, recuperate, then start your life again. Please do it for Eva. She's been missing you. And it's not just your family who loves you and is worried

331

about you. When Helen Churchfield saw you running off, she ran all the way to me to get help for you.'

Rachel needed to sit up straight to absorb this. 'Helen did that? She put aside all her fears for me? I don't want to spoil things for anyone. Helen will soon be a bride. She and Thad deserve to be happy, not worrying about me. As do Jowan and the family. And you too, Flint.' She wiped her damp face with the heels of her hands. 'I'm so sorry I've made you miserable. And I'm sorry I've forgotten about dear Eva. I'll go to see her very soon.'

Flint kept a hand on Rachel's back. He could feel some energy returning to her. If he couldn't have Rachel and her love, if he could do nothing else for her, it would ease some of his own heartache if she regained her former strong spirit. 'You don't have to keep apologizing. Shall I take you home now?'

'Yes, I'd really like to go home. Is Helen there alone? How do you think she'll be?'

'She was shaky but seemed in charge of herself, I thought. She insisted I hurry after you. Johanna Treneer came round to see what the fuss was about. She offered to walk Mrs Churchfield home but the lady said she would be fine.'

'It sounds as if Helen coped very well.' Flint helped her to stand then stayed at her side, both facing the way back. 'She shouldn't have any trouble getting to the church for her wedding.'

They fell silent, knowing they were sharing

the same thought. Their own cancelled wedding day was not far off. The sad fact bubbled up and grew in the air all around them.

'I'm sorry,' Rachel said, deeply apologetic.

'Don't be. If it's not what you want any more...'

She glanced at him, looked away and sought his eyes again. They were soaked with sorrow and so beguilingly light brown. 'I really did want to marry you.'

'At the time, but now I understand, of course.'

Why should he have to understand anything? They had not spoken of love but she had been deeply committed to the lifelong union they had soon been to undertake. 'I was looking forward to becoming your wife. For you and me, Eva and the baby, your mother too, for us all be together, a new family.'

'But not now, of course.'

She hated the *of course*. She was making Flint sound as if he was a commodity only to be used in certain conditions, low and undesirable, just there for nothing-else-for-it situations. 'I cared about you,' she said forcefully, angry with herself.

She was looking at him but he kept his eyes ahead. 'That is good to know.'

She hated it that he accepted the consolation nobly. A little earlier, not only had he understood about her wrong relationship with James Lockley, he had made excuses for her. He had guessed all along and didn't think at all badly of her. He was such a good, considerate man. No, he was more than that. She had told him just now exactly what he was and it was a whole lot of things all tied up in a single word – wonderful. In her miseries she had forgotten that was how she had come to think of him.

'I still care about you, Flint.'

'I'm so glad, Rachel. Perhaps we can stay friends. It will be good for Eva's sake.'

She wished he'd turn to her. She wanted to see him, see his eyes, to look into him.

Her burden of hopelessness, degradation and hurt were peeling away, disintegrating and evaporating into nothingness. The grief of her lost baby was still as raw, but all her old warm feelings for Flint ignited in her and flowered stronger with every new second. She pushed away the dreadful thought at how her fragility had nearly cost her this special bond with him.

'Flint...'

Her tone was different. It made Flint move his head and study her. Was that more than caring for him he detected in her calm features? He admired her pale loveliness, ethereal and haunting in her vulnerability. It touched him so deeply he almost cried, to plead that she'd let him love her. Only Rachel would ever do for him; she was the only one who could enhance his life, make him complete. 'What is it?'

'Would you do something for me?'

'I'd do anything for you, Rachel.'

'And I you, Flint, I really would.'

His brow showed furrows of puzzlement. 'What does that mean?'

'It means I'd like you to stay with me when I get home, then for us to stay together for good.'

'Are you sure?'

'Completely sure.'

His perplexity broke into the beginning of hope. 'Even to...?'

She slipped her hand in his. 'Yes, my darling Flint. I really do want to marry you – and this time for all the right reasons. Let's go back and make fresh plans to form that new family.'